The Book of Air

Joe Treasure

Clink
Street

London | New York

Published by Clink Street Publishing 2017

Copyright © 2017

First edition.

ISBN:
978-1-911525-09-7 - paperback
978-1-911525-10-3 - ebook

For my father Wilfrid Treasure, craftsman and house builder

And they that shall be of thee shall build the old waste places: thou shalt raise up the foundations of many generations; and thou shalt be called the repairer of the breach, the restorer of paths to dwell in.

(Isaiah 58:12)

Agnes

This is how I write my name when we've made paper and sharpened our pens. Agnes child of Janet. When we copy out our texts in the study. But this is not a text. What is it then?

Our paper in the study is not like this. Not smooth as butter. And not bound like this into a book. A book that is not a book, having no words in it. None until I write them.

Because here are the words. And where do they come from? Out of my head on to the paper.

There are four books. Everyone knows this. Everyone who is not too dull even to learn the Book of Moon when they are six summers old. Four books. The Book of Moon, which is for all the people of the village. The Book of Air, which is for those clever enough to study and with the time to leave off field work. The Book of Windows which is for one or two maybe in a lifetime. The Book of Death which is for no one living, not until the world is soon to end. Four books. What book is this then?

I found it two days past, in an attic at the Hall, behind a big iron box that had a use maybe in the endtime. I was hiding from Roland. He searches for me and wins a kiss. A childish game I thought it was. But since the turn of the year his kisses have grown stronger. His lips press harder on mine, and mine on his until I begin to feel his closeness not only on my mouth, but deep down in my belly.

Should I strike those words out? I would be ashamed for Sarah to see them. But why should I strike out words not meant for her? If I think of Sarah I must strike out all the words. I should suck the ink back off the paper, and leave it as pale and smooth as an onion, which I know can never be done. This book has pulled these thoughts out of my head, and if

1

Sarah saw them she would tell the Mistress who is mean and shrivelled, and the Mistress would have me flogged.

The men were looking to see where the roof leaked and left the ladder up. And so I climbed into the attic. And so I found this book. If the roof hadn't leaked, if I hadn't climbed the ladder, the world would still be as it was. If Roland's kisses hadn't filled me with longing and made me want to hide so I couldn't be found. But there I was. And there was the book softened by cobwebs in the grey light. Though I gasped with fear to do it, I slipped it in the pocket of my apron. And down the ladder I crept, and down the staircase, with my eyes closed, as I do sometimes when I imagine myself a person of leisure, trailing my fingers down along the ancient handrail, turning at each flight, until I feel the wooden dog that lies carved on the final post, looking over his foreleg to see who might come in at the front door.

My mother calls me now to bring in wood and boil water for the beans. Our cottage is smoky already from the fire and I have no appetite for supper, but I must go, or see her disappointed in her wilful child. And still my hand keeps moving, dipping the nib, forming the words as I think them. A fifth book. But there are only four books. I think of my dead father, and my gran who once sang me to sleep, and all the dead before them, gone without names, back and back to the endtimers who left us Talgarth Hall and all its treasures, Maud, Mother Abgale, Old Sigh and others long forgotten. So is this the Book of Death? It might well be, such power it has over me.

Jason

I've been wandering. I sleep and wake and have difficulty telling the difference.

I was dreaming of the future. I got up from my bed and the place was full of strangers – the staircases and passageways – and no one could see me. I was a ghost in my own house. I opened a door and I was in the orchard. And then you came to me, Caroline, bright and fresh as though you were still alive.

I open my eyes and the world ends all over again.

Was Maud in here again during the night trying to feed me cabbage soup? I hear them down in the kitchen making a racket with pans and knives – Maud and Abigail. They were in the yard earlier, chopping wood and talking to the chickens. Abigail talking. Maud doesn't talk. I scare her, but she comes anyway. I saw them together on the landing, Maud with an oil lamp, Abigail stroking her hair. She dresses like an old woman, Maud does – headscarf, wellies, layers of cardigans – though she can't be more than seventeen. Nice enough looking if she ever cracked a smile.

Abigail's not exactly a stylish dresser, but there's something about her, the way she holds herself – she knows what she's worth. And she's scared of nothing. She put a wet flannel on my face when I was burning up, pressed it to my mouth. A shock of water, ice cold in the throat. When was this? Last night? A week ago? It can't have been that long because I seem not to be dead yet.

'I'm sorry, Jason, to see you in this state.' She spoke in a murmur, looking away, almost as if she was talking to herself. She didn't want to agitate me, perhaps. At first I couldn't make my voice work to ask her who she was, but she told me anyway. 'My name is Abigail.' An oddly formal way of speaking she has. And she rinsed the flannel and pressed it again to my face.

'Do you know me?' I asked her, and she said, 'This is your

house, Talgarth Hall. Your room. We put you here to bed.' I asked if it was day or night and she said it was early evening and Maud was milking the cows.

'Whose cows?'

She smiled at that and said, 'The cows don't much care whose cows they are.'

Was that one conversation, one facecloth? Or does she come every night?

Maud doesn't make conversation, but I know it's her even in the dark. She smells of soup. I swore at her when I first arrived. I think I did. I was in my own fog and whatever I said didn't come out right. What the fog was she doing in my house? How the fog did she get in? If she knew what was good for her she'd fog off out of here before I called the police. I would've been on my face if I hadn't had the door to hold on to. She backed off up the hall anyway, poor mute Maud, as if I was about to hit her.

Call the police! That's a laugh. You couldn't get the police out to deal with squatters even before, even when everything still worked. Before the world caught the sweats. No wonder she kept her distance. What planet had I dropped from?

That's when I started singing – strange noises I'd never thought of making in my life. You'll understand this, Caroline, even though I can hardly make sense of it myself. You know how it goes, how the virus takes you. You've been through it. Here's how it went for me. I was of the multitude of the heavenly host. But I was also myself, and more entirely myself than I'd ever been, with a cry for you, Caro, and for all the dead. *Come back!* A cry of joy, because for that moment I believed I could reach you. I had to let go of the door because my arms were impelled to move. Only the legs let me down. The impulse was there, shuddering through the joints, but I couldn't stop the legs from buckling. I had my eye on the newel post at the foot of the stairs – the carved greyhound curled up with its snout under its paw. If I could get that far the world would be saved. It didn't feel mad. It felt powerful.

I'd wondered what it would be like when it got me, when it reached this stage – the blessing. It's what everyone thinks about, even if they don't let on. They lie awake at night, terrified, curious. And then they find out. And that's them done. Countless times I've woken in a panic, stared at the ceiling, heart pounding, wondering how it would take me, how the blessing would feel from the inside. And now I know.

Oh, Caroline, you found out earlier than most.

I was on my knees, but still singing, when the other one came down with a shotgun, turning on our oak staircase – Abigail, hips swaying in her long skirt. And sick as I was, with the barrel pointing at my chest, I felt a shot of adrenalin, God help me – life prodding me in the heart. In the groin. *It's not over yet. You're not sodding dead yet.*

But what about Abigail? Why didn't she pull the trigger? I've asked myself that. Or kick me out, at least? She could see I'd caught it. She would have recognised the signs. Why bring sickness into the house and tuck it up in bed?

They must have found Simon where I'd left him, curled up on the back seat of the Mercedes fast asleep. I know he's all right because I hear Abigail talking to him. *Come down with me, Simon, and I'll boil you an egg.* Her voice drifts up the back stairs from the lower corridor. *Take this jug to Maud and help her fetch the water.* She's calm with him and kind and doesn't ask him questions. *You needn't be scared of the chickens, Simon. They'll lay you another egg tomorrow.*

See, Caroline, she's talking about the future. Strange word. We used to know what it meant, then suddenly we had no use for it. It's too late for us, Caro. But if Si remains untouched, I suppose there might be one after all.

Agnes

I've been to the Hall today to cook and clean, to fetch in water, keep the wood pile high, feed the geese. I went on as if everything was the same but nothing was the same. Roland came to find me in the kitchen while I was using the grinder – a machine from the endtime with a screw that holds it to the edge of the table and another that grinds the meat when you turn the handle, sending it out in little worms of lean and fat and gristle.

'That's a clever thing,' he said.

'Yes,' I said, 'they were clever who made it.'

'And when it breaks, what will you use then?'

'Why should it break?'

'Not this year or next. Maybe not in your lifetime. But when.'

'I suppose whoever comes after will have to cut their meat small with a knife.'

'And when all the knives have been sharpened away to nothing, what then?'

I shrugged. I don't see the point in thinking about what might happen or not happen that can't be helped.

'We dig with metal spades, don't we Agnes?'

'Us that have them.'

'And with wooden ones if not. So which are better?'

I told him I didn't have time for riddles.

'The metal ones, of course,' he said. 'But do we know how to make them?'

I said if he was just going to talk nonsense he should fetch more wood in, but he stood behind me, holding me at the waist. 'Too cold outside,' he said, 'warmer here with you.' He mumbled these words against my neck like a child, and I softened towards him. But his hands began to go their different ways, one up one down, until I felt their warmth inside as well as out.

I made to shake him off. For a moment I felt the force of his grip, so I gave him a prod with my elbow and twisted away from him. 'Your sort can waste the day,' I said, 'but us cottagers must work.' He scowled at me. I had spoken more bitterly than I meant to. He called me a preener. I said, 'I needn't listen to you, you're just a boy.' And he stalked off to sit in the murk. What had I done to deserve such language but save us both from shame? He might be a child still, but I am not.

They say Roland's mother died while he was still struggling to be born and there was nothing to be seen of him but his head as purple and wrinkled as a cabbage fit only for pickling. And he had burdened the world for no longer than a week when they found his father face down in the river below the village, his coat snagged in trailing willow branches. He'd slipped from the bank reaching for hazelnuts. So they always told me, though I've never seen hazelnuts in February.

So Roland is an orphan and may live at the Hall and pass his time in book learning, except he has no taste for book learning and would rather mope alone. And I who long to master the secrets of the Book of Air must wash his sheets.

Are these thoughts mine? Here they are looking up at me in my own words. Am I angry, then? I am angry with mother sometimes. She is calling me now to feed the pig. I am angry with the pig who lies in straw and grows fat on my peelings. But the pig will have its throat cut to give us pork, and since the day she birthed me mother stands crooked for the pain in her back and hasn't so much as sneezed without pissing herself, so why should I be angry?

And I have my book, this book which has no words until I write them, which lies open like a meadow on a summer evening for me to lie down in.

Today at the Hall, while I scrubbed and swept, the thought of it burned inside. Before I left the cottage this morning I put it in the box under my bed where I keep my father's things –

the wren he whittled for me when his last sickness began, his best knife, the silver chain his own mother once wore around her neck. The knife is from the endtime and is of great value. Its blades slide open on tiny hidden hinges. The chain is just as old but even more precious because it came from my grandmother who sang to me, but died when I hardly knew what death was. My father gave it to me when it took all his strength to reach it from his pocket. I love these things. But I have never hidden my box with such care as I did today.

And thinking of my book while I worked I felt as though a hole had opened in the sky and I was falling into it. It was all I could do not to tell Roland. I thought of following him to the stables and saying I have a secret, bigger than your father's death.

But instead I chopped kindling for tomorrow's fires and listened to the children in the schoolroom chanting from the Book of Moon, and the Mistress telling them that this was how everything will end for each one of them when the last breath rattles from their throats and they are lowered into the pit.

I knew that the older ones were in the study and I chopped faster so that my work would be done and I could join them. I never hear Sarah read from the Book of Air without a leap of joy.

When I reached the study I was in a sweat from chopping wood in spite of the cold. Sarah nodded that I should take my seat between Megan and cousin Annie. Roland was there, having bored himself with brooding. Megan smirked and giggled as I sat down, but Sarah silenced her and encouraged me with a smile.

The study is a temple, Sarah says. But the temple is not a place. Not this room in the Hall, across from the kitchen, with its ancient table smooth and flat for writing on and its big windows with the grass outside where the sheep graze after haymaking. The temple is a state of readiness, a balancing of the pen, a clearing of the mind like a field for planting.

She was explaining again about the four meanings of the Book of Air. That the book itself, and every utterance it contains must be read four times, each time different, to be truly understood. First as the story of Jane for whom everything was new, second as the story of the endtimers and their ancestors from creation to destruction, third as the story of the world and what makes it – fire, water, earth and air – and last as the story of our life in the village, how it must be ordered and endured. And that only when all four meanings can be discovered at once and held in balance, as our bodies when we are healthy hold the elements in balance, can we claim to be true readers of the Book.

She read a text for us to write, holding the page like a petal gently between finger and thumb to turn it. It was the story of how Jane met Rochester when his horse slipped on the icy road at dusk while she was out walking, and the spark between them was ignited. Though she had lived in his house for months, working as governess to the orphan child Adele, he had been away all that time and was only just come back. And so she helped him to his feet. And what do we learn from this? That women, though slighter than men, are stronger in character and must lift men up. And that life is a clash of elements, fire and ice, earth and air.

But all the time I was thinking of the ink that I must steal from Sarah's cupboard and carry from the Hall in the pocket of my skirt. For once I didn't mind that I must stay behind after the others to dust and sweep. When Sarah's teaching was done, Roland was first to leave and Megan followed, smirking at me from the doorway because she was free to walk with Roland if she liked but I must stay and work. Annie took my hand. She looked at me in her mournful way and said I should knock on her cottage door when I had time. She lives with her father, Morton, who keeps nine cows and so they live better than most. I said I would, of course, but something dark about Uncle Morton will keep me from knocking. My mother shrinks from him too who has known him all her life. But mother shrinks from everyone.

Sarah had locked away the Book of Air in its cupboard. When we were alone, she asked me was I troubled by anything, and I said no. 'Your letters are quick and neat,' she said. 'I'm glad you make time to come.' And she gave me such a smile. I glowed with pleasure that she should say such a thing to me.

It was dark when I was done with my cleaning and stood outside in the passageway. The children were long gone from the schoolroom. If the Mistress sat in there alone she sat in silence. I listened for the rocking of her chair on the floorboards but heard nothing. She had gone to bed early, I thought, with her cats, which mean more to her than the people of the village. I felt the weight of the ink against my leg. I have a glass bottle from the endtime that I stole from the kitchen. It has a metal stopper that twists on to the neck so it won't splash under my skirt but I think everyone must see it when I walk. And I'm afraid if I fall it will break and the stain will seep through.

I heard the floorboards creaking. Someone moved in the darkness and a low voice made me jump. 'Soon you won't be able to call me a boy anymore.' It was Roland.

I guessed what he meant before he told me.

'It's my time,' he said. 'The men will come for me tonight.' He held my hand and I let him.

'Aren't you afraid?'

'Why should I be afraid of what all men must go through if they are to be men?'

I saw him shrug and turn his head away, but I thought he was afraid even so. There were footsteps above us on the landing and he gripped my hand more tightly. I felt his breath on my face and his lips feeling for mine.

'Don't,' I said.

'Soon, though, Agnes? Say we can talk.'

'I don't know. It'll be different when you're not a boy.'

'It'll be better,' he said, and I felt his smile.

He pressed against me with his hand on my skirt, and I thought he would feel the ink bottle. So I slipped away from him and out of the Hall, and walked under the stars towards the village. I was at the bridge before my heart had stopped its racketing.

Dear Roland. It's half a year and more since his voice

cracked and a dust of hair settled on his chin. Who noticed but me? Having no parents he is everything and nothing.

I dare say it will be no worse than my own outing just before the break of summer when the women took me up on the moor at dusk. There were two of them. They came dressed as Reeds, veiled in green as Reeds must always be, and stuck about with rushes and meadow flowers. I knew who they were, even so, old neighbours whose men have died, though I knew not to speak to them by name. We call them Reeds, the Mistress says, because it was the name of Jane's aunt who had to keep her in order when she was young and wild and hadn't yet learnt her place. The Reeds left me on the moor for a night and a day and a second night to drink mossy water and scavenge for berries. I was hungry, but not as hungry as Jane when she ran away from Rochester's house because she'd found out he had a wife. It was comforting to me to know that in suffering this I was remembering Jane's greater suffering. I was lightheaded as the second night came on, and I fancied I could hear Rochester calling to me from far away, but I knew it was just the wind in the bracken. Before dawn I saw the Reeds searching for me to fetch me home. They stirred in the half-light like stunted trees in a gale and I thought the moor had found a new trick to play on me, but I saw soon enough who they were and stood to show myself.

I thought they might feed me, but first they showed me a secret and swore me not to tell and I've told no one yet.

And so I became a woman.

I was afraid at first when they came for me at home. I told them I wasn't ready. But I had bled every month since the last year's end and had passed my fifteenth year so they knew it was time. And what was it after all but heat and cold and hunger, and a secret to be kept from men and from children.

Jason

I'm still here, Caro. How come I'm still here? It never takes this long. *From the sweats to the pit, three days and that's it.* Must be a symptom no one talks about – three days, but the last day feels like weeks, months, while your mind shuts and opens, and every opening hits you like a hangover. You'd tell people, except your head's on fire and your throat's closing up. Am I right, Caroline? Was it like that for you?

And I feel so old. I'm forty-two and I feel like an old man. It used to take time to get old.

From the sweats to the pit. The kids took to chanting that in the street. There was a ragged pack of them playing their chasing game the day we got out of London, Simon and me. They were playing as if their life depended on it, and not one of them untouched – jabbing the words at each other. *Three days and that's it.*

We hit a road block near Chiswick. Hard men in gas masks, playing at soldiers, keeping the neighbourhood clean. Waving their guns at microbes. The real soldiers had buggered off weeks before. Or keeled over. Same all over London, same everywhere. Containment was the word they used. Didn't last long. You need police to run a police state.

But they kept us waiting as if they were the real thing. A couple of cars ahead of us, a van behind, all the engines turned off to save petrol. It was quiet enough to hear the hum of the wind. Across the street, a terrace of houses and a pub on the corner, the Green Dragon. You felt the eyes watching through lace curtains and window bars – whoever was left – or just the windows watching.

And all the time I'm thinking, they'll recognise Simon's face. They'll work out who he is. For a couple of days his picture was on the front pages, the TV, all over the internet – not everyone's forgotten. They'll ask for ID and see my name and make the connection and shoot us. Or I'll say I haven't got any ID and they'll shoot us anyway.

A woman appeared in a doorway – she was wearing a pale blue sari, some silvery detail along the edge of the fabric, and she was so elegant you'd think nothing could touch her. But the moment she let go of the door and stepped into the street you could see she had the staggers. Her bag hit the pavement and vegetables spilled out – a tight white cabbage, peppers the colour of sunlight, five onions shedding translucent skin, all rolling towards the gutter. See, I was paying attention. We all were. Jesus, Caro, there must have been acres of vegetables rotting all over Kent, all over the south of England, and we were craving the stuff. I wondered if she was buying or selling, but I wasn't getting out of the car to ask. I was heading west, ready to take my chance on the road. I figured there'd be food enough if we didn't get knifed picking it. Fresh meat too, walking around on four legs, hens starving in their sheds with no one to let them out.

The van driver wasn't waiting though. I watched him in the mirror, a big man manoeuvring his belly from behind the steering wheel and out on to the road. He must have been mad or desperate – anyone could see those jokers were itching to use their guns.

Remember what cities used to sound like – sirens and diggers, music blaring from car windows, jet engines. All gone. There was nothing to cushion us from the sudden burst of gunfire and screaming.

It woke Simon. One minute he's curled up like a cat, next he's all attention, peering out through the window. He'd seen enough death, God knows, but here was a new twist – the woman on her knees, the loose end of her sari held to the van driver's neck before he'd even stopped twitching. It took me a moment to register that she wasn't trying to save his life – it was too late for that. For her too, it was too late. She was dying of what she'd been dying of already. Remarkable the steadiness of her hand, though, as she printed crimson petals on the wall of the pub. Her legs could hardly hold her. I stopped to watch her stoop and rise five or six times, the delicate touches of silk transforming arterial blood into images of poppies and begonias and drooping pomegranates, and a hint of a red pot as she finally sank towards the pavement. The gunmen were dumbstruck, motionless behind their gas masks. It catches you like that, the blessing, every time.

So I watched. But you can't predict when the urge to live will kick in. Before I'd had time to think, I'd swung the car into a U-turn, skidded up an empty side street, gunfire jabbering behind us, and I was finding a new route to the motorway.

We'd passed the exit for Slough before I realised I was soaked in sweat. The road was abandoned, we had most of a tank of petrol, the Mercedes would take us wherever we wanted. But my heart was racing, panic rising in my chest. A normal reaction, maybe – to the guns, to the murdered driver. But you know when it's hit you. Once you've got the sweats, the rest follows – the staggers, the blessing, the burn, the pit.

Some people think you get it from looking. You watch someone with the blessing, you can't not watch, and the disease enters through the eyes. That's the cunning of it. Cunning bollocks. It's a contagion like any other – it's carried on the air and you breathe it in.

So what is it, then, this strange opening to impulses and talents never guessed at – a consolation? Or a twist of the knife, a glimpse of what we might have been even at the point of death, to make us all mad with grief?

I saw him last night, Caro – Simon, on his way to bed. It wasn't a dream. I think it was last night. I know it was evening because of the way the bathroom window across the landing catches the light from the hills. Abigail held him by the hand, keeping him at a safe distance, though he didn't seem inclined to come any closer. It was nice of her to bring him to see what's left of me – his Uncle Jason. Simon's gaze was curious and sad.

I tried to wave, but he was gone before I'd worked out how to get my arm from under the bedclothes. I tried to smile, but my face doesn't always do what I want it to.

He put me in mind of Penny at that age. Whatever Simon got from his father and whatever the world has done to him since, it was my little sister Penny who gave him that look, like the world's a puzzle and why won't you tell him the answer. And my mind was invaded by thoughts of Penny until I was in a turmoil of anguish and rage. And I made myself think about you instead, which quelled the rage, though not the anguish.

Death's become so ordinary I imagine I'm numb to it. Then it catches up with me and I can hardly breathe for the pain. Caro, Caroline, you were really something. Every day we were together I knew I was in luck. And then the luck ran out – mine, yours, everybody's. I tell myself your death is nothing. Penny's death, the biggest thing in Simon's world – nothing. To weep over you, to tear our hair and rend our clothes in grief – an idolatrous obscenity.

But we do it anyway.

When I sang in the hallway, when I cried to you to come back, it was my soul crying to yours. It was reading to you must have put the idea in my head. Reading's never been my thing, but when you got sick there wasn't much else I could do. For some of the book you were delirious, but I reckoned you'd read it so often that it didn't matter, though it was new to me. So I got to know about Jane Eyre, the orphan who grows up to be a governess, and Rochester who's ready to marry her even though he's secretly married already, and Rivers the preacher who takes her in when she runs away and nearly starves on the moor. And you were awake enough to correct me when I pronounced Rivers' first name as if he was a saint. 'Not *Saint John*,' you said, *Sinj'n*.' I thought you were raving – something about sin or sinning. But you said it again. 'Sinj'n, Sinj'n Rivers.' And then I got it. And I knew I wasn't wasting my time. So I kept on to the end. I read myself hoarse, while the sun came and went. I read until the lines of text buckled in front of my eyes. Then your temperature dropped and strange things began to happen to you and we had a row – the last thing we did, the last words we spoke before the blessing hit. We both knew you were dying and we were yelling at each other about a made-up story. You could hardly stand, but you were swinging punches at me and kicking my shins with your bare feet and screaming in my face and I was screaming back. It was ugly.

And it was my fault. Entirely and utterly. What was it made me so angry? I felt robbed. It wasn't a ghost story – I'd worked that out. Yes, all right, weird things go on in the house – ghostly appearances, eerie laughter in the night, Rochester's bed's set on fire – but there's an explanation for all of it – not the drunk servant Grace Pool as Jane thinks at first, but Rochester's mad wife Bertha locked away upstairs in Grace's care. Not a ghost story, then, and not a fairy tale full of magical events. Not until right at the end, when Jane's miles away across the moor with Sinj'n Rivers, and Rochester calls to her and she hears him. The way I saw it, your Charlotte Bronte had pulled a trick. She'd come up with this pathetic piece of magic to sort everything out. I was furious because I was exhausted and I was furious because there was no magic trick to bring you back.

It was three in the morning, a dead hour in a fucked up world, and I had murder in my heart.

I've seen couples fight over some stupid things – what kind of shower fittings they want, the colour of the bedroom carpet – but, honestly Caroline, this was the stupidest. Wasn't it?

Neither of us could bear that you were dying.

Now it's my turn to die, in this room that we fixed up to be our haven from the world, when there was still a world to return to whenever we liked. It's pretty much the way it was when you were last here. The door could open and you'd step in from your bathroom across the landing and you'd slip into bed beside me. That photo of you is still there in its silver frame, the one with the silver lilies up the side – you on the front at Brighton windblown and grinning. Your books are still on the shelves either side of the chimney breast – paperbacks mainly, holiday reading – and an old laptop of yours on the desk in the corner.

We used to hear the road from up here, faintly, when there was traffic – delivery vans shifting gears towards the rise, labouring engines, whatever noise got through the filter of trees and across the lawn. Enough to tell us the world was still out there. But never so much that a rising wind wouldn't drown it, or a herd of cows passing on the moorland road.

First time I brought you here, I was trying to impress you, showing you all this – look at me, lord of the manor, by which I didn't mean that part of London where I pulled off my property deals, but the real sodding medieval McCoy – and you were impressed, being a wide-eyed middle-class girl from the suburbs. 'Not actually medieval, of course,' you said, peering out of the car. 'Eighteenth century, mainly – though that odd-shaped turret must be earlier.' I drove us under the arch into the stable yard and you were excited all over again by the stables and outhouses. 'Lovely Victorian brickwork,' you said.

All of which I already knew, though I didn't say so. You'd learned this stuff from books, but I knew it with my hands – the soft surfaces of brick and stone, the crumbling texture of lime mortar, the invisible ripples of the laths behind the plaster, light everywhere, and the settled shape of things because it was all going to be here forever.

It was early summer and the sheep from the farm next door had been let loose on the lawn. We could hear them nibbling below the bedroom window. Sometimes in the dark they sound like old men hacking over their ciggies in pub doorways. Then the crows start up. Then cats and foxes and God knows what. Give me a police siren any day, or a domestic at chucking out time. Not that sleep was what we'd come for. 'How about double glazing?' I said, and you said, 'You mean so we can enjoy the peace and quiet of the countryside?' And we both laughed. We had a good time, didn't we, Caro, even though you'd had the best education taxes could buy and I was just an ignorant capitalist.

We were going to have fun fixing this place up. We were going to raise children here. Five at least, I told you. 'You'll get two like everyone else and like it,' you said, but you laughed as if my idea was appealing in a scandalous kind of way. And I wasn't joking. I wanted a riot of kids. I wanted them tumbling through the woods, climbing the trees, chasing each other up the backstairs and down the big oak staircase, ransacking the attic. I'd be rioting with them – helping them build their tree houses, organising go-kart races on the lawn. Now look at me, Caro. I can hardly move. I'm done for. Put to bed in the turret. It took all their strength to get me up here, Maud and Abigail, with me stumbling between them. They'll have to carry me all the way down again when my time's up. Didn't think of that, did they? They forgot I wouldn't be walking, wouldn't be around to dig my own grave.

Agnes

I've sent word that I'm sick. I've waited all morning to be fetched from my bed and made to answer to the Mistress for what I've done. I'm not sick but only in need of sleep. I may be sick if this shaking is a sign of sickness. I'm in need of sleep but cannot sleep. I'm not sick. It's fear that makes me shake, fear that I shall be punished, fear of the Mistress. What if I'm shut out from the Hall for ever and must find other work? What if I'm never to sit in the study again, or ever to see the Book of Air? My biggest fear is that Sarah will not forgive me.

I wait, but still no one comes.

I went last night to the Hall when mother had gone to bed. I waited in the stable yard in the shadow of the outhouse wall, crouching against the damp ivy. After a while the Masons came as I knew they would. They came into the yard with a cart, two riding, two walking, their features blackened and muffled. One of the riders stood up in the cart and tapped the window with a bean stake. The curtain moved and I saw the pale blur of Roland's face behind the glass. Then nothing, except the snorting of the mare and the stirring of branches, until Roland appeared at the kitchen door. He started at the sight of the Masons, but they covered him at once in a black hood and bound his arms. Then they hoisted him up and slung him on the cart like a side of pork, throwing some sacking over him.

If I had turned to the wall and waited for them to go, if I had turned away and they had found me there, I might have suffered only a sharp word. I should have said I was there to save the chickens from the fox. Why not? I might have remembered the chickens scratching in the yard, or the axe left outside to rust in the dew. I might have been restless, called from sleep by the wind, a small slip not worth a flogging. There's no harm in walking out at night for a purpose. When we hear that scroungers have been seen in the village, mother has me stay out with her sometimes to watch the vegetables and beat pans to scare them off.

I didn't turn to the wall. I watched. And when the Masons left I followed.

I know who the Masons are when they are not Masons, as I knew the old women under their veils when they came for me. We all do, though we never say so. Three of these Masons I knew for certain. Peter who sees to the tanning and is as broad as a tree. Tal, fencer and cottage fixer, narrow and clever with his hands. The third, Uncle Morton, Annie's father, who I never see but I feel a shadow fall across my heart, though the worst I know of him is a scowl and an angry word. He grew up fatherless like me, and helped raise my mother who was four years younger, so I should think better of him, but cannot. Morton's limp would show from any distance. It could be black as the pit and you would hear the uneven clop of his feet.

But there was one I didn't know.

They turned out of the yard by the orchard and set off along the moorland road. They made slow progress, and the cart made enough noise creaking over the rutted track that I was able to straggle behind, keeping near the hedge, shadowed by hawthorn and dogwood. I followed to the uplands where the sheep graze. After a while the ground fell away and they reached a river bank where they drew aside into the grass.

A strange island had grown in the middle of the water. It might have been a shed for a single cow but made all of hazel wands and with walls of woven cloth. It twisted in the current and I saw that it was tethered upstream, one rope to each bank, and sat on the water like a boat. Not like a boat in shape, but like the bed the Mistress sleeps in, which is its own room hung with curtains to keep out winter draughts. A bed then such as Jane might have known, only that its frame was not carved and jointed like furniture from the endtime but crudely twined together, and not in an upstairs chamber of the Hall but out here among the summer grazing where no bed should be, bobbing strangely on the flood.

The mare sneezed and lowered her head to eat. The Masons were in the water, with Roland, unhooded now and naked to the sky, riding like a corpse on their shoulders. They were up to their waists before they reached the middle and moved unsteadily, feeling their way. Pulling the curtain back they lay him on the bed and covered him with a quilt. The bed rocked on the water, and upstream the rushes swayed where the ropes cut through. They murmured to him then, songs we use to put babies to sleep, chants to fend off scroungers. They drew the curtain around him and waded back to dry themselves at the cart, leaving Roland to sleep, if sleep was possible. I thought I heard him snoring, but it might have been the water rushing between us. I slept, cold as I was with only the bracken to warm me.

I had a dream of flying and my book that I write in now was on my shoulders. The blank pages fluttered like wings. There was a blaze of cowslips and poppies on the ground and I flew down towards them.

I woke and it was deepest night. A slip of moon showed between clouds. Its light touched the branches of Roland's bed where they were stripped of bark, and came to me over the water.

I closed my eyes and found my dream again. But the book was now a weight that pushed me down towards the meadow, and what had been flowers was a lake of fire. When I was about to fall, I woke with a start and saw a flame above the water and an answering flame below it, and between them the narrow shape of Tal wading from the bank. The flame was the torch he carried, a clutch of branches dipped in tallow. He pushed on towards Roland, steadying himself in the air with his free arm.

I thought it was a mistake when his torch dipped and the corner of the curtain was suddenly alight. I opened my mouth to cry out, to warn Roland, to call Tal by name, though he was black-faced and muffled as a Mason and his name lost to him. But there was a strong hand on my mouth and the warm breath of a stranger at my ear and my body was pressed to the ground with a man's weight. I watched the curtains flare into bright colour, and then the frame itself, a winter tree bursting in an instant into blossom. And the stink was of apple logs burning on a winter fire.

But the smoke hadn't yet reached me from Roland's floating bed. It was the stranger's breath I smelt. Not quite a stranger, then. It was the same stink that lingers on the backstairs, that drifts in the upper passage where the half staircase leads up to the red room and the turret. Sometimes I hear his footsteps. The boards creak and I turn to the wall, because the backstairs are for the Reader to come and go unseen. I have never been in the turret, though I leave food outside the door when I am told and gather empty dishes. This is what I know of the Reader – his quick tread, a glimpse of him in the shadows, the food eaten or not eaten. And the smell, like wood smoke and flowers together.

His name is Brendan. That's what the older villagers call him who knew him before he was the Reader, when there was another Reader. I'm afraid of a flogging, but I'm more afraid of Brendan. He knows what I did. It was dark, but he must have known me. He put his hand over my mouth, and his mouth to my ear, and he pressed me into the bracken.

The bed was a guttering candle before Roland tore through the blackened rags to leap into the water. I heard the grunt as the Reader pulled himself off me, and the sound of his heavy tread in the bracken. The Masons, the three of them I knew as neighbours, waded into the river to pull Roland to the bank. Then they offered him naked to the moon. I saw in that moment, frightened though I was, that the Masons had put him to sleep as an infant, but he had leapt from his burning bed as a man, a man like Rochester who survived the flames when his mad wife set fire to his bed while he slept.

Then the cart was gone, taking Roland with it, and the Masons and the Reader.

Jason

Abigail's here with mashed potato in a bowl, onion and bacon chopped up in it, and an egg custard. It's the first time she's come with food. I knew they'd been cooking. The smell reminded me of hunger. She tells me she put the bacon through the mincer so I wouldn't have to chew it. The old mincer you picked up at a local flea market – worth more now than a warehouse full of hi-tech food processors. When it comes to it I can't eat much, but Abigail's pleased with me. She seems to want me to live. She says we should eat the bacon while we've got it. She found it in the freezer. The electrics came and went for a while, she tells me, then just went. But it's cool in the basement so there's a lot hasn't spoiled yet. She wipes my chin where I've dribbled. Then she wrings out the flannel and puts it cold to my face. I smell the onion on her hands. She has a bosom you could drown in. All wrapped up in a cotton dress buttoned to the neck, but comfortably there. A strong face that you think doesn't do emotion, until you learn to read it. She wears a headscarf, three corners gathered in a knot at the back of her head.

She asks me if the house is really mine and how long I've had it.

'Nine years,' I tell her, and find I can talk. 'I bought it after the o-eight crash. Not because it was a bargain – I would have paid a lot more for it – but because the owner was up to his neck and couldn't say no.'

I don't know why I tell her this. Because it's my story, I suppose, even though every part of it has lost its meaning.

'You really wanted it, then,' she says.

'Always.'

'That's a long time, always.'

She offers me some custard, moving the teaspoon towards me. I open my mouth and it slides cool and sweet on my tongue.

I ask her why they brought me here, to the turret, to the highest bedroom in the house.

'Because you said we must.'

'I did?'

'You kept growling and saying *Up!* In the hall and on every landing. *Up! Up!* She laughs remembering, and covers her mouth, but not before I see how her smile lights up her face.

It was because of you, Caroline, I wanted to be here – in the bedroom you liked best, on its own little landing across from its own bathroom. OK, you said, a houseful of people, friends, visitors, five children, whatever, but at night they'll all be elsewhere, somewhere below us, and this will be our haven, our retreat.

There's a noise like music. I open my eyes and I'm alone. I didn't see Abigail go, so I must have slept. I think it's the radio, but are there are no radios. I sit up, put my feet on the floor and wait for the dizziness to pass. I get myself to the window.

And here's our view. I've dreamt of it, longed to see it, felt I might never see it again. More than our view – our place. Lawn as big as a field. The gravel drive running down towards the road. We used to be careful, remember Caro, turning out of our drive, or crossing on foot into the lane to stroll over the bridge into the village, in case some tanked up yokel chose that moment to put his foot down. What chance of that now? The road's dead. The river has all the life now, obscured by trees but winking where the sunlight catches it.

I look to the right, westward, and there's our orchard skirting the lawn, and beyond that the moorland road cutting back to the north and out of sight. The other way, to the east, the old church stands as it has for centuries in its graveyard on the riverbank among yew trees and willows and the straggling edge of woodland. On our side of the road, the meadow, where I see now there are cows grazing and, just visible from here, the High Wood – our own little piece of ancient forest – and somewhere in among all those trees the fence that marks the eastward edge of what's ours. What's mine. What might be anybody's now, I suppose.

The music comes again. There's a horse-drawn cart passing the church into the sunlight. It moves along the road, flashing between trees, and turns in at our gate. A pole rises from each corner to support a green and yellow awning, which flaps in the wind. I hear the wheels of the cart on the gravel drive. The musician is sitting on the edge, leaning on one of the poles. It's a clarinet he's playing and he sways it about, lifting it for the high wailing notes. A monkey swings from the awning. There are other animals roped to the back of the cart – two horses, a donkey and some goats. The cart is stacked with cardboard boxes. The woman driving has a straggle of blond hair and wears riding boots and jodhpurs. Hard to gauge anyone's height from this angle, but the man waddling behind with the goats looks peculiarly squat.

They pull up fifty yards short of the house. The musician lowers the clarinet and shouts something. I don't catch it at first. Then I do. 'Living or dead?' And he plays another flourish. He's been raising his head, turning from side to side to view the windows. Now he looks towards the front door and raises his arms in what might be a wave. Beside him, the woman drops the reins and raises both hands. 'We mean no harm' she says, 'What's happening here?' Down out of sight, Abigail must be pointing the shotgun.

Living, breathing people. It's good, right? There aren't many of us. I get a sick feeling, even so.

Now they've made contact, the voices are quieter. The woman's talking. She lowers her hands and climbs down. The musician too springs down on to the gravel. What right has he got to be so smiley? Where's he been? Hasn't he heard?

'Peace and joy,' he says.

I've hardly the strength to move from the window, but I move anyway. The thought of dressing defeats me, so I pull the duvet off the bed and wrap myself in it. I shuffle across the landing to the bathroom. The sight of the shower is a stab of grief – the travertine tiles you chose and loved, designed to make modern luxury look like it's stood for centuries softening in the Tuscan sun. I sit on the toilet, shivering under my quilt, my feet cold on the bleached boards, and stare at your paint job. Caroline, the plans you made. You were going to fill the house with colours – posh paints with names like *String* and *Mouse's Back* and – this one – *Rectory Red*. You pulled me in here when you'd given it a second coat. 'Look,' you said, 'I told you. It gives the porcelain such a lift.' You were right too. You were always right. One look at the wall and I've lost it. It's not that you did it well. There are places where the emulsion's bled on to the skirting, and the whole thing needs a third coat. I'd have got someone in, but you couldn't wait. You never could. You were an enthusiast. And now it's the most beautiful paint job in the world. I weep until the wall's a crimson blur.

I feel my bowels convulse. There's fire inside me. Then everything loosens in a shuddering rush. The walls darken and close in. I'm inside myself, contained by my own intestines. When my vision clears and the walls recede, I'm drained and hollowed out. Dazed as though from physical labour, I take a minute to breathe. Then I fold a plump cushion of toilet paper from the roll and, shifting my weight sideways, wipe myself. And more paper, until I'm dry.

I twist round to reach the chrome lever and press it. I feel the spray from the cascade underneath me and hear the steadier hissing as the cistern refills. And only now I remember that it's a long time since I flushed a toilet. No one's had mains water for months. Some miracle has occurred, some intervention by the god of plumbing. Or history has been thrown into reverse. The cities are repopulating. The lights are flickering on across the country and around the world. The internet is waking from its strange dream of paralysis and silence.

The miracle, I realise, is only that up in the attic there's still water in the tank. It could hold enough, maybe, for a few days of normal use, which means that Abigail and Maud haven't turned on a tap since they've been in this house. And I find myself wondering again who they are and where they come from.

I make slow progress down the backstairs. My body is a dead weight lugged from step to step. There's pain in my joints – hips, knees, ankles – left over from the fever. A door bangs below and there are quick footsteps. A figure comes into view. Light from the window catches the dark tangle of hair. It's Simon. He looks up at me, a doubtful frowning look, head tilted, mouth opening and closing like a fish. He says, 'There's…' Then he does that thing with his mouth again. He makes a noise in his throat, sniffs a couple of times and out pops the missing word – 'people'. It's a hard word for him.

'I know, Si. How about that!' And gripping the banister I sit down on the stairs.

Simon doesn't always know whether to breathe in or out when he talks. 'Funny… people.'

'Bust-a-gut funny,' I ask him,' or pack'm-off-to-the-farm funny?'

He tilts his head and his frown deepens.

'Ha ha or peculiar?'

He shrugs.

'You mean they're both?'

'Zackly!' It's one of Penny's words. For an insecure person she expressed a lot of certainty – *exactly, obviously, don't be ridiculous, that's insane.* And it slips effortlessly out of Simon's mouth.

These people, Simon, did they seem nice?'

'The one with the mmm-blowy thing did. He's called… Jangle.'

'Jangle! That's a weird name.'

Simon gurgles with laughter. 'I know.'

I can't remember when I last saw him laugh.

'Uncle Jason?'

'Yes, Simon?'

'Are you all… better?'

'Well I got this far, didn't I?' I pull myself up again, take the last few steps to the turning where he stands. 'Show me these people.'

The low door at the foot of stairs opens, the one that leads to the stables, and Maud comes in with a bucket. There's fruit in it, pears and apples. She stops when she sees me and stands motionless for a moment. Simon signals a greeting, a little wave of the fingers – he's learned already that the effort of speaking would be wasted on Maud. And she signals back and glances up at me again, eyes unblinking, before ducking her head and hurrying on into the kitchen.

Through the open door I hear Abigail's voice, hushed and anxious. 'What is it, Maud?' Then raising her voice she says, 'Is that you, Jason?'

I feel clumsy that I still depend on speech, and clumsy in my physical weakness as I shuffle into the kitchen, pulling the duvet around me.

'You should have called if you needed something.'

I'm looking at the visitors. They're getting to their feet now that I've appeared, and it's not deference to the owner of the house. The woman speaks first. 'Are you sick? You look sick. Doesn't he look sick, Aleksy.' She turns to Abigail. 'Has he had the sweats?' She's a bit bashed about, but striking, even so. God knows what she's been through.

'And the rest,' Abigail says. 'Five days ago at least and he's on the mend.' She looks at me as though there's something she wants me to understand. 'This is Deirdre,' she says. 'Deirdre's on her way to the coast.'

'Five days? Nobody lasts five days.' She's twitchy, this Deirdre. With me in the room, she doesn't want to settle. She takes a long pull on a cigarette. She's a classy smoker, all cheek bones on the in-breath, head angled self-consciously to blow. Between puffs her hand is poised at shoulder height, cigarette aimed at the ceiling. She might be thirty – probably less, given the rate at which we're all aging.

I ask her, 'Why the coast?'

'I thought maybe Ireland. They say Ireland's better.' I hear the accent now – subtle, like posh English softened at the edges.

'How better? Like people don't die in Ireland? Nowhere's better.'

'Five days? Are you sure?' She's talking to Abigail.

'How are you planning to get to Ireland anyway? Do you think the ferry's running?'

'No one lasts five days. Aleksy, tell them.' Aleksy is built like an ox, but short – less than five foot. The monkey sits on his shoulder foraging in his hair.

'I'm here, aren't I?' I say. 'Jesus Christ!' I don't know why I'm so angry. Don't even know what I mean exactly – here in the room while she talks about me? Here alive? Here asserting ownership of my kitchen? All of these.

Aleksy has been working up to saying something, preparing his hands in a judicious gesture, controlling the involuntary movements of his face. 'A new miracle every day. We live in a time of miracles. Five days and still alive? Who can say? A survivor? It's possible.' He settles on a chair, sitting on the edge so that his feet touch the floor.

'You're both well, then?' I ask him.

'Untouched, thank heaven. Who knows why? Polio I had as a child. You work with animals from Africa, they said. Of course you get sick. But they were peasants who said this and knew nothing. That was a long time ago. Fifty years. And then comes the virus – I watch them go down with it, this one and this one, gymnasts and jugglers. Clowns too. All young and full of health. Dead now, their beautiful bodies scattered across Europe, and me still here – no sense to it, no justice.'

The clarinet starts up in the hall, a wild howling like jazz and not like jazz.

Aleksy nods towards the door. 'Django. He don't talk so much. Music is his consolation.'

'A friend from your circus days?'

'All gone. The circus is gone.'

Simon, who has been hovering by Abigail's skirt, slips out through the door in pursuit of the noise.

'We picked Django up on the road,' Deirdre says. 'I stopped for a pee and there he was, sitting on a branch practically over my head, tooting away. Scared me half to death.'

'But a gentle boy,' Aleksy says.

Abigail is pouring water from the pan into the tea pot. 'Maud found tea in the village,' she says, 'and some vegetables still good – potatoes and onions mainly. None of the locals are left. There are more things we could bring. We should wait though, in case anyone comes back.'

'Who'd come back now?' I ask her. 'Where would they come from?'

'You came back.' It's striking the way she says this – more an affirmation than a challenge. 'And Deirdre and Aleksy have come. We don't know who's on the road. All those cottages were home to someone.' The colour rises in her face. It's awkward for her to assert herself in argument.

She's right, up to a point. How can we know who else is out there? We settle into silence. There's everything to talk about, and nothing. Our stories are all different. Our stories are all the same – we watched the others die and here we are.

In the early days of the virus, remember Caro, people couldn't stop talking about it. Then suddenly we couldn't bear any more talk. We'd overloaded on novelty. Words were too thin to bear the weight. People stared blankly at each other. Only their eyes spoke. *Will you hurt me? Have you got something I need?*

'Look, Jason. Deirdre brought these oat cakes.' Abigail shows me the plate of them, fresh from their wrapping and still in their plastic tray. 'She used to have a shop.'

'Local farm produce,' Deirdre says. 'French and Italian cheeses. Pickles, preserves, antipasti. Oils and dressings. Organic wines. I built it up from a pick-your-own operation and a farm shop selling vegetables.' Tears come to her eyes and she wipes them impatiently with the back of her hand.

'All she can load on the cart,' Aleksy says, 'she brings with her.'

'Not that much, Aleksy. The odd jar of this or that.' She smiles pathetically at Abigail as though a lie and a smile would save her neck if Abigail meant to rob her. 'I left in a hurry.'

Abigail blinks, not understanding, not thinking of herself as powerful.

The clarinet stops. There's a murmur of voices on the staircase.

'Deirdre had a stable full of horses, Jason,' Abigail says. 'Isn't that right, Deirdre? And taught children how to ride.'

Deirdre nods tearfully and starts talking about the names of the horses that were stolen on the road, what colours they were – bay or piebald – how many hands. None of which means anything to me. But I know now what Abigail is telling me, why she's interested – she thinks Deirdre's an asset. She's practical, Abigail. She's got this kitchen sorted. There's a stack of logs by the stove, jugs and buckets for water, bowls of vegetables. She's been going through the knives – they're laid out on the draining board, including a lot I don't recognise. Practical, and familiar with this scrappy, sweated existence where nothing's piped or wired or transmitted, where nothing comes to your house that you don't lug in through the door. I can see it's not new to her. But what does she know of people? Deirdre would look good on a horse, I can see that, and maybe she'd know what to do if a horse got sick – I know I wouldn't – but she's too twitchy for my liking. Her hand shakes when she lowers the cigarette to her mouth. She sucks too hungrily on it. What will she be like when her supply runs out? What will she feed on then? The rims of her fingernails are already ragged and bleeding.

Through the window, I watch the chickens scratching in the stable yard.

Aleksy clears his throat. 'You shouldn't wait for the villagers,' he says. 'What is property? The Mercedes on your drive. Very nice car, very smooth, but worth less than one of Deirdre's goats. Time now to reassess, reallocate. Our duty is no longer to the law but to nature.'

Deirdre shrugs, smiling awkwardly at Abigail, as though embarrassed by a precocious child. She sucks on what's left of her cigarette and stubs it out before exhaling.

The monkey, who has climbed down from Aleksy's shoulder, stands on a chair to study the microwave, watching his reflection in the glass.

Aleksy gestures with his head. 'The cows down in the field are yours?'

'We've been milking them,' Abigail tells him, 'as many as we can. They were desperate. We've got more milk than we know what to do with.'

'Of course. So now they're yours. And now you need hooks.' He registers our blank looks. 'For mowing, making hay.'

Abigail says, 'Scythes.'

'Scythes, yes. Too late this year. This year you scavenge. But next summer…' He makes a sweeping gesture, one fist at shoulder height, the other at his waist. 'When the sun shines and while the rain holds off. Another job for you – to search the barns, the sheds. A job for Jason when his strength returns.' He shows me his teeth. 'When the miracle is complete.'

Simon comes in pulling the musician by the hand.

'Hello, hello, everyone.'

So this is Django. He looks at me and I see something – a flicker of recognition – but his eyes move on to Abigail and Maud. He lifts his clarinet. 'Love your staircase. Great acoustics.'

I've changed my mind about Deirdre. Twitching and nail biting are sane responses to the world. Screaming would also make sense, or sitting in stunned silence. Not sane is admiring the acoustics.

Deirdre says, 'Django, this is Jason. A survivor, apparently. Had it five days and getting better.'

Django studies me and I find I'm afraid. He's recognised Simon. He knows who we are. But nothing changes in his expression, and he turns back to Abigail with the same steadiness. He's young – early twenties, younger maybe. He wears a bowler hat, jacket striped like a deckchair, skinny trousers rolled above the ankle, big boots. The country's piled with unworn clothes and Django's looted an Oxfam shop. He's a buffoon. So what is it in his eyes that gets to me? Openness. Benign curiosity. People don't look at people like that, not any more.

I shuffle out into the yard to take a piss. Abigail's inclined to follow but I tell her I'll be all right. I rest against the wall with my legs shaking. Then I make a slow ascent to the turret and stumble into bed.

Abigail's unpacked your copy of *Jane Eyre*, Caro, and left it on the bedside table. The old book falls open near the end, near the part we argued about – Jane rescued from exposure and starvation on the moor, taken in by the saintly St John Rivers and groomed for a missionary life in India. What choice has she got, with Rochester outed as a would-be bigamist? She'll cope with everything St John demands of her, the punishing work, the brutal climate. Everything except marriage. Everything, in other words, except sex with the sanctimonious Rivers – a duty he'll perform as rigorously as any other – no doubt about that. And even this, eventually, she'll agree to if he keeps pushing. Yes, all right then, yes, if that's what you really want. Whatever. And then, at the moment of crisis, this...

I heard a voice somewhere cry 'Jane! Jane! Jane!' Nothing more. 'Oh God! What is it?' I gasped. I might have said 'Where is it?' for it did not seem in the room – nor in the house. It did not come out of the air – nor from the under the earth – nor from overhead. I had heard it – where or whence for ever impossible to know! And it was the voice of a human being – a known, loved, well-remembered voice – that of Edward Fairfax Rochester; and it spoke in pain and woe wildly, eerily, urgently.

I was so angry when I read that first time. Now I'll call out to you, Caroline. And I'll say sorry, sorry for my anger, sorry for everything. And you'll hear me from impossibly far away, from the other side of the virus, from beyond the blessing, from the bottom of a communal grave near Blackfriars Bridge. *Wait for me. Oh, I will come.*

Ridiculous fantasy. Girls' stuff. And all I've got left of you.

Agnes

I meant to burn this book, tear it to light our cottage fire, such danger it has led me to. I meant at least to put it by and write nothing more in it. But my life has taken a new turn, and I feel its pages pulling my story out of me.

After the Reader had caught me spying on Roland, I lay in a fever of fear and agitation. At sunrise, mother looked in at my bedroom door. She said, 'They'll be wanting you at the Hall. The fires won't be lit.' I hadn't slept but that would have been nothing if my spirit had been stronger. 'Tell them I'm sick, mother,' I said. But she looked fearful and shook her head. She doesn't go to the Hall unless she must. 'Then tell Bessie next door,' I said. 'And tell them to let the geese out.' When she'd gone down, I heard words coming in through the window and dreamt soon after that they were speaking about my wrongdoing.

Later I woke to hear someone climbing the stairs and it was Annie. Her hands smelt sour from her milking. She put her hand on my forehead and said I was hot. 'Does your head hurt? Is there aching in your joints?' I thought I might cry, she spoke so kindly, and looked with such sweet concern. I wanted to tell her everything I had done, but there was a deep pain behind my eyes and my throat was sore, so I found it easy to lie back and say nothing.

'I'd take care of you if you'd let me.' I heard her breathing then and felt her milky hand on my face. When she spoke again there was more breath than sound. 'If you told me your troubles, I could maybe tell you mine.'

And I thought, what does she know of troubles? I slept then, and when I woke she was gone.

I hoped Roland might come, but he stayed away. He's a man now, of course, and not so free to come knocking on doors.

It was the Mistress herself who came for me at last. It was early morning and still quite dark. I had stayed home for three days and had slept off my fever. She brought lamb stew and told me that I should eat. She spooned the broth from the stew into my mouth and asked why Janet had not fed me. I might have said Janet has been more of a child than a mother to me since my father died. But I did not want the Mistress to pity me or to think I wanted pity.

She said if I was not too sick I must wash and dress and go with her at once to the Hall. She fed me, I thought, because she would not have me faint under the whip. But why wash for a flogging?

The sun was rising as we left and mother was in the yard. She whimpered at the sight of me, the Mistress gripping my arm, and she turned away to scratch the sow. I would have cried to her but she was as much in need of comfort.

When I was a child I would crawl into her bed to tell a dream but she would hum and stop my mouth. She said that dreams escaped at night from the place of madness and must be locked away again. And those who could not lock away their dreams were to be locked away themselves. And she would look at me with such fear in her eyes that I schooled myself to say nothing of dreams when she was there to listen. I saw that fear in the twist of her shoulders as she turned to the pig.

The air was moist, with a fresh sprinkle of rain. I knew I should be anxious for the grass, which would soon enough be ripe for cutting and in need of sunshine to dry it. But the grass meant nothing to me. Bessie next door was early at her spadework. She nodded at the Mistress and said she thought the sky would clear by noon. She caught my eye with a smile meant just for me as if to say this day would pass just like the rain, which I knew in my head but could not feel in my heart. I caught the laughter of the women fetching water below the bridge and wished it was only water I had to carry.

The Mistress led me in silence through the gateway and up the drive to the Hall. She is old, the Mistress, hunched and narrow, and sour as a cider apple. Already I'm taller than she is.

I could have knocked her to the ground. But I walked meekly behind and knew I would stand as meekly for a beating.

The damp breeze grew stronger, and all across the lawn the grass dipped and straightened. Already the feathery heads reach higher than my knee, with pale pink flowers showing among the green. As I walked up the drive, half a step behind the Mistress, the near growth leaned out heavy with seed to wet my skirt.

She took me under the arch into the stable yard where the geese came to welcome me. The young children who waited to be called to the schoolroom were playing their circle game. 'Sweat to pit, sweat to pit, free daze, you're it.' I would have joined them if I could. If I could be a child again. The children were silent, seeing the Mistress come. The geese followed me, to settle by the kitchen door with their necks twisting together and their soft warm bodies rising and falling like one living thing.

I thought she would make me wait while the village was called and I would be shamed in front of all my neighbours. The cellar door was open as we passed into the kitchen. Perhaps, I thought, if I offered to clean the cellar, gather up all the dust and cobwebs, that would be enough. If I scrubbed the stove. But the Mistress took me to the foot of the stairs. She said I was to go at once to the upper passage, up the half stairs to the turret, and knock on the Reader's door.

There are no windows on the half stairs and only two doors. One leads to the red room, which has been locked and empty for as long as I can think, the other to the Reader's room. In all my years working at the hall, I had never seen inside it. Only the Mistress sweeps his floor and changes his bedding. I leave food outside the door when I am told to and pick up the dishes, and sometimes the food just as I left it except for what the mice have eaten. And I take his piss bottle to the yard and empty it into the barrel for the leather making. Always I am quick up and down the half stairs, careful not to turn my back on either door, afraid that the Reader will come out of one, or something worse than I can name out of the other.

But this time the door was open. I could see a candle and

the Reader's face. I paused on the landing not daring to breathe, dizzy with the scent of apple wood and grass seed. I felt he was watching me and my skin was all spiders at the thought.

When I came in he asked me where I had been and I said, 'Sick, sir, at home.'

He held a pipe to his mouth. It glowed in his fist and he breathed out the smoke. Some of the men smoke leaves this way, but I've never known smoke to smell so sweet. His voice rumbled when he spoke. 'Should I light more candles?'

I said he might let the sun in and save his candles.

He laughed and said he had worked late and sat later, struggling with his thoughts, and had not noticed the dawn. He was out of his chair and across the room to the pull the curtains open. He turned with the sunlight coming in and winked.

So this is the Reader, I thought. All my life he has been somewhere to the side of me like a smudge on the eye. I have caught sight of him in the shadows of the upper passage, turning away to murmur with the Mistress. He has ridden at night, this way or that, sometimes through the village. I have dropped my eyes at his approach. I have thought of him as old. But his face is open and alive.

He winked a second time, and I saw that it was not meant but only a twitch in his face. Otherwise his gaze was steady. 'So you've been sick. Sick from thinking?'

I waited, not sure what I should say.

'From thinking what you've done? Or from thinking what might be done to you?'

I said 'no sir', or 'yes sir', or both of those one after the other.

'What will be done to you, do you suppose?'

'I shall be punished.'

He thought about that and winked and sucked on his pipe. 'You live with your mother Janet?'

'Yes sir.'

'Can I see your cottage from here?' He moved his head to show that I should join him.

I passed his armchair and his desk and his bed, feeling as if a rope tethered me to the door and tightened at my chest. His room was higher even than the rooms on the upper passage, and I could see right across the lawn and over the river to the cottage chimneys. When I pointed to our cottage he stood behind me to see where I was looking. I felt his breath on my neck, and thought of his weight pressed against me in the bracken.

'And you work here at the Hall?'

'I do sir.'

'And study sometimes with Sarah. She talks of you.'

I felt the tears come in my eyes.

He moved so he could see my face. 'What's the matter?'

'Is she angry with me? I know she must be angry. Will she let me study? I'll take a flogging if I can only read the Book of Air.'

'Why would she be angry?'

'Because…' I said and for a moment said nothing else.

He waited for me.

'Because I hid below Roland's window. Because I followed the horse cart.' I found I was slow to name what I had done.

He watched me, and his good eye would have been enough to make me say anything if he had watched a moment longer. But he smiled. 'You hid below Roland's window. Who would flog you for that?'

I didn't know how to answer him.

'Do you love Roland? Do you feel called by him? Is that why you watch by moonlight while he sleeps?'

'No sir.' Though the room was cold, I felt my face burning.

'What do you think of Roland?'

'That he should study harder.'

The Reader made a noise like the noise mother makes when she wakes herself with her snoring. A cloud of smoke rose from his mouth and I saw he was laughing. 'And what does he do when he should be studying?'

'He wanders alone. He sits in the murk, sometimes for hours.' I felt bad telling tales of Roland. I know he's drawn to the murk because of his father. They say his father was seen to sit there all day and all night before he died.

'Roland is disappointing. But what about you?'

I held my breath, waiting to hear what words he had for me. I waited until I was afraid I would faint.

He said nothing but breathed out smoke and let it rise between us. Only when he tilted his head and said 'Well?' did I know that he meant me to answer. 'Tell me what I should think of you.'

I was silent for a moment. Then I knew what I wanted to say. 'You know there are persons of earth and stone and rock who will be found where you left them, like Rochester?'

'Are there?'

'Yes, and there are persons of air who are as hard to hold as Jane. Well I am a person of air.'

He looked at me strangely and I felt it was something I shouldn't have said about myself.

'And Roland?' the Reader said. 'What about Roland?'

I said I didn't know.

'A person of earth or a person of air? Neither I think. So is he like Rochester's mad wife, who set fire to his house and died in the flames?'

I shook my head. I hadn't thought about this.

'Not a person of fire then. He is cold perhaps and goes where he must go.'

I thought of our kissing on the backstairs. 'Not cold,' I said. 'Not cold like Sturgeon Rivers.'

I write the name according to its sound, as we do in the study, because Jane's spelling of it contains a mystery lost to us. And writing it, I imagine Sarah at my shoulder, hear the smiling voice with which she praises good work. But there is nothing to praise in this. Ink and paper misused in remembering events of significance to no one but me, that I said of Roland that he isn't cold, and that the Reader agreed and sucked smoke from his pipe and that I was afraid.

'Not yet like Sturgeon Rivers, no,' he said. 'He's only a

summer brook, a trickle to dip your foot in.' He seemed no longer interested in Roland.

His eyes made me uncomfortable, so I looked away. There were shelves on either side of fireplace filled with strange and beautiful things – glass bottles of different shapes, some with paper covers printed with words and pictures, delicate pottery in bright colours, metal objects intricately formed. He looked at me still, as if I was a thing he'd never seen before, a flower vase dug up in a field for him to put on his shelf.

'Take something,' he said.

I shook my head. What could I take, and what should I do with it? Put it on the cottage mantle for the neighbours to gawp at? Hide it with my father's knife? Then I saw something I wanted. It was a bottle of plastic from the endtime – white but so thin that when I picked it up the light showed through it. I imagined the ink trickling in at the neck to darken it. I turned the stopper to see that it fitted snuggly. Its sides settled under the pressure of my hand. It had no weight. It was perfect.

'This,' I said.

'Take it.'

To stop his looking I named the Book of Windows and asked if I could see it.

He was silent for a moment and I thought he would rebuke me. Then he said, 'If you like,' as if seeing the Book or not seeing it didn't much matter. He led me to the desk where there was a box about the size of the box Tal carries his tools in. Not wooden, like Tal's, but metal shiny as moonlight with a black panel on the front. The Reader rested his pipe on the table, and the panel gave back its flame like a mirror. He put his finger to one corner. There was sharp sound and the front swung open as if pushed from inside, and I saw that the mirror was a pane of glass, dark, smoke stained.

'It's beautiful,' I said and reached a hand to touch it.

'Oh the box. Yes they loved boxes – black, silver, the colours of the night sky. And to put what in? No one knows. Some so thin they close on nothing, on a breath of air flat as paper. And there, saying nothing, are all the letters of the alphabet tightly packed. But always, outside or in, there's a window. But to look at what?'

'Doesn't it say in the book?'

'Somewhere, perhaps.' He pointed through the open door to the object inside. 'There it is.'

It might have been a slab of cheese lying on a plate.

'Tell me, Agnes. What do you know about the Book of Windows?'

'That aside from the Book of Death, about which nothing can be said, it is the deepest of all the books, the most difficult to master. And that only the Reader – '

He waited for me to find the words and the courage to speak them.

'That only you, sir, among the people of the village now living can read it.'

'What else?'

'That it contains the highest wisdom of the endtime, all Jane's knowledge boiled and rendered to its essence. That its pages come loose in the hand like summer pears.'

'You know what everyone knows.'

'I know what the Mistress taught us.'

'And it's true enough for the schoolroom.'

I felt I had disappointed him.

'There are things, Agnes, that the Book of Air can't tell us.' He closed the box with a click, and stood for a moment in silence. Then he looked into my face. 'Tell me, Agnes, do we believe that the endtimers solved the mystery of Calling?'

I could barely answer.

'That they had learned to speak at a distance, to cry out to one another and be heard, to assert a presence, as Jane wrote, independent of the cumbrous body?'

I nodded.

'Jane promises us that knowledge. She teaches us to ache for it.' The words were no more than a rattle in the Reader's throat. 'But she nowhere tells us how it might be done.'

'Sarah says – '

'That we contain Air and are contained by Air?'

'Yes sir.'

'That nothing is or can be in the world that the Book of Air leaves out?'

'Yes.'

'But not this. For this we have to search in other places.'

'In the Book of Windows.'

He looked at the silver box, then at the trees away beyond the lawn. 'Perhaps.'

A simple word. My father would say it if I asked him to carve me a finger doll or take me with him to count the sheep. A shrug. An opening and closing of the lips. A falling note straddling promise and disappointment.

And the Reader said it no less lightly, as if the outcome was nothing to him, while I gaped, breathless and unbalanced.

Because if not in the Book of Windows, where did he mean?

When they brought me back from my outing on the moor, the Reeds told me book learning isn't everything, old women muttering in the shadows who would make a mystery of ringing a chicken's neck if it was all the mystery they had. But for the Reader who has read the books all through to say this filled me with fear, to leave this possibility that the highest knowledge of the endtime was to be searched for elsewhere.

Our conversation was over. I was back in the kitchen with some unwashed dishes in my hand, having drifted like a sleepwalker along the corridor and down the stairs.

Fear, yes, but excitement also. He said 'perhaps' and I don't know what he meant by it.

The fire needed lighting, so I went in the yard to fetch wood. Passing the shaded corner where the woodshed joins the back wall of the house, I thought of the secret the old women showed me after my time on the moor. It was to this place they brought me. It was the dead time of the night, and I was so tired and hungry I could no longer be sure whether I was awake or dreaming. There is an ancient pot, blue and yellow with painted flowers, big enough for a child to hide in. They dragged the pot to one side and uncovered a flagstone browner than the others with shapes and letters on it. They lifted the stone, and it was not a stone but a rusting block of metal. Underneath was a space, four brick walls going down into darkness, the size of the pit we dug last winter for Annie's baby sister. We lay on our bellies on the ground and looked down into the darkness, and I saw our own faces staring back at us. One of the women lowered a lighted candle on a dish until it touched the water where my face had been, and the other dropped sage and flower petals. I lay between them, staring down at the flame until the smoke stung my eyes. There were holes in two of the walls, black circles as big as saucers. I imagined myself the size of a thumb and wondered where those holes would take me.

When I spoke, my voice whispered back at me. 'What is it?'

The Reeds took it in turns to answer, and the echoes were more voices.

'A place of reflection.'

'A place where fire and water meet.'

'The Grace Pool.'

The candle floated to one side and I saw my own face again, not as steady as at first. 'Is it a secret?'

'From men and children, yes.'

'Does Sarah know?'

'Sarah knows book learning but book learning isn't everything.'

'Will I see it again?'

'When you must.'

'When your thoughts rise up in your throat.'

'When you have to speak but are afraid to speak.'

'And will I hear an answer?'

They said nothing, but lifted out the candle, put the cover back, and dragged the pot back into its place.

And there's another secret told. All these secrets inside one great secret. Until someone reads what I write and I am taken in front of the Mistress and all the secrets are out.

The Grace Pool is the proper place for secrets.

So today, with my head full of the Reader and my first sight of the Book of Windows, I stopped with my kindling to see if the pot had been moved. Looking at it, I felt my thoughts rise up in my throat and wondered if I should go back tonight with a candle and sage. Would I have the strength to move the pot and the metal flagstone under it? I was lost in these thoughts and didn't hear the others until Megan spoke.

'We missed you.'

I turned, and they were all there, just come from the house into the yard, Megan and Roland and cousin Annie. I know not to trust Megan's smile and I thought, of all of them, she was the least likely to miss me. With one hand she touched Roland's arm. Not even a hand, just three fingers tapping lightly on his shirt. But I saw then that she would tie a rope round him if she could and drag him after her.

Annie, who has light skin and hair the colour of wheat, looked paler than ever and hollow in the face as though some worry gnawed at her.

'Sarah has been asking after you,' she said. 'I told her you had a fever.'

'Thank you.'

'And you're well now?'

'Much better.'

'You look better,' Roland said, 'and you've been to see the man.'

I knew he meant it as a question, but I didn't know how to answer him. Why the Reader had sent for me was partly a secret between us, that he had caught me spying, and otherwise a mystery to me.

The geese came waddling towards us over the cobbles.

'I've been shutting them up at night,' Annie said, 'and letting them out in the morning, but they're glad to see you back, I think. Look how they come to you.'

It was true, they gathered close about me, treading on my feet and twining their necks over each other.

'They like you best.'

'They do,' Megan said. 'They treat you like a sister. Don't you think they do, Roland?' She poked his arm to get him to respond. 'Don't you think they treat her like a sister? You don't suppose some gander flapped in at her mother's window one night?'

Roland smiled though I could see he tried not to. 'They like Agnes best because she's the kindest of us, and the cleverest.' He looked at me when he said this and then at the ground, and the smile had gone from his face.

I would have said that geese know enough to care more for kindness than for cleverness. But just then Peter came in at the yard end leading the horse and cart with Tal's son Daniel trailing after, and we went our different ways, me towards the kitchen, Megan and Annie to the fields, and Roland to skulk somewhere out of sight. From the kitchen door, I saw Daniel blush when the girls passed him and turn after them to say something, but no sound came except a kind of grunting. He's clever with his hands, Daniel, just like his father, and more than twenty years old, but he can't look one of us girls in the eye, and it's a torment to him to speak, though he talks easily enough to the horses.

I looked again at the blue and yellow pot. The stones around it were green with moss. It might have stood there growing roots since the endtime. Even if I had the strength to move it, would I find the Grace Pool, or nothing but a patch of ground with worms wriggling?

Jason

Sometimes I check out without warning. Time passes and I can't quite put my finger on what I've been doing. I sit in a field to shake a stone from my boot and find myself in an empty cottage sorting through a drawer of kitchen knives. I stoop for the log basket, stand with the water slopping at my feet and see I've lifted a bucket from the spring. I have vivid moments when I reel from the smell of the earth on my spade, the smell of midday warmth on cobwebs and tomato plants gone to seed, or dazzled by moonlight on wet leaves. Other times the world is a blur. Objects lose their edges. Colours wash into one another.

Last night I found myself on my knees staring down into the inspection chamber in the yard. I must have only just dragged the cover off because it was still rocking beside me on the flagstones, and I felt the memory of its weight in my arms and shoulders. That huge Italian pot you liked so much – I'd moved that too. There was nothing to see, but I found myself weeping for the whole intricate system of waste pipes and soil pipes that used to rush our used water through the building's secret cavities to gather here and be funnelled away into the septic tank – all abandoned now to mice and spiders.

And today I'm alerted by the sound of someone else's weeping, and find I'm at the top end of the yard, working in the old outhouse, the one with the broken wall and the rotten roof timbers, sorting bricks, tossing the cleanest into the wheelbarrow in the doorway.

I imagine for a moment that it's you, Caroline, up in the house. You're alive and I'm dead and you're weeping over me.

These bricks are beautiful. The old lime mortar crumbles off them and they're good as new, grained with soft colours and warm in the hand. I'm working on a composting toilet. It's my project and I'm going to do it right, with a ventilator shaft and an insect filter, enough capacity that it won't need digging out all the time, boxes for ash and sawdust – all that, and sweet-scented flowers under a skylight – a palace of a latrine.

I should be working on the house. It's drizzling. I remember now the heavy rain in the night, and the steady dripping somewhere along the top corridor. I took a candle and put a pot down to catch the water, an old pillowcase inside to deaden the splash. Later I put a ladder up to the trapdoor and got as far as poking my head inside, but found I've lost my sense of balance – had to get back to floor level again until the spinning stopped. I need to get up on the roof, though, or the place will rot from the inside.

She hasn't stopped weeping. It's Deirdre. Who else would make so much noise over a bit of grief, an average day's hopelessness?

She's up in her bedroom, wailing at the open window. It's like a drill in my head.

I leave the outhouse, toppling the barrow out of my way, step across the spilled bricks and cross the stable yard to the kitchen door. Aleksy comes in from the fields with a spade over his shoulder. He hurries to catch up with me, his weight barrelling from side to side as he walks. The monkey appears on the roof of the stable and chatters down to meet him. 'Onions must be planted,' Aleksy says. 'Also beets.'

'Good of you to take the time.'

He raises his free arm in an expansive gesture. 'And why not?'

'Because you're on your way to Ireland.'

'Like you said, a pipe dream. You know she was born there. But if Django stays, Deirdre will stay also. She's fallen for Django, which is too bad.'

From somewhere inside comes the sound of the clarinet. The monkey clambers back on to the roof and finds an open window.

'You see. Even Rasputin has fallen for Django.'

'So you plan to stay.'

'With your permission.' He makes a gesture of old world gratitude, which is overtaken by a spasm before I can work out whether the politeness was meant ironically or not.

Deirdre arrives in the kitchen from the hallway as we're coming in through the back door. Her eyes are red and she's chewing on a finger. She isn't smoking, so I assume she's worked through her stash. I expect a revelation, an unmasking. *That Simon* – she'll say – *I've just worked it out, he's the boy who was on the news, I knew I'd seen that face before.* So her words take me by surprise. 'We've had a break-in.'

'What do you mean, a break-in?' I ask her. 'There's no one for miles.'

'We don't know that.'

Abigail's on her knees at the stove, sweeping out the ash. She doesn't stop working.

'And why you say *break*? Break what?' Aleksy's question is just a pointless quibble, but it echoes mine, so we seem to be ganging up on her. 'What's to break? Who now locks doors at night?'

'Everybody.' Deirdre looks at me and at Abigail. 'Don't they?'

Aleksy shrugs. 'Sometimes people must go out to piss.'

'Then they should lock the door afterwards. We could all have our throats cut.'

'And you go at night sometimes down the back stairs and out into the stable to talk to your horses. I hear you telling them secrets about your lovers.'

'No you don't, Aleksy. You're disgusting, making things up like that.'

Abigail rises, tucking some lose strands of hair under her scarf. 'What's missing, Deirdre?'

'My wallet.'

There's silence while we all take this in. Abigail looks at me, puzzled.

Aleksy is the first to speak. 'You wanted to order pizza?'

'I'll help you search for it,' I say. Deirdre irritates me but I'm not joining Aleksy's gang. 'Why don't we start in your bedroom and work from there. It can't have gone far.'

Aleksy's muttering. 'Yes certainly, start in bedroom, end in bedroom. Why should I care? Onions must be planted.'

Abigail looks relieved, glad for my help. She stoops again to her sweeping. They're subtle, these shifts of light across her face, but I begin to find them more eloquent than the gaping and grimacing that most people use to express their feelings.

I lead Deirdre into the hall. Django is kneeling on the floor, breathing into his clarinet. He's made a start on sorting stuff into piles, boots and shoes in one corner, clothing in another. The monkey's in the clothes pile with a pair of trousers on its head. Simon is laying leather belts neatly side by side.

I rest my hand on his head as I pass. 'All right, Si?'

He nods without looking up.

Django raises his head and peers at me through a pair of glasses that make his eyeballs bulge. 'They'll be ready for you, Jase,' he says, 'when the old eyes begin to go.' He takes them off and slides them across the floor to a heap of spectacles by the staircase. Seeing Deirdre, he gets up, head tilted in sympathy. He reaches into the inside pocket of his blazer and pulls out a bunch of wild flowers. Yellow petals spill across the oak boards. 'I picked these for you.'

Deirdre snorts, but takes them and looks pleased.

Abigail has given her the first floor bedroom at the back, overlooking the stable yard, the room with the four-poster bed. There's a heap of bedding. Clothes spill out of bags and suitcases and trail across the floor.

'I left it there,' she says, pointing to the dressing table. Clustered on either side of the mirror are bottles and jars – perfumes, powders, creams. She pushes them around as if to tidy them, and screws a lid on to a jar. 'I try not to use them.' I know what she means – there'll be no more when this lot's gone. She puts Django's daisies down on the chest of drawers and looks around. 'I'm sorry. I know it's a mess.' She starts sobbing again.

'It doesn't matter. Let's try and sort this lot out. It's got to be somewhere. Maybe in a pocket.'

'But I know it was just there, by the mirror.'

'Even so. Think of it like an investigation. That's what my dad used to say if I lost something. Eliminate the suspect from your enquiries – this shelf, or this corner of the room. He liked cop shows – The Bill, Juliet Bravo. Search each place carefully, he used to say, and you won't have to keep coming back.'

I'd forgotten that about him. It takes me by surprise to be reminded of it now. He was calm and orderly in everything he did, my dad, the same way he'd do a job, dusting thoroughly before opening a paint tin, meticulous about washing brushes.

Now I've taken charge, Deirdre doesn't resist. We straighten the bed. Then we start on the clothes, folding them, or putting them on hangers. She's got some classy looking stuff. Linen jackets, silk blouses, bits of flimsy underwear lying on the floor like pressed flowers. A surprising number of useless strappy shoes. There are three pairs of riding boots that look as if they'll keep the weather out, and a couple of waxed jackets.

Deirdre says, 'When did he die, your dad?'

'I don't know – it must be thirty years ago,' and I shrug because it was an ordinary death, after all.

'Oh, you must have been young.' She sits suddenly on the bed. I see the energy go out of her. 'This is pointless. So many more important things to do. The wallet's gone, and what use is it to me anyway?'

'It's unsettling to lose things.'

'Yes, but you lose one thing after another that you thought mattered and you're still alive. And maybe all that matters is water, enough food to keep you from starving, shelter from the cold. But you're not an animal. You cling to something that tells you that you're not, not *only* an animal at least, not yet. We're the lucky ones, that's what Abigail says. We made it through. Through to what, though? To wash at a trough without soap. To grub for vegetables in gardens abandoned by the dead. She guards the tinned food like gold. Keeps it locked in the cellar and hangs the key round her neck. Did you know that? Drink your milk, she tells me, like I'm a child. And I do, though it feels like an assault on my stomach – the richness of it and no substance to fill you up. I'm hungry and bloated all at the same time. Aren't you?'

'Not that hungry. There's something off with my appetite since I was sick.'

'I'm ravenous. I'm constantly ravenous for something. And even the milk is a luxury we won't have for long. We don't even know if the cows will make it through the winter. Have we found them enough hay and silage?'

We sit side by side staring out the window towards the yard and the scrubby hillside.

'And we'll never get milk like it again anyway, whatever happens.'

'Why not?'

'They're milkers, Jason. We're not likely to find a Friesian bull round here. The only bull we've found so far is a Welsh Black. Maybe there's a Hereford somewhere, or a Charolais, but we wouldn't want a Charolais.'

'Why not?'

'Too big. Too many birthing problems. Either way, the next generation's going to be some kind of cross. Better for beef, not so good for milk.'

'Beef sounds good.'

'Yes, and there'll be calves to eat, if the cows are healthy and things go right, and rennet for making cheese. But so much uncertainty. No antibiotics. I've never helped a cow in labour. Have you? And next summer we'll need to make our own hay or they'll all die anyway before we see another spring.'

The jackdaws are gathering on the stable roof.

'At least you've still got your house, Jason. What have I got?'

'You've got my house too. For as long as you want.' I'm surprised to hear myself say this.

I'm back sorting bricks. Maud and Deirdre have brought the cows into the yard for milking. The cats appear, one squeezing under the stable door, another padding, lean and furtive, from the kitchen. Someone will put a saucer down for them, or they'll balance on the rim of a bucket to lap up the cream. No one knows where they came from, what kind of lives they've had. They just moved in, like Deirdre and Django and Aleksy. Soon someone will give them names and they'll be part of the family. It comes to me with a jolt that this isn't so far off what I imagined. A gathering of people – children, friends, whoever shows up. It's what this house was going to be for. Like the Jesus bus of my childhood but with indoor plumbing and no Jesus. It was the one thing they got right on the Jesus bus – that there was more to life than mum and dad and two kids watching TV in a semi.

From the age of fourteen I had an idea of how I wanted my life to be and it started with this house. The first time I saw it, it made some claim on me.

The bus was parked on the side of the road and the grown-ups had sent us out to pick blackberries, five or six of us, straggling along the verge. This was a few years after dad died. Three years, it must have been. I had the saucepan. The girls had plastic bags or held their skirts up. I saw the orchard and thought of blackberry and apple pie. For us lot, food wasn't something that appeared in the fridge by magic. It took effort. Vegetables came out of gardens and allotments. Not ours, obviously, but somebody's. A few quid for mowing someone's lawn meant a pack of sausages or a frozen chicken. Some copper piping pulled off a skip had a price if you knew where to take it. We didn't steal. Stealing was against the Eighth Commandment. Shoplifting was a sin. If you came back with money you hadn't earned there'd be trouble. It never occurred to us to break into someone's house, or try the door of a parked car. But a handful of carrots with the mud still on them? All part of God's bounty. No different from mushrooms found growing in a wood. The Lord was providing and we weren't asking awkward questions. We were townies, travelling on the Jesus bus, in search of the land of Canaan. We knew what derived from man and what derived from nature. Beyond that, subtle distinctions of ownership went over our heads. So the hedge gave us blackberries and, when we scrambled through the hedge, there was a wilderness of apple trees, boughs bending towards us, the sun reaching down through the leaves, and so much fruit we didn't know where to start.

We spread out but Penny stuck with me. She was a clown when she was young – all grins and scabbed knees – and she'd have followed me anywhere, and I should have given her more time, but she was my kid sister and I thought she was a pain.

There was another girl too. Tiffany. She couldn't have been more than five – a chubby thing all bundled up in a bigger kid's jumper. She kept hold of Penny's skirt and set up a whine. 'Wait, Pen, wait.'

Penny was saying, 'We haven't got all day, Tiff,' all bossy, as though we had somewhere to get to.

That's when I saw this house, and people round a table on the lawn. I told the girls to shut it. We'd reached the edge of the orchard. I was reeling. Was it the people that had this effect on me, or the building? Or what the building added to the people – a sense of solidity? I knew about eating outdoors – we did it all the time, as long as it wasn't too cold or tipping down. But this wasn't squatting on a kerbstone or huddled on the steps of the bus. These people had real wooden chairs and a wooden table and reached for sandwiches from a china plate. The front door was wide open and the lawn was just another part of the house, a room with invisible walls.

Penny had started kicking the trunk of a tree as though she could make it rain apples. After each kick she'd hop about clutching her foot and muttering, 'Broody Judas'. She was performing for my benefit, but I couldn't take my eyes off the house – how rooted it was, nature creeping up its stonework, sending tendrils up the drainpipes and along the sills. And I said, 'That's what I want.'

Something in my voice got Penny's attention. 'What Jase, what? What d'you want?'

'That house. I'll have it an' all.'

'You gunna steal it, Jase?'

'I'm gunna buy it, and I'm gunna live in it. Like those people. And have my tea on the lawn.'

Little Tiffany was staring up at me, awestruck. 'Can I come?'

'How do you mean?'

'When you buy it, Jase, and it's yours, can I live in it too, with you and Pen? Can I, Jase? Please?'

The two of them looking at me like that, wide-eyed and earnest, made it seem real, like I'd sworn an oath.

Twenty years it took me.

Agnes

After that first talk with Brendan – he tells me I am to call him Brendan – I took my book at night to the river, upstream beyond the orchard. I meant to throw it in. I thought I would never have the strength to shut my mouth about the book and about Brendan too. To keep silent about this to him, and about him to everyone. It made my head turn and turn like the big staircase in the Hall to think of the lies I must tell. For a while I held the book close and felt my heart thumping against it. Then I swung it behind me, meaning to hurl it into the stream. But at that moment a barn owl shrieked and in my surprise I slipped from the bank into the water. I clung to a handful of cow parsley. When I pulled myself out I was covered in mud and wet to the knees, but the book was unspoiled because I had held it safe above my head. I knew then that I would never destroy it.

I went instead to the Grace Pool. The pot was heavy to move and I was afraid to try. I crept away with my thoughts unspoken. I think there is no such place. I was asleep when I lay down in the courtyard with the Reeds, or it was the herbs they dropped in the candle flame that put the idea in my head.

I should have left the book in the attic. It would have lain there for some other person to find, or until it rotted, and no danger would have come to me. I should have left it with the other treasures. One other thing was of great value and beauty, but I wasn't tempted by it. A black pipe it was, something like the pipes Tal whittles from bamboo shoots to play tunes on, with holes for his fingers, but longer, as long as my arm, and the holes covered with little rings of metal. Some of them moved as I touched, so I was afraid I had broken them. I blew in at the end, but heard only the rush of my own breath. There were

55

other things too. There was a small leather case not much bigger than my hand neatly packed with little tiles of plastic, each a different colour, with words and strange designs. I've seen more like these since in the turret, laid out on the shelves beside Brendan's fireplace. But I left the leather case and the pipe where I found them. Only the book I brought away with me.

How did they make their paper so smooth and pale, with nothing to snag the nib and suck the ink into puddles, and so much of it, sheet after sheet, each one perfect? Sarah has taught us how to scrape the inner bark from willows and mulberries and dry the long threads from hemp stems, grinding them in the pestle with rushes and leaves of iris. We boil rabbit skins for gum. Stirring all this together in clean spring water, we move our hands and wrists this way and that to catch it evenly in the sieve. We press and roll the pulp and let it dry. And so we make paper. All her life Sarah has done this and knows its secrets as well as anyone in the village. And still how calloused our pages are. Our neatest letters send out tendrils, growing bigger than we meant them.

I would write in this book only for the pleasure of making letters.

The day after our first talk, Brendan sent for me to come from the yard where I was feeding the peelings to the geese. And the next day, from the study. He sent the Mistress, who looked over her glasses at me, and spoke as if I was a child caught sniggering in the schoolroom. The other girls looked at me then, Megan breaking into smiles that were less innocent than they looked, Annie pale and anxious. Roland stared at his hands, thinking perhaps that he was the one who should be sent for, not me. Sarah let go of the page she'd been reading and looked hard into my face as if it would tell her why I was wanted where I had never been wanted before. And the next day another message. And each time I climbed to the turret. Sometimes Brendan had a question, about Roland, or about my mother or about how things went on in the village. Sometimes he wanted nothing but to be brought some nettle tea or a piece of bread. Sometimes he'd have me sit by him and talk about

Jane, which I always love to do.

One time, as I came down the big oak staircase, trailing my fingers along the handrail, I found Annie sitting at the turn, hugging the shadows.

She said, 'Is he kind to you, Agnes?'

'Kind? Why shouldn't he be kind?'

'Is he though?'

I shrugged. 'He's kind enough.'

She got up on her knees then and gripped my hand until it hurt. 'They're not to be trusted.'

'Who do you mean?'

'Men. They can't help themselves.'

I laughed, but only because I felt awkward hearing her say such things. 'We only talk, Annie.' I sunk down on my knees beside her. 'We sit and talk. He asks me about mother sometimes, and about the Book of Air. We talk about calling and how Jane could have heard Rochester from so far away, a day's journey at least.'

'Isn't Sarah's teaching enough for you?'

I laughed again, because she looked so earnest. 'Annie,' I said, 'we only talk.' I left her there at the turning of the stairs.

Another day I was sweeping the upper passage and reached the half stairs and there were his boots on the narrow landing and I looked up and there was all of him. And his whole face was a question so deep you'd need a bucket with a long rope to fetch up an answer.

'You're here,' he said.

'Yes sir.'

'Before I sent for you.'

'This is my day to sweep upstairs.'

His strong eye settled on my face. 'So you didn't hear me call?'

'Did you call?'

He peered at me and his weak eye began its dance. 'Surely, Agnes, a cry vibrated on your startled ear, in your quaking heart, through your spirit?' He was saying Jane's words, but making them his own.

'No sir.'

He smiled and I wondered if he was teasing me. It made me uncomfortable to hear words from the Book of Air so lightly spoken.

That evening as I walked home from the Hall I saw someone standing at the foot of the drive. The gatepost is half buried in ivy and clematis and overhung with oak branches, so I wasn't sure it was Roland until he reached out towards me and pulled me into the darkness.

He said, 'What does he want with you?'

'Nothing. Just to ask me things.'

'And you do what he asks?'

'I mean questions. He asks me questions.'

'All that time alone, reading and thinking, all that time to study the Book of Windows, and he has to send for Agnes to answer his questions?'

'Only to have someone to talk to. He knows so much more than me. He knows more than anyone.'

'Does he though?' The words were little more than breath against my ear. 'Does he know this?' Roland kissed me then, and the feel of his lips and his boyish smell were so familiar, and the shape of him so comfortable against me, that I forgot for a moment that we are no longer children to romp in the Hall and snuggle in corners. I would have stayed longer, cushioned in ivy with his mouth against mine if his hands hadn't gone to work. If they hadn't known so exactly where I ached. How unfair it seemed to be divided against myself, and Roland risking so little and me so much. I squirmed away from him, catching my skirt and headscarf in branches of blackthorn.

He turned his back and kicked at the undergrowth. 'I don't know why you're so unkind.'

'You know why,' I said, pulling the thorny strands from my hair.

'I know. Brendan has turned your head and made you think you're too good for the rest of us.'

I looked at him where he stood, proud and angry, hugging

himself because I wouldn't. And I thought, I shall go home and cook supper and write about this is in my book, just as it happened. And I thought, how strange to be here in this exact moment of my life with this boy who likes me, and to be thinking how to hold it in words for no one to read. As if I had taken a step back from this moment to see how it looked, or as if I had wandered outside of myself and had lost my way.

Roland had taken something from his pocket and was fiddling with it.

I asked, 'What is it?' I was sorry to be fighting. We'd always been such friends.

He shrugged. 'Just something I found at the Hall.'

'Let me see.' It was a machine something like scissors, the two arms hinged like the handles of scissors. They didn't cross over, though, and become blades, but met in a tangle of notched wheels, all rusted now.

'What was it for?'

'They had metal tins with sealed lids. They used this to cut the lids off.'

'How do you know?'

'I've found some of the tins. You can see where they've been cut.'

'And how did they put the lids back?'

He looked up at me with amusement, as if I'd asked a stupid question and he was glad of it. 'They didn't.'

He took the thing from my hand and walked off into the orchard, and I went home to mother and the pig.

And so the days passed. Roland didn't visit. We passed on the staircase or in the stable yard. But he kept away from the kitchen. The rain held off and I helped with the haymaking, following behind the men as they swung their mowing hooks, to gather the grass. I chopped wood for the fire, fetched water, worked in the kitchen. When I could, I crossed the hallway to the study and listened to Sarah's teaching and wrote the texts, with the sweet smell of the mown hay coming in at the window. But in every word spoken to me I heard a question. I had become a mystery. I saw Megan grow more giggly with

Roland. Annie would come in looking heavy and sullen and say nothing, or come late, or look ill and ask to leave early. Then she stopped home and it was just the three of us. I thought Annie stayed away because she had no one to talk to.

Then a day came when all the villagers were called to the lawn and the Mistress told us that Annie was going to have a child. I blushed to hear this. I was ashamed for her at first, and then for myself. I thought of all the times she had offered to confide in me and I'd thought only of my own trouble.

The Reeds brought her out from the Hall and pushed her to her knees. Ada, who is as thin as a stick, was one of them. The other I didn't recognise until she set about cutting Annie's hair. Then I saw it was Miriam, who makes ewe's cheese and is clever with orphan lambs. She touched Annie gently and we could all see she was sorry for what must be done. She had made a start when Annie tipped forward without a word and was sick into the grass. Miriam waited until the retching stopped, then lifted Annie upright and went on with her cropping, while the Mistress told us that it would be worse for Annie because she would not say who the man was.

'And why must this girl be punished?'

We all knew to be silent until the Mistress answered her own question.

'Because we are not cattle and we are not scroungers and we are not vermin, but people of the village. And by the fire that got me I will have you live as though Jane our first Governess listened at every door and watched at every keyhole.'

Meanwhile Miriam worked on until there was nothing left to hide Annie's skull but a ragged stubble.

I wanted to speak. I burned inside to say this was wrong, that a man had hurt Annie and we must repay her by hurting her again. But the words twisted themselves into a knot in my throat until they made no sense. I glanced at my mother, who stood beside me, but there was a dead look on her face as though she had taken her thoughts elsewhere.

We stood among the racks where the hay was drying, vetch

and meadowsweet and grasses of all kinds, yellowing in the sun, while Annie was caned. The Mistress struck her on the hands, so as not to harm the baby, and not as hard as she might have done I thought, but hard enough even so. I looked at Sarah. She was pale, whether with anger or fear I couldn't tell. I was thinking, what would they do to me if they found my book? I shivered and went hot and felt my insides turn to water. Below by the river a cow was calling to its calf, and I thought how simple to be fed hay and be milked and to have no choices, and I wished there was more noise, enough to drown Annie's cries. Above me something moved quicker than I could follow. A house martin, I thought, swooping from the eaves. When I looked again I caught a movement of a curtain high under the gable. I felt something like shame to know that Brendan was watching, but for what reason I can't say.

When the caning was done, the Mistress said, 'Because she has no man to speak for her, Annie will stay with us at the Hall for a time.'

Annie had sunk to her knees and was hunched over, with one hand on the ground and one on her belly. She looked about to see what this meant. I thought at first it was kind of the Mistress to offer Annie a room, but the whisper among villagers spread a different understanding of her words. I saw the fear grow in Annie's eyes and felt it rising up inside me, crushing the breath and lifting the hairs on my scalp. Annie wasn't to live like Roland, lounging at his window above the stable yard, or like Sarah, looking out at bedtime to see the gathered hay pale in the moonlight. She was to be locked in the red room.

'If she's good and quiet,' the Mistress said, 'we shall keep her only until the baby quickens, and then back home she'll go, if Morton will take her.'

We all looked at Uncle Morton then. I could see nothing in his face but a sort of impatience to be elsewhere – in his field, perhaps, picking raspberries, not having his time wasted. I think he never learned to be a father, losing his own father so young. While we waited to hear what he might say, there was a disturbance behind me and Daniel pushed between mother and me to stand in the circle. His mouth opened but no words came. Then he said, 'I'll...' but nothing more, while he sniffed and made that grunting noise that always means he's got a word stuck in his throat.

On the other side of the circle, Tal took a step forward as though he meant to rebuke his son, but the neighbour who stood next to him put a hand on his arm, and he said nothing.

Daniel's words came out at last in a splutter. 'I'll... speak for Annie if she'll let me.'

There was a commotion and then silence, while we waited to hear what the Mistress would say. Annie fixed her eyes on the ground. The Mistress gave Daniel a sharp look. 'You're saying you'll take her?'

Daniel sniffed twice and said, 'Yes.'

'Tomorrow then. In the afternoon, before milking.'

And it was decided.

Next day, when the time came, Daniel looked dazed with excitement. Like all the women, I had woven ragweed in my hair. At first it didn't feel like a wedding day, there had been so little time to look forward to it. When the men tied Daniel's blindfold and pushed him into the circle to search for Annie, he played his part well, but Annie shrank from so much attention and could hardly move to avoid his arms. We helped her of course, the women, pushing her this way and that, until at last we allowed her to be caught, but it was a troubled kind of joy I felt, seeing Annie without a hair on her head long enough to tie a ribbon. She led him still blindfolded to where the Mistress waited. And they were brought face to face in view of the Hall with the sun sinking pale and watery above the orchard.

And so they were married. When Annie loosened Daniel's blindfold there was such joy in his eyes and he held her with such pride that her own face lit up with pleasure. We all crowded round to hug and kiss her and she wept to find herself so loved, and I wept too. Even the Mistress took her in her arms and whispered some words, perhaps of consolation, and all her shame was washed away. Only Morton seemed unmoved.

Then Daniel led her down across the lawn to the gateway, and across the road and over the bridge to his mother's cottage and their bridal bed. And we were left to dance, and those too old to dance to cheer themselves with gin. We danced long and wild because it was a day no one would stop us, and Tal played his pipe and Peter beat time on a cow skin drum.

Mother sat for a while to watch. If she ever danced in her life I never saw it. Now any labour hurts her back. Standing hurts her too, and stooping, and sitting too long in one place. Bessie talked to her and I saw her smile and was glad. Then Sarah sat by her and took her hand. Roland and Megan went and sat in the shade of a beech tree and seemed very fascinated with each other, so I danced until the trees and the sky ran all together. When I paused to let my head stop turning, I looked for them but they were gone. I went to the spring, splashed water on my face and on my neck and stood while it ran down my back.

Sarah came and knelt beside me to drink. 'You're often alone,' she said.

'Yes, I suppose I am.'

'Because you want to be?'

'Sometimes.'

'Roland and Megan were here, but I don't see them now. Why don't you find them?'

'I'm not sure they want to be found.'

'All the more reason.' She stood wiping the water from her lips with the back of her hand, and then gathering with her fingers the drips on her chin. She saw my confusion. 'For their sake, I mean,' she said. 'Because they're your friends.'

'Are they?'

'Yes. And it would be an act of friendship not to leave them too long alone together. You see what happened to your cousin.'

'Annie was a different case. Roland and Megan can marry if they want.'

Sarah looked at me closely. 'And you? Is it what you want?'

I found I was in a state of agitation, to be asked this question, and to have Sarah ask it. For a while we stood saying nothing, watching the villagers on the lawn. Then Sarah spoke again.

'There are things I should have said to you, Agnes, and I've stopped myself.'

'What things?'

'The Reader…'

'What about the Reader? He sends for me and I go. We talk. That's all. Could I refuse him?'

'Refuse to talk? No.'

'What then?'

She hesitated. 'You know why the man must be led blindfolded to the woman in marriage.'

'Because Rochester was blinded in the fire but Jane married him anyway.'

'Yes, and why else? What did Jane mean by telling us that?'

'That men are made to look about for danger and to see what time is best for planting and for gathering the crops, but in matters of love...' I stopped, not wanting to talk about love.

'In matters of love, Agnes, their eyes will mislead them.'

'But Brendan….'

'…is a man like other men.'

'He asks me questions. We talk about the books.'

'Well then. No harm can come of that.' I could tell she didn't mean it. She looked again at the dancers, squinting her eyes against the sun. Then she said, 'Except that while you talk with Brendan your friends are forgotten.'

'I'm here now though, aren't I? And where's Roland?'

'Yes, where?'

'With Megan, not wanting to be found. And I must see to the geese and shut the hens up or the fox will get them.'

'But first you must find your friends.'

They were the first hard words that had ever passed between us, and I felt very sorry for myself as I walked away from the spring.

I heard Megan laughing as I came close to the stables, not like someone opening her mouth to laugh at a joke, but with a noise in her throat like bubbles rising. I pushed the door open and walked in across the straw, shocked by the sudden darkness and warm stink of horses. There was a murmur of voices and a rustling of straw or clothing. A horse stirred and snorted. I said Megan's name because it was her voice I'd heard.

There was a sigh and she rose up from one of the stalls. As my eyes became accustomed to the gloom, I saw she was tying her scarf behind her head, and I saw Roland stand up beside her.

'Megan, Sarah wants you,' I said.

'I bet she doesn't, though.'

'She sent me to fetch you. She was drinking at the spring.'

Megan peered at my face to see if I was lying, or to show she didn't care whether I was lying or not. Then she walked past me, brushing straw from her skirt, and out into the yard.

Roland said, 'Did you miss me at the dancing?'

I didn't answer but turned to stroke the horse that had put its head towards me. It was Gideon, who is strong but always gentle.

Roland came close and patted Gideon's neck. He said, 'Do you think it was a scrounger was to blame for Annie's baby, like they say?'

'Is that what they say? How horrible.'

'Horrible that they say it, or that she did it?'

'Do you think it's true then?'

'I think the scroungers must be worked off their feet doing all the wicked things they're blamed for.'

'So you think it was a villager and she wouldn't say?'

'I wonder sometimes if the scroungers even exist.' I thought he was joking, though he sounded solemn when he said it, but he had rested his head against Gideon's mane so I couldn't tell. Then he burst out laughing to see me so confused, and walked away into the yard.

I felt that Brendan was there in the stable before I saw him. He was standing behind me, in the low doorway from the house. He asked if we had all enjoyed ourselves. I thought he must have heard Megan giggling with Roland, or Roland laughing about the scroungers, but saw that it was Annie's wedding day he meant.

65

'Not much,' I said.

He watched me with his good eye and asked if I was angry.

I shrugged. I might have said no, but found I had enough anger to choke me.

'Have I offended you, Agnes?'

'You watched,' I said.

'Shouldn't I watch?'

'You watched Annie's flogging from your window.'

'You watched too,' he said, 'and you were closer. I saw you there with the others.'

I couldn't explain my anger. Why was my watching different from his? So I shut my mouth and scraped at the straw with my foot.

'Come tomorrow night,' he said.

'Come where?'

'To the Hall. I mean you no harm. Come after dark.'

'I don't come to the Hall after dark.'

He looked at me, his weak eye flickering, and I could tell he was thinking of the time I waited under Roland's window. I had never been punished for spying and he was thinking of that too perhaps. He meant me no harm, but he could do me harm if he wanted. 'You're right,' he said. 'It would be safer to meet away from the Hall and the village. Meet me in the ruin. Tell no one.'

'I must tell my mother.'

'Tell Janet there is work for you at the Hall and you will sleep here for two nights. Dress for a long ride. She knows to say nothing.'

And it was just as Brendan had promised. Janet heard my story and maybe she believed it and maybe she knew it was a lie. She kept her mouth shut anyway, though her face clouded over, and she turned away to stir the soup.

I must go now to the ruin. It's time. But I am afraid to go. The ruin is a place of danger. Even in daylight I would be afraid. It stands on the margin of the village and the forest. It belongs neither to us nor to the scroungers. People say it was once as grand as the Hall and more beautiful, with windows as colourful as a summer meadow and huge bells that rang all across the valley. The bells are still there, they say, half buried in the ground and overgrown with brambles. This was where the Monk lived.

Everyone knows the story of Maud and the Monk but I don't know if it's true.

At the full moon, the Monk would ring the bells and Maud would slip from the Hall at night to meet him and they would dance. But one night she was seen running across the lawn, and next time the bells rang she was locked in the red room. For three nights the bells rang, but Maud didn't come. And on the fourth night the Monk tore out his own heart and ran away into the forest. Over the years he withered and grew a tail like a rat. And he lives still in the forest, swinging by his tail through the shadows. And they say that if you stand in the ruin when the moon is full, you'll hear the jangle of the bells.

I'm afraid I'll go to the ruin and Brendan won't be there. More than ever I feel in need of my father. My heart cries out to him, but he is beyond hearing.

Jason

Someone's calling my name. I wake up and don't know where I am. Then the grey shapes settle around me and I'm in my bed in the turret.

I dreamt I had a child. I'd lost her and she was crying to me, crying from across the sea. I was on a ship trying to reach her. The deck tipped up and I was hanging above the water.

'Jason, are you awake?'

There's someone standing in the doorway. It's Deirdre. The others are in other rooms, asleep or doing whatever they do at night. Outside the wind howls and the rain is driven against the glass. Everything else is gone and this is what's left.

Deirdre carries a lighted candle in one hand, two wine glasses in the other. There's something insubstantial about her, some softening at the edges that makes me think she isn't really there. But it's the candle flame dipping and straightening that sets everything in motion, and a draught rippling the fabric of her dressing gown.

She says, 'I wanted to thank you for helping me earlier.'

'We didn't find the wallet.'

'But you made me feel better about losing it.'

She steps into the room, shutting the door behind her with her naked foot. So light you'd think the air would lift her. She's got a bottle under her arm. 'I've always hated losing things.' She leaves the thought hanging and walks unsteadily to the window. 'You sleep with the curtains open?'

'I like to see the sky.'

'And when you're not in bed?'

'Everything else – the orchard, the cottage roofs among the trees.'

'You don't mind being watched?'

'This high up?'

'They'll see your candle.'

'Who? Who are you talking about?'

'We've no idea who's out there.'

'In this weather?'

'Beggars and scavengers – half-wild already before everything crashed, before the lights went out. Ready to take whatever we've got.'

'What if there are good things happening? People better equipped than us, with generators and access to petrol, getting things organised.'

'You're a hopeless optimist.'

The rain comes on heavier. I hear it rattling the slates, washing into the gutters. It's filling the downpipes and slopping from the hopper heads. I've got to get up on a ladder and clear the leaves out, see where the slates have slipped. I know what water can do. It's somewhere in the attic already, trickling along the undersides of the rafters, collecting in pools between the joists. A ticking clock.

Deirdre has filled two glasses with red wine. She sits on the bed to hand me one. The candle flickers on the bedside table, catching a draft from the window.

'I'm sorry for waking you.'

'I was dreaming of the sea.'

'It's because of the storm. I can't sleep. Doesn't it excite you? Drink with me.'

'Why?'

'So I don't have to drink by myself.'

'Is that what you've been doing?'

She shrugs. 'I found the bottle in one of my bags. One thing at least Abigail hasn't got her claws into.'

I sit up and take the glass. Her face softens. She clinks my glass with her own, and winces as they collide more noisily than she intended. She pulls out a handkerchief and dabs at the bedding.

'Sorry. Sorry. Poor sheet.'

'It's not important.'

'Poor glasses.'

'They look all right.'

'This time. But for how long? And nowhere to buy more of them.' She reaches out to draw my hair back from my face. 'How are we going to cope?'

'With plastic and cracked mugs, I suppose, and plenty of booze.'

'From where?' Her hand is rough and scented with wood smoke.

'We'll make our own. We'll grow hops or cider apples. We'll use potatoes and set up a still. We'll find ways of getting drunk. People always have.'

'When did you last have a haircut?'

'Can't remember.'

'I'll give you one tomorrow if you like.'

'Tomorrow I'm finding the leak.'

'You said it made you dizzy, going up the ladder.'

'Yes, but I'll get over it.'

She lifts my left hand towards the light. 'Do you always wear this?' She's looking at my wedding ring.

'I take it off to work. My fingers swelled up when I was sick and I thought it was stuck for good. Now it's so loose I'm afraid of losing it.'

She turns it on my finger. 'Is it just the light or is there a thread of silver in it?'

'It's white gold.'

'Just round the edge, like a wave. You'd hardly notice.'

'My wife chose it.'

'You've got blisters.' She winces as she touches them.

'I'm not used to digging.'

There's a flash of lightning. Deirdre pulls back, startled, looking out at the sky. We're both waiting for the rumble of thunder. When it comes, she says, 'Are you hungry?'

'No.'

'Neither am I really. We'll get so bored of eating the same

things we'll forget to eat.'

There's more lightning and we wait again for the thunder.

'The thing about the wallet... I know you all thought I was making a ridiculous fuss. And you were right. What is it all – credit cards, business cards, club cards, loyalty cards – worth nothing now. Driving licence, gym pass, lovely crisp twenties from the cash machine. And what's it for?' She blows her nose into her handkerchief. 'Maybe it was Aleksy, now I think about it. He's obsessed by me. It's his room we should have searched, not mine.'

'How long have you known Aleksy?'

'A couple of weeks. Which makes him my oldest friend.' She shivers. Do you mind if I close the curtain? There's a draught from the window.'

'If you like.'

'Or I could get in beside you. It's a big enough bed. And we could watch the sky together.'

'Are you sure that's a good idea?'

'How English you are.' Her smile wavers in the candlelight. 'I saw the way you were looking at me before. In my room. How you touched my things, folded my underwear. You have good hands, in spite of the blisters.'

'I didn't like to see them on the floor.'

'I bet you wouldn't mind seeing them on me though.' She stands up from the bed and turns, pulling her dressing gown open. 'What do you think?' She poses in the candlelight, head turned, decorated in nylon, satin, lace – playful and embarrassed, enjoying her embarrassment, enjoying mine.

I say, 'Tell me about Aleksy. How did you meet?'

'You're jealous of Aleksy?'

'Should I be?'

Her face hardens and she covers herself. 'Ah, I get it. You're *deferring* to Aleksy. You feel you should get his approval, maybe. Well when you two have worked something out, be sure to let me know.'

'Where did that come from?'

'How about if you wrestle for me. I get a ringside seat and the winner throws me over his shoulder.'

'Christ, Deirdre, that's not what I meant.'

'I met him on the road, all right! He helped me pull the cart out of a ditch. It was his fault, because his car backfired and startled the horse. A couple of miles later, there he was again – he'd run out of petrol. I gave him a lift. We're not married. I'm not his *woman*. I'm not anybody's. When did the rules change?' She starts to cry – deep wrenching sobs.

I reach out to her and she slumps beside me on the bed.

'It's OK.' I'm holding her, stroking her hair and she's clinging to my neck.

'You shouldn't drink if you're sick.'

'I'm not sick.'

'I heard you earlier. After dinner. I heard you outside, out in the rain, throwing up. Afterwards you sat by the fire. Your hair was wet.'

'Too much garlic.'

'Really? I didn't notice. Abigail does her best with what she's got.'

'Yes, but she's a salt and pepper kind of cook. Now she's hiding the salt and using garlic instead.'

'While stocks last.'

'It grows wild in the woods. It's the salt that's irreplaceable. And the pepper. And sugar, chocolate, coffee, olives, oysters, crisp dry Muscadet…'

'Don't.'

'Everything's ending.' She mumbles this at my chest. I feel her breath against me. 'You can have me if you want, Jason. I mean obviously. That's why I'm here.'

The wind rattles the window.

'Or am I too pale for you, too white?' She giggles nervously. 'I could never get a tan. Five minutes of sun and I come out in freckles. I used to slap it on. Lovely brown legs out of a bottle. But you won't notice in the candlelight. We're all beautiful by candlelight. Pain and sweat and struggle and hunger, that's our life from now on, and more beauty than we can bear.'

'Your legs are fine.'

'Because I'm probably not your type. I suspect you have a thing for exotic women.'

I lift her head away from me and look into her face. Green eyes, she's got, and ash blonde hair, dark at the roots. 'How drunk *are* you?'

'One glass, that's all. Maybe two. I meant because of the boy, because of Simon. Not that you can afford to be picky – given the way things are, I mean.'

'He said something? Because you probably didn't understand him.'

'Yes, not much of a talker is he.'

'He's a good boy.'

'Who said he isn't?' Deirdre shrugs, drinks from her wine glass, looks out at the driving rain. 'So what was she like?'

'Who?'

'Simon's mother. West Indian, was she? Afro-something-or-other? Gorgeous anyway, judging by his looks, which, no offence, he didn't get from you.'

'I don't think you've been paying attention.'

'Oh I've been paying attention all right.' She moves closer, and her words are warm against my face. 'But my own tastes are not angelic. In either sense.'

'How do you mean?'

'You'll get the idea.'

'Aren't you afraid?'

'Probably. I'm afraid most of the time.'

'Simon's not mine, you know.'

'Adopted?'

'I'm his uncle.'

'His uncle? Wow. Of course. Who's left but orphans, widows, mothers of dead children?'

'I assumed Abigail had filled you in.'

'Let's not talk about Abigail.' Her mouth tastes of wine. Her hands are behind her, busy adjusting and unclipping.

Then they're in my hair and on my chest. She makes a noise in her throat. I'm assaulted by loneliness. It doesn't stop me, but it's there anyway, holding my mind separate from my body. Sorry, Caro. Sorry for you, dead and gone, bulldozed into the ground. Sorry for me, doing this, like everything else now, alone. Sorry, but there's comfort in the contact, and my heart settles to it. It was racing back there with all that talk of Simon, and Simon's parentage. But it's all right. Deirdre doesn't know. So Django doesn't know, and what I see in his eyes is just his way of looking.

'Ow, ow. It's OK. Don't stop. Ow.'

'Sorry. I hurt you.'

'They're just a bit sore.'

I draw back and raise my head to find her eyes. I heard her in the garden throwing up, and I know it wasn't the garlic. 'Are you pregnant?' The question feels arbitrary, the way it comes to me. I expect her to laugh, and she tries to, but her expression is evasive and gives me the answer. Even by candlelight I see the flush of colour on her neck. She settles on a defiant stare.

'So that's what this is about.'

'What? You think I need a man to take care of me?'

'Don't you?'

'You know nothing about me – what I'm capable of. Just because my moods are on the surface you think I must be feeble. But I can take care of myself. I managed fine before I got here.'

'I don't doubt it.'

She climbs off the bed, wrapping herself up, and stands at the window. 'It wasn't easy on the road, you know, with the cart, and the goats to slow me down. There were times when I was pretty much a sitting target. And don't think I couldn't have just chucked some food in the Land Rover instead, don't think I wasn't tempted.'

'You had petrol?'

'Almost a full tank.'

'So why didn't you?'

'Because getting to safety is nothing if you've got no way to live. Fat lot of use your car's going to be.'

'So you made the right choice. Congratulations.'

'You make it sounds so easy. You haven't a clue.'

'About what? I know what's been going on. I've dug my share of graves. I know what it's like to survive on what you can steal, what you can fight for. Tell me what I'm missing, Deirdre.'

I think at first she isn't going to answer. When she does, her voice is almost drowned by the storm. 'So these two men stopped me on the road. They wanted to know what I was carrying on the cart.'

'When was this?'

'Weeks ago. Before Aleksy. One of them just began unloading my boxes on to the verge. A fat ape he was, with a nose like a pig. The other one said he wanted to see what was in them before wasting his time, and he took out a knife and started cutting them open. I assumed he was the boss. So I told him he could have me if he left the stuff. While he was unzipping his trousers I asked him what he'd been – you know, before – and he said a city trader. He seemed sort of harmless, quite nice in a way, except he stank. Next thing we were doing it right there on the verge. He hadn't finished before the ape pulled him off me and said it was his turn. The trader swore at him and I said that wasn't the deal, but the ape hit me and started anyway. The trader's knife was just there, in the grass, where he'd left it. I got the pig-faced bastard in the thigh. Then I went for his back. I hit a rib, felt it jarring all my up my arm. He got off me then, or the trader rolled him off.'

'And then what?'

'What do you think? The trader finished the job.'

'Unloading the boxes?'

'Not that job.'

'Jesus Christ.'

'He's the father, probably. Though I can't say for sure.'

I want to ask her how this ended. Did the trader keep his side of the bargain or what? But she's finished talking. She looks out at the storm for a minute. Then she covers her face. After a while I hear small bleating noises.

She's a mess, but I'm no better – just a different kind of mess. We're none of us any better. Abigail drives herself like an ox. Maud's lost the power of speech. Django, if he was ever normal, has retreated into his own world. Aleksy struggles with a repertoire of blinks and twitches.

'You'll be all right.'

'How the fuck do you know?'

'We'll take care of you.'

'We?'

'Me and Abigail.'

She's staring out the window again.

I used to think of myself as walking forward into the future, constructing the future I was walking into. I used to think of myself as not wasting energy thinking of myself as one thing or another, but just doing what had to be done. Now I seem to stand sideways on, watching some version of me that isn't quite me. I notice myself feeling things. Or not. Or more than one thing at a time. Now, for example.

I pull my trousers on and go up to her at the window. 'Deirdre... talk to Abigail.'

'Fuck off, Jason. No, don't touch me. I don't want your hands on me. Just fuck right off out of my life.'

'Tell her you're pregnant. She can help.'

'The horses are mine, by the way, and the goats, and most of the edible food is what I brought – whatever Abigail thinks, hiding it in the cellar like it's her personal hoard.'

'Get some rest, Deirdre.'

'I was all right on the road and I'll be all right again, don't you worry.' She's reached the door and stands with the bottle in her hand. 'Once a month in the missionary position, that'll be Abigail's idea of sex, if she ever lets you into her capacious knickers. Because Abigail's idea of sex, in fact, is snuggling up with Maud. Or hadn't you worked that out yet? They just let you stay to dig holes and shovel shit.'

'Sleep it off.'

'Sleep the fuck off yourself. And then you can pack up your pretentious wine glasses in your chav wet dream of a car and you can leave us all the fuck alone, because we don't need you here.'

She slams the door behind her and it swings open again. The catch is worn – something else that needs fixing that I haven't time to fix. Her footsteps are unsteady on the backstairs. I hear her stumble and swear. For a moment there's nothing louder than the storm. Pulling on a sweater I go out to the landing and listen while she gets to her feet again and makes it down to the first floor. There are other footsteps, another voice murmuring comfort – Abigail seeing her safely to bed, or Aleksy thinking he's in with a chance.

It's only when I turn again to my door that I see Django sitting with his back to the wall. There's barely enough light to see his expression, but it's one I've seen before. He does compassion like a mime-artist, head to one side, mouth and eyebrows arched. He holds his jacket open.

'It's Deirdre who needs the flowers,' I tell him. But it isn't flowers this time. A box of chocolates, perhaps. He pulls it from the inner pocket and shows it to me. It's a copy of the Bible. So that's all he's got. No secret knowledge, no plan of vengeance, just the promise of salvation.

'It's a new heaven,' he says, 'and a new earth.'

'But the same old rain.'

Beyond him, further along the corridor, water drips into the cooking pot. Either we pay attention, or we abandon the place to the slow invasion of nature, the seep and drip of water finding the weak points, until a dozen winters have split it open like a fallen trunk for woodlice to crawl through and rodents and nesting birds. Which is what's happening – here and everywhere. It starts with a cracked slate or a choked gutter or someone smashing a window in search of food. The heat's off, the damp's rising. The works of man are rotting from the inside.

Agnes

I would say where I am, but I hardly know how to. I am put to bed among the ruins of the endtimers, and Brendan nearby in another room. They call this the O. I can call it neither Hall nor cottage nor forest.

I have climbed three flights of stairs to a pile of sacking. There is a broken window and the branch of a tree reaching above my head. I am half afraid to lie down in such a disordered place. At home my mother sleeps across from me. I think I shall never rest without the noise of her dreams. I remember the box of treasures hidden under my bed – my father's best knife and the little bird he carved with it, and the chain he had from his mother, as fine and supple as a thread of water lit by the moon.

Brendan was waiting in the ruin, as he promised he would be. I mean our ruin at the edge of the village. I never knew there were so many more ruins, so many broken walls.

It was hard at first riding with no reins or stirrups and nothing but Brendan's coat to cling to. The wind was rising and there was a great commotion of leaves and creaking branches. We travelled eastward and had soon left the village far behind. I think I slept, perhaps only for a moment, perhaps for longer. We passed cottages with fallen roofs. Towards dawn, we came down into the heart of a ruin vaster than I could ever have imagined, pieces of wall and sloping timbers all overgrown, extending beyond the road on either side, until they were lost in woodland and mist.

We came to a stream and Brendan stopped to let Gideon drink and rest. We sat on fallen stones and ate some bread and boiled pork.

He asked me what I thought about being in the forest and I said I would be afraid to be there alone. He said, 'Afraid of what?' and I said, 'Of scroungers and wild beasts but mainly of the Monk.' He said, 'The story of Maud and the Monk is good for a winter evening by the cottage fire' and I felt foolish then for believing it.

He asked me questions about myself. Do I like cleaning and cooking at the Hall? Am I frightened of the Mistress? Has she beaten me and do I fear to be beaten? Then he asked about Janet. Was she well and happy when I left her? I told him I have never known my mother well or happy since my father took sick, and scarcely before then. I asked him what of his parents and he said he had been an orphan for as long as he could remember and brought up at the Hall when there was another Mistress, long dead now, and Sarah was a child but already more clever in learning than any of them. It moved me to hear her praised, and to know that she understood the Book of Air when she was younger than I am now.

I should not have argued with her at the spring. I let her see me sullen and petulant and am sorry for it.

Later we talked about Jane and the names of Jane inscribed on her Book and whether they are truly her names, or the names of the copiers who made the book, or not names at all but words of some other meaning lost to us. John Murray and Currer Bell and C Bronte with two points over the e, like no other e written. And the strange spelling of Air that Jane uses only of herself and that must never be repeated outside the Book's green covers.

I asked why the Book of Moon has pictures, which is because it must be understood by everyone chosen for death, which is everyone living. I knew the answer to this, but asked because it comforted me to hear Brendan say it. But when I asked why the Book of Windows can be understood by so few it was Brendan's turn to be silent. I notice he is reluctant to speak of it. Perhaps it is because he thinks it so far above my understanding, but I think it is because it makes him feel sad in some way. When mother says one of us must feed the pig, and groans with her hand at her back, I go silent sometimes and stare out into the darkness because I would rather be somewhere else where there is no pig to be fed and no Janet, though I don't know where. This is how Brendan looks when I ask him about the Book of Windows. His sadness stirs me because there is the same restlessness in it. Since we left the village he has seemed younger to me.

He turned then and caught me looking. 'Trust no one,' he said.

'No one, sir?' I asked him.

'No one except me.'

'And Sarah?'

'Sarah will break your heart. You should find a boy to love.'

'But not to trust?'

'A boy with a strong back for digging and strong hands, but gentle when he should be.'

'And I shouldn't trust him?'

He didn't answer, but said, 'I have brought you where the villagers are afraid to come. Today or tomorrow you will see things you'll never forget.' And he spoke to Gideon and we climbed on his back.

The road we travelled on was thick with brambles, but roughly paved along its centre with patches of tar, like the road through the village. We turned off on a track that curved downwards and we were in a vast dried up riverbed. Its sloping banks were thick with trees and underbrush. The wind, finding this opening through the forest, howled along, pushing us forward. Gideon stumbled into fissures and caught his hooves on roots.

After a while the riverbed rose and curved and I saw ahead the slender stilts that lifted it up towards the roof of the forest. It wasn't a river, then, but an ancient causeway, so wide that you would have to shout to be heard from one side to the other. As we came above the canopy of branches, the sky grew lighter ahead of us, and the sun broke above the trees. I saw in the distance answering flashes of light, stretching into the sky in lines as straight as a ploughed field.

Everyone has heard of the towers of the endtime, and of Old Sigh who flew down from a burning tower to save the Book of Moon. But were they truly a hundred times the height of a man, these towers, and with a thousand windows, as some say? I never believed so. But now I have seen them with my own eyes.

I slept then against Brendan's back and dreamt of Old Sigh. When I woke, the towers were all around us, sprouting from the forest.

My father once stood on a cliff's edge. He told me this before he died, that he had run away from the village, westward towards the setting sun. It had been a hard winter and a wet spring and the vegetables were rotting, my father said, and the cattle sick from standing in mud, and the villagers were hungry. He came to the edge of the world and saw the sea a long way down, like a river with only one bank. He told me about the seabirds wheeling and the waves white against the rocks and the feeling that he might topple. Riding among those towers with Brendan I felt that I might topple upwards, tumbling past those windows into the black sky. So many windows, it would take Tal a lifetime and more to patch them up. And how would he climb to reach them?

We stopped by a ruined house and Brendan jumped down from the horse. He stamped on the ground with his boot and it rang with a hollow sound, scattering the birds and sending the forest creatures scuttling. There was a grinding and knocking from underneath. Brendan stepped aside and a door swung upwards and fell back against the ground.

I clung to Gideon's neck and Brendan told me not to be afraid, it was only Col. I had never seen a scrounger, not to look at, only once or twice a ragged creature running in the shadows. This one called Col looked human I suppose as he climbed out of his hole on his stiff joints, except that his eyes moved about like a dog fearing to be stepped on. Brendan gave him a fresh joint of pork and Col gave Brendan a bag of leaves. 'Tobacco for the pipe,' Brendan said. It seemed a poor bargain.

I know what labour goes to fattening a pig, and Brendan stood knee-deep in leaves.

I wanted to ask the scrounger if he grew this tobacco himself and where he grew it. But the door was already shut against us and I heard barring and bolting from inside. These scroungers, I thought, steal from us and steal from each other and live in loneliness and fear. And they are as far from planting a crop as I am from flying, and yet here is this tobacco that burns sweeter than any leaf in the village.

I was thinking about this, and thinking what a small mystery it was compared with the size of the forest and the quantity of broken walls among the brambles, and the height of some of them that rose through the trees towards the canopy of winter branches, when Brendan laughed. He must have seen the way I looked about, because he said, 'Does it frighten you to be so far from the village?'

'A little.'

'And excites you a little?'

'Yes.'

He was in the saddle again and prodding Gideon back on to the path. 'And does it make you wonder, Agnes?'

'About what?'

'About everything. Why did they build so high? Did you see, Agnes, even their roads were made to climb above the forest. I was told as a child that calling was so common among them that they could sit, each in his own tower, and know the thoughts of all the others. Is that possible? Did they sense each other like birds that wheel all one way and then another without warning? Was that how they were killed, do you think, Agnes – not by a fever that lurks in the blood and travels from one body to another in sweat and stale breath, but all at once, in a single convulsion of minds, each agitated beyond endurance by the knowledge of his neighbours' suffering?'

He looked so young, asking these questions, as young as Roland, and he asked them so eagerly that I laughed, and he laughed too.

I had no answers, but I had my own questions. 'Were the four books known to them, or were they only for us who came after? And if so, what did they live by? Were the scroungers all villagers once, as they say, and why did they leave to live so desperately? Or were they made to leave, and for what offence?'

And we both laughed again as if we'd witnessed a wedding and were giddy with dancing, though our laughing made no sense.

'This is where we stay,' Brendan said. We'd turned in at a doorway wider than any in the village. It led it into a barn high enough for hornbeams to grow tall, and near the frame of the roof pieces of sky where the glass of the endtimers had long ago broken for the wind to blow in. We passed window frames large and square like no windows at the Hall with broken angles of glass at their edges. I saw odd letters carved above them among the ivy and the shadows of other letters. The windows opened on rooms you couldn't see the end of for the darkness or things growing that love the darkness.

We came to a broken window that was boarded, and a boarded doorway next to it. Brendan climbed down to knock.

'We'll eat here,' he said, 'and they'll find us a bed. They call it the O.'

We heard bolts grinding and the door opened. A scrounger looked out at us all smiles, and there were more scroungers inside. Brendan took me by the hand and pulled me in. He pointed at me and said my name and people said, 'Ho there.' He pointed at the man who stood by the door and said, 'This is Trevor.' Then he pointed at a girl and said, 'And this is Trevor's girl, Dell.' It seemed strange for Brendan to be naming people as though they were just that day from their mothers' wombs but no one else found it strange because they laughed or smiled and made space for us to sit.

To the back of the room there was a window with no glass and thick bars across it, but the light came mostly from higher up where parts of the roof and walls were missing.

The girl called Dell gave me a cup to hold and filled it from a jug. I'd say she was my age or more, but not a woman yet because her hair was loose and unscarfed. We sat, me and Brendan and Trevor and more scroungers. We sat on chairs, some of wood, some iron, some cushioned with the stuffing spilling out of them, and everyone was talking and Dell filled everyone's cups. Across the room a man sang. He worked with his hands at a curved box and I heard the notes of his song and other notes that rose from his fingers.

Brendan gave Trevor a sack of eggs and a paper of butter and a loaf and he passed them to Dell, all the time laughing and talking. I saw Brendan hand something directly to Dell – a delicate cup no larger than a goose egg with flowers marked on it, a treasure from his shelves, and I saw her blush and stare sideways before slipping it in her apron and turn back to her work, and Brendan turn the other way to laugh at something Trevor had said. For a while it was as if there was no one in the room but Brendan nodding and smiling in his place and Dell in every other place with her jug. Then I put the cup out of my mind and the room filled up again with talking.

Sometimes the scroungers talked to me or Brendan and sometimes to each other, but I could make no sense of what they said. I wondered if this was French they were speaking or German that Jane learned to speak. But after a while there were words I knew like friends that walk at night from the shadow of a tree.

When I had emptied my cup, Trevor spoke to Dell and she would have filled it again, but I asked for water instead for fear of getting drunk. I was drunk already, I think, on the strangeness of everything. Trevor nodded at me, holding his own brimming mug in the air between us, and said, 'Here's licking a chew kid,' and I thought lick and chew must be his words for drinking. But he said it again when Dell filled his mug, and this time I heard 'Here's luck and achoo kid' as if he meant to bring luck by sneezing.

When it began to grow dark, Trevor said something to Dell. She put her finger to the wall, and lamps hanging from the ceiling flickered and glowed like little moons. Trevor saw that

I was startled to see them work without oil or tallow. He leant towards me and said it was the Jane Writer. I felt suddenly warm to him, to think that Jane was with us. I know Jane is in everything and everything in Jane, but I felt I had left the Book of Air a long way behind, and it comforted me to meet it again so unexpectedly.

I said the words back at him – 'Jane Writer' – and he smiled and nodded, his face shining with pleasure.

'Here though,' he said, 'I'll show you.' He rose, not quite steady on his feet, and led me out into the big room where we walked among the trees and undergrowth. There was a noise like a swarm of bees. We moved towards it, and it was louder, like cartwheels on a dry road. I was a little frightened to be here in the dark with a scrounger, and the mystery of the Jane Writer ahead of us. He unlocked a door and I was almost deafened with the sound. I don't know what I expected to see. Not this monstrous yellow beetle that squatted, shaking and growling, on the floor. Holding Trevor's arm, I edged back and eyed the thing from behind his shoulder.

'It can't bite,' he said with a laugh. 'It's a machine is all it is. Drinks like buggery, mind.' He chained up the door again and he led me back the way he'd come. 'Dell and I keep the old girl going with petrol,' he said. 'From the underground tanks. Not everyone's got the lungs to suck it out. Or would know what to do with it if they did.'

It was only later I understood what this might have to do with Jane. We'd eaten the meat and vegetables Dell had cooked up on the fire, and Trevor said, 'Time for the pitchers.' The others made a clatter then with their mugs and started calling out, 'pitchers, pitchers'. I thought at first it was more drink they wanted. But there was no need to shout for that with the jug passing round so freely.

The people stood, those not too drunk to stand, those who weren't sleeping, and followed Trevor through a doorway. Dell went round with a tray, gathering mugs and dishes. I waited to see what Brendan would do, if he would stay with Dell. I felt a pang of fear that he would. But he followed Trevor and the others, so I caught up with him and asked him what these pitchers were and hadn't there been enough drinking for one night.

He said. 'It's the pictures. Stay close by me and say nothing until you've seen them.'

There are pictures in the Hall and every page of the Book of Moon is a picture, but there was excitement in Brendan's voice and I knew I was going to see another wonderful thing.

Trevor led us through abandoned rooms, some no more than high walls standing among the trees. We climbed a long metal staircase and walked down a narrow twisting corridor until the walls opened into a sloping room where the seats faced all one way. The others knew to sit without being told. Brendan took my hand. 'Sit here,' he said, 'beside me.'

We sat in darkness with only a few stars visible among the highest branches and heard a noise behind us like insects buzzing. In front, where there had been a wall, blank except for the cracks, there was light, and against the light there were words, people's names that came and went quicker than I could read, quicker by far than anyone could write. I wondered who these people were. Then where the names had been I saw sky, bright but cold as moonlight, and I had no more questions because I was dumb inside as well as out. There were buildings and people walking, and everything sharply shadowed, but pale where the moon touched it. It was as though a huge window was thrown open and I was pulled from my seat to lean out impossibly. Men walked with hats like soup dishes or flowerpots. I seemed to fall in among them and float.

And all this time noise like the bellowing of cows late for milking and the wailing of the wind in a chimney and the thunderous sound of galloping horses, but not quite like any of these. And not like women wailing at a burial, either, or singing at seed time. It turned my insides to milk, this noise, and churned them into butter.

The men were dressed in white like at a wedding. One of them ran from me, turning with fear as though I meant to do him harm. There was a crack like a metal nail struck with a hammer and the man fell.

I seemed to be with him in the street, and then inside a house grander even than the Hall. I turned back to see if he needed help but could see only Brendan beside me and others, the light stirring on their faces like moths. I felt my eyes pulled back to the strangers through the window.

But my hand reached for Brendan's hand and gripped it hard. It was a comfort in that darkness to feel it so large and strong.

When they took their hats off, the men were sleek-headed like otters and with hairless chins, and pale as if they never saw the sun. They sat with women at tables. The women turned their heads and their ears sparkled. They grew huge until the space was filled up with their faces. Their mouths moved and sounds came like the chirping of sparrows or the croaking of mating frogs.

And I knew that this was not now or here. These were no scroungers beyond the wall. This was a glimpse of the world of the endtimers and I was in the presence of some great power that lingered after them. We had the Book of Air, but Trevor and the scroungers had the Jane Writer. I remembered how Jane as a schoolgirl longed for a power of vision which might reach the busy world, towns, regions full of life, heard of but never seen. Was this the fulfilment of her longing? Was this how she had taught the endtimers to call to each other at a distance? My mind, in turmoil, settled again on the visions and I forgot to think, forgot that I was sitting with Trevor and Brendan and only watched the people move and shrink and loom again in front of me.

Out of all these faces, some became familiar. A man with hooded eyes like a lizard whose lips hardly moved when he spoke, a woman more beautiful than anything I can think of even with an upturned wash bowl on her head, but so pale I thought she might faint. And I began to recognise words. Someone spoke of drinking and they filled their glasses and drank. There was talk of a ring, and a ring passed across a table.

A man sat at a desk, his hands busy at his work. He was in charge, always sitting while the others came and went. I could see he was more important than anyone. His eyes were white. His face was round and dark like an eggplant. He turned from his work, though his hands never stopped, and his mouth opened and he sang a lullaby. A kiss is still a kiss, a sigh is just a sigh. Tears came into the woman's eyes and shone in the light from the moon. Later when the lizard man heard the song, he rested his head on his arms. I ached to live in this hall and have that great round face hush me to sleep.

And while I was still wiping my tears I heard it – what Trevor had said. 'Here's looking at you kid.' The man with hooded eyes looking at the woman, lifting his glass as Trevor had lifted his mug. I heard it for the first time. It was about looking and it was what we were doing, me and Brendan and Trevor and the others. Here's looking. A text as deep as any in the Book of Air and as hard to understand, that's the thought that came to me. I gasped at the strangeness of it. I sat among scroungers and wanted nothing better than this – to be wide awake dreaming, everyone together, the same dream.

Jason

There's so much I never got round to telling you, Caroline. So much I kept from you. Because I was ashamed, I suppose. Of what? It's hard to say. Shame isn't logical. It's a smell that clings to you and maybe no one else can smell it but it's there anyway.

It was Derek's idea, the Jesus bus. Mum had taken me to the pictures as a treat for my tenth birthday, and McDonald's afterwards. We'd seen *Back to the Future* and it scared the crap out of me. There's this bit where Michael J Fox is trying to get his dad to make out with his mum at their high school dance and it's just not happening. He's got this photo of the whole family back in the future, and him and his sister start to disappear. And I thought that's my life. Dad's gone already. Who's next? Mum? Penny? I could hardly eat my Chicken McNuggets thinking about it.

Next day Derek came round. Mum was at the end of her tether, what with me moping and Penny acting up as usual and Dad not there to help. So Derek started in about this idea of his. He was going to buy an old double-decker, put some bunk beds in it and a kitchen and hit the road. There were other people interested, apparently. 'How about it, Flo?' he said, 'Give up everything you've got and follow Jesus, like it says in the Good Book.' If there was one thing my mum couldn't resist it was the word of God.

We'd never have gone if my dad had been alive to say no. Derek would never have dared suggest it. Our little terraced house wasn't much but Dad had put a lot into it over the years. Derek didn't have so much to give up. He owed more on his flat than it was worth. I heard Dad say once that Derek's flat was under water. I thought of him in flippers and goggles, catching fish in a frying pan.

They both worked on building sites in those days. Derek was theoretically a plumber, my dad said, by which he meant that he knew about plumbing in theory but was bugger all use in practice.

He used to do the rounds with his pamphlets, and he'd stop off in our kitchen for a cup of tea. And then he'd get going on one of his stories about fighting communism in Korea and finding God.

'Don't mind Derek,' my dad would say, 'Derek's a talker.'

Finding God changed his life, Derek reckoned. 'After that, it was no more boozing for me, no more taking the Lord's name in vain, no more Korean tarts.'

I wouldn't have minded hearing more about the Korean tarts, but my mum would say, 'Ah well, what's done is done,' or, 'least said soonest mended,' and offer him another Jaffa Cake.

He had a way with words, Derek did, but as long as Dad was there he was just television, a programme you'd watch while it was on and then not think about until next time.

Dad was a painter and worked for himself, which meant he worked for whoever would pay him the hourly rate. He loved paint – it was the icing on the cake, he said, the final touch that pulled everything together – all the different stages of the job, the plastering, the carpentry, the tile work – and transform them like magic into a room. People say if you can piss you can paint, but my dad was a craftsman. He'd cut a line along a glazing bar, hand steady as a surgeon's. His gloss would settle on a door like dew on grass – without a single brush mark, the dimples fading before you'd stopped looking.

He fell off a ladder and broke his neck. He was painting a ceiling at the top of a stairwell and had a heart attack, but it was the fall that killed him. Next thing I know we're having prayer meetings in the lounge. That summer Mum put the house on the market and we caught the bus.

It was all right for me, Caro, the Jesus bus. As long as we kept moving. I missed out on a few years of school and what might have gone with it – friends my own age, football. I never got any qualifications, but it didn't hold me back. I made enough to buy this house. I got you. For Penny, though, it started too soon and ended too late. In her mind, I don't know if she ever escaped. What was she learning all those years? Hard to imagine. Hard even for me and I was there for some of it.

To start with at least we had Walter, which was better than nothing. We'd sit in class on the top deck and he'd say, 'They are all gone into the world of light,' and he might be remembering old friends from his missionary days, or he might be doing English. English was the poems Walter had learned at school. There weren't any books on the bus, apart from the Bible, so he did it all from memory – Wordsworth, Tennyson, Browning, Kipling, Masefield. He recited bits of Shakespeare but never told us they were speeches from plays. We'd get no warning that a poem was on its way. It would just start coming, and something in the sound would tell you – the first rhyme or just the way the words knocked against each other. We learned from Walter that the quality of mercy is not strained, and that the child is father of the man, and that the old order changeth, giving place to new. Then he'd get back to history – or geography, which was history with maps drawn on the blackboard – and we'd learn how the old order of British rule had given place to shabby arrangements about which there was nothing interesting to say.

He lived in the past. He was sentimental about a British working class that no longer existed. He admired doers – men who got their hands dirty or fought in the front line or understood the customs of the Punjab. And he'd get misty-eyed over Indians who'd worked with him in Jalandhar. One in particular, called BJ Chaudhry – a name that would come falteringly to his mouth, followed by silence or a growl of throat clearing.

Mornings on the Jesus bus we studied Walter's brain. We listened. We wrote things down. We answered questions to show we were awake. Then we were free.

Free to get up to no good, usually, until someone collared you to clean the bus, or scrub a bucketful of spuds, or help ___ek with the chemical toilet, which was just for emergencies but filled up pretty quick even so. I learnt fast and was good with my hands, so I'd be sent on the roof to patch a leak, or underneath with gaffer tape and wire hangers to keep the exhaust pipe from rusting off. When Derek had a job on – fixing someone's boiler, say – he'd take me. I spent half my childhood up a ladder or with my head in a cupboard or my arm down a drain. Plumbing was Derek's trade, but we'd turn our hands to whatever would earn us folding money.

We kept moving. Stopped where we could – lay-bys, backstreets, patches of waste ground, windswept moors where sheep grazed and sullen ponies stared into the rain. There's only so long you can park a double-decker bus with a stove-pipe poking out the window before someone's hammering at the door, telling you to move on, or sniffing around with awkward questions. But wherever we showed up, there were people to welcome us, odd jobs for us to do. We were on the grapevine, you see, Caro. Celebrities for Christ. We'd done what they talked about doing – we'd given all that we had and followed *Him*. That was worth a food basket, or five quid over the odds for unblocking a sink. We were the Jesus bus and a donation was the next best thing to getting on board.

The grown-ups had taken to complaining about it – all this moving. They'd grumble when they thought we couldn't hear. It began to come up during prayers. Derek would open the Book in search of guidance. *Go to the great city of Nineveh and preach against it.* But where were we to look for Nineveh? *I will live in thy tabernacle forever.* And wasn't the Jesus bus our tabernacle? Cheryl, who was Tiffany's grandma, hated the cold. It played hell with her veins. She'd been a streetwalker, she told us, before she let Jesus into her heart, but she'd never done drugs, not like her daughter, Tiffany's mum, who was still on the game round King's Cross, God help her. All that standing was murder on the legs. And you couldn't wrap up warm, even when it was freezing, or they'd never see what was on offer. *They shall enter into my sanctuary.* Tiffany would have a different life, thanks to the Jesus bus, Cheryl said, but it was hard even so, not to be able to put your feet up by the fire of an evening and watch a bit of telly. *And the Lord appeared unto him and said, Go not down into Egypt. Dwell in the land which I will tell thee of.* Yes, but which land was that?

It was all right for Derek. He liked driving the bus. He liked wrestling with the gearbox on the hills. It took muscle to turn the steering wheel. He'd get called a thieving gyppo, like the rest of us, or a pikey, or an asylum, but he got respect too. He was a prophet with plumbing skills. What more could you ask for?

He was a believer, Derek, I'm not saying he wasn't. But God's plans had an uncanny way of falling into line with his own convenience. So when his back started playing up and it got hard for him to steer the bus along those backstreets and country roads, his revelation at Bible study shouldn't have been such a surprise. But it got everyone's attention. Even in mum there was a shift from one kind of stillness to another.

Mum. My mum, Penny's mum. She was there, more or less, on the bus with the rest of us. And she did her share of the work, though maybe not so much mothering. It seems to me now that she held the bus together. Arguments ran aground against her silence. She wasn't calm, exactly. She was a light bulb that flickered from time to time as though it might go out. The less she said the more the others waited. 'What do *you* think, Flo?' someone would ask. 'I'm right though, Flo, aren't I?' And they'd wait while she flickered off and on again. If I ever doubted that there was a world of the spirit more real than this one, I only had to look at her. For all his visions, Derek seemed too heavy-footed to get anywhere near Heaven. My mother was already halfway there.

So who was looking out for Penny? It wasn't so bad as long as the bus kept moving. But everything changed when we parked in Lloyd Morgan's field and the tyres went soft and the weeds grew.

Agnes

The worst thing has happened. I thought the worst would be a flogging, or to be sent from the Hall and never study with Sarah again, but this is worse.

Mother is dead and I am locked in the red room.

I'm not the first. Were there others when I was young? Before I can remember, there were others, I know that for certain. Before I was born. I dreamt just now that they spoke to me one after another while I lay in bed.

Yesterday I was with Brendan at the O. We'd been gone from the village for two days and I thought we would come back and find everything the same.

I was comfortable against Brendan's back as we came near the Hall and lost in my own thoughts. But something was wrong. I felt it in his body even before he spoke. He pointed and there were flecks of light away on the moorland road.

'Go home,' he said. 'If something's happened, Janet will tell you.'

I slid to the ground. Brendan took me by the wrist and held me hard. 'Remember, Agnes. Tell no one. Trust no one.'

I nodded and he let me go.

What gives a cottage life when work is done and the candles are out? When you walk past on the street what tells you all is well with your neighbours? Do you feel the warmth of their breathing or hear through the walls the snorts of sleep? I don't know if the silence I heard was truly different, but I knew I was alone. When I opened the door to our cottage it was the pig I thought to hear first, but heard nothing. I stood in the kitchen, wondering. Someone came in at the back and I thought a scrounger was come to murder me. Then he spoke and it was Roland. 'Everyone was looking for you,' he said, 'but they've gone now to the moor.'

'Then someone is dead.'

'Where were you?'

'Where does my mother say I was?'

'You should come with me. Most people have set off. The men will be digging.'

'I can't hear the pig. Listen, Roland. She roots around in the straw under the staircase. Did mother leave her out in the yard?'

He looked at the floor then and told me, 'Your mother is dead and the pig strung up in Morton's shed with its throat cut.'

'Dead of what cause?'

'You should come with me to the moor. They'll be finished digging soon enough. You know she must be buried by daybreak.'

'You go,' I said, 'and you can tell them you found me sick and I'll be there soon.' I couldn't be with Roland. He was angry with me, and I couldn't blame him. He had more reason to be angry with me than he knew. I wanted not to be with anyone.

When he was gone, to quiet myself I went and sat in the murk. It's a mournful place and fitted my mood. I stared out through the glass towards the broken walls of the ruin where they say the Monk once lived. The river beyond it was dark and the birch trees looked pale against it. I thought of drowning and wondered how my mother had died. I heard the warblers in the reed bed and the wind hushing them, but I had no one to hush me. No one to say, Sleep Agnes, let the old day rest behind the hill. And so I pulled the door closed to be more alone. It moved as stiff as an old dog and whined like a dog too. I knew then that the murk hadn't always been like this, scabbed with rust and mossed over, yellow tendrils straggling across its floor, the leather chairs dry and cracked showing their insides of twisted wire and wool like a ewe caught in a hedge. It once gleamed like a scrubbed kettle and people sat happy in it. Perhaps it even moved, as people say, all by itself, its metal wheels carrying it out along the drive and over the bridge into the village, to the cottage where I used to live with mother and must now live alone. Or out past the ruin and into the forest towards the towers of the endtime and the O where the Jane Writer hums.

I remembered that in the pictures there were closed carts, much like this, that moved with no horses to pull them.

Then it came to me that while I was off enjoying strange pleasures my mother was left alone to die. It was as though a hand reached inside and squeezed the breath out of me. I knew I was to blame. I hunched over with the pain of it, resting my head on the wheel. I rocked back and forward again, hitting my head to see if one pain would drive out another. When I stopped, I felt the broken skin and saw the stain of blood on my finger. And I found I was angry. Wasn't it always like this, Janet sapping the joy out of everything, making me feel bad? Why had the earth taken my father and let her live on, sad and useless?

After a while I took the moorland road and came on the villagers gathered for her burial. The men had done digging the pit and were laying the kindling for the fire. Faces turned to me as I walked through the bracken. The torchlight moved on them so that they seemed to scowl and grin and scowl again.

Mother's body lay beside the pit, wrapped in a sheet. I walked towards her and the villagers moved aside, but when I came close Peter stepped up to block my way. His coat smelt warm and mealy from baking bread. Morton limped to join him all cow dung and stale milk. I said I wanted to see my mother, I wanted to see her face before they shovelled earth and stones on her. Peter looked away and said something I couldn't hear. I pushed at him but he held me. He mumbled about the pig, and spat into the bracken, and said she wasn't fit to be seen.

'What, though, about the pig? Why is the pig killed?'

It was Morton who answered, his face near mine. 'Janet cut her own throat, Agnes, as she sat with the pig for company.' It was an unkind thought that didn't need saying. I thought it was bad luck for Annie to have a father like that, and worse luck for me to have no father at all, and now no mother either.

I said I wanted to look at her, and I would. I knelt to pull the sheet back and saw her dead. One eye stared at nothing. The other eye was gone and the whole side of her face eaten away – the flesh like summer fruit ready for stewing, and what teeth she had left showing like plum stones.

I felt someone kneel beside me and saw it was Sarah, and was glad to have her, so kind and beautiful, beside me, and to feel she had forgotten our quarrel. She helped me to my feet and held my arm to keep me from falling. The men were airing the flames with leather bellows. The Mistress stood at the pit to say the words of the Book of Moon and all the voices in the village stumbled after, low with dread. When they said goodnight to the stars, the sound roared in my head. A mist came over my eyes – not tears, but as if I saw nothing but my own blood. When they spoke of air, my lungs emptied and all the air departed from the moor and I thought the world was done with breathing.

They passed round fennel tea to stave off sickness. But my mother had drunk fennel tea as often as anyone in the village and she had died anyway. Her body was leaky and stiff but would have limped on if her thoughts hadn't killed her. No tea could protect her from her thoughts. I waved the bowl aside when it reached me.

The men lowered her into the pit and watched while the fire singed her sheet and smouldered and dwindled and I watched with them. The smoke caught in my throat and made my eyes water and when I could see again the fire was gone and the hole had sunk into blackness. Everyone fell to coughing. Some coughed to keep death away but I coughed because the wind blew against me and my mouth was full of ash. The only fire now was in my head – to think I would never see my mother again, to think I had wished her dead, or wished myself away from her which was as bad. The wind had carried off the smell of burning and brought in its place the sweetness of heather. I saw the dark shape of the hill against the sky, heard a blackbird and a meadowlark, felt the villagers' impatience to be gone. It was time to gather wood and carry water. But I couldn't stop myself from speaking.

'What words are there for Janet?' I said it quietly at first but then again louder so everyone would hear. 'What words for my mother?'

The Mistress looked at me sharply across the pit and spoke sharply too. 'We've said all the words that are to be said.'

'So what was her life?'

'Her life was what all lives must be.' For a moment she looked lost – this wasn't the schoolroom for me to be asking her questions. Then the familiar answer came to her. 'Life is a fire that burns itself out.'

'But there was no fire in her. It was smothered years ago. What did you do to her to make her that way?' I was looking at the Mistress, then turning all about to shout at the others. 'What did you do to her?'

'Gently, Agnes,' Sarah murmured. 'These are private words.'

'Every day, though, I have spoken to her – about the pig or the garden, about the coming rain or when the rain would stop – and felt I was blowing on embers, emptying my lungs to breathe a spark of life into hers.' I didn't know what I wanted to say, only that I must speak or be stifled by my thoughts. 'The fire in her was gone out. Even before my father died, she was only half alive. What cruel thing happened to make her like that? Why did she never speak of it? And now she's gone what will be remembered of her? Will we write her story? Jane is kept alive among us. If Jane why not Janet?'

I stopped speaking because I knew that the next word would be my book. But I had already said more than I should. Sarah's hand was tight on my arm and I saw in the growing light the fear in my neighbours' eyes. If Jane why not Janet? The whisper of my words was like a breath of wind in the bracken. I saw Roland turn away, staring hard at some distant object. Beside him, Megan looked at me open-mouthed, not yet daring to be pleased. It was the old women who came, three of them moving forward from among the other villagers, Reeds now not women, though they had no time to dress and veil themselves. I felt Sarah's reluctance to give me up. Then her grip loosened and it was the women who held me.

'Where is Brendan?' I said. 'Brendan won't let you take me.'

'The Reader doesn't concern himself with you,' the Mistress said.

'He loves me though. He'd tell you if he was here.'

'These are wild words, Agnes. You must be taken care of while the madness is tamed.'

They made way for me, my neighbours, shuffling aside with their eyes cast down. Only Annie pushed herself towards me. She put her arms round my neck and I felt her tears on my face.

And where was Brendan all that time? In his chair by the fire, lifting the delicate pages of the Book of Windows? Or stretched out in his bed? Is he there now, ten paces from where I sit? I could shout out to him but would he come? I could call him silently, but even this close, tied as we are by our journey and everything we saw and everything we felt, would he hear me? I don't think so, for all his studying, though I love him harder than I had thought possible.

Jason

I've been with Abigail to check some of the farms out along the England road. There were three dead in the house at Abbeymill, their bodies ripe and buzzing. We wrapped scarves round our faces and dug them a shallow grave behind the barn. They repaid us with a clutch of spades and rakes and hoes, three axes, some rolls of bailer twine and a good sharp saw, besides what we found in the kitchen – mainly knives and a haul of tinned food. At Higdon we rounded up some geese. Abigail enticed them into their house with grain, and we dragged the whole thing up on to the cart. There was the old woman shrivelled in her bed under a cloud of flies. Next thing I knew I was standing in a trench with Abigail leaning down to pass me a shovel. She said, 'Where did you go?' and I couldn't tell her because I didn't know.

We stood in silence at the graveside. When I was a kid they used to say, *I am the resurrection and the life.* But what would those words mean now?

'It's sad,' I said, 'to be buried by strangers and no one left to remember you.'

Abigail nodded. 'Sadder still not to be buried at all.'

'What will it be like for us?'

'We'll have family, friends, children.'

Riding home on the cart I ask her where she grew up and she says, 'West of here.' There's a hint of Welsh in her accent but some London as well. She's hard to place. We're both watching out for signs of life, signs of danger. We glimpse a couple of survivors dodging into a barn and feel them watching through the slats as we pass. Young or old, male or female? Hard to tell. Further on there's smoke rising from the corner of a field and a smell of roasting meat. A head appears from behind a wall and we hear voices. Then our view is obscured by trees. A soft wind dries the sweat on my shirt and stirs the branches overhead. In the distance church bells is going – faintly and without any pulse. I hear the sound filtered through birdsong. I lose it and find it and lose it again, so I think it's only in my head, until it's unmistakably there, an uncertain heartbeat. It has me listening to the birds – soft hoots and cries and elaborate repeated trills. A fantastic jumble of sound that ought to be cacophonous but is utterly, bewilderingly beautiful. And so much of it, coming from so many directions at once that you forget to notice. I hear it like a building, one course laid on another, up and up, but so light that it floats. I'm lightheaded, I think, from the day's work. And at its centre now this metallic resonance. And something else scurrying round it – Django's clarinet.

I asked him yesterday what kind of music this is that sobs and wails and isn't quite jazz and isn't quite anything else, and has its own way of tugging at you. I asked him if it was gypsy music or what, and he took the reed from his mouth long enough to smile and say 'If you like' and started up again.

At the far end of the wood we reach the church in a burst of evening sunlight. I pull the horse to a stop and get down. Abigail follows me into the porch. I lift the latch. When I open the door, the monkey scampers out and chatters off among the gravestones. There's that Anglican smell of hassocks and musty hymn books. Beyond the pews, beyond the chancel rail, Django is sitting on the altar, legs hanging, the flared end of his clarinet making shapes in the air. Behind him, in the stained glass, bodies in loincloths rise from their graves to join God or to be pitchforked into everlasting torment. I turn the other way, towards the tower, pushing through the velvet curtain. Between a rail of cassocks and a stack of chairs the bell ropes dangle, and there's Simon in a haze of dust jumping and swinging.

'All right, Si?'

'I'm...'

'Django taking care of you?'

'Django says I'm...' His neck tightens and he sucks in breath through his nose. He's doing his w-face, which makes him look as if he's about to hoot like a baboon.

'Whizzing through the jungle?'

'Not that.'

'Walking on the moon?'

'Not that either. Django says I'm...' And his neck tightens again.

'Have you eaten?' Abigail asks him. 'Did someone feed you?'

Simon lands on his feet, totters but stays upright, and walks over to Abigail. 'You have to listen to me.'

Abigail smiles at this. 'You have big lungs for a little boy.'

'I'm not little. Django says I'm... wonderful.'

Abigail's still taking this in and Simon is looking at her with big solemn eyes, when Deirdre pushes through the curtain. Aleksy follows, gasping for breath.

'Did you see someone?' Deirdre turns from me to Abigail. 'Is that why you rang the bell?'

Abigail asks her who she means, who we might have seen.

'Looters, scroungers. You didn't see them?'

'No,' I tell her, 'we've seen no one.' Abigail looks at me, surprised at the lie, but I'm not inclined to feed Deirdre's fears. 'It wasn't us rang the bell. It was Simon.'

'Well I hope you're going to smack his bottom,' Deirdre says, 'teach him a lesson he won't forget in a hurry.'

Abigail takes her hand and she stops moving about. 'There's no harm done, Deirdre.'

'Maybe not, but you shouldn't ring the bell, do you hear, Simon? Not unless there's danger. Tell him, Jason.'

'Hear that, Si?' I said to him. 'You shouldn't ring the bell.'

Simon's fighting to say something. His lips are open and I can see his teeth. He feels the injustice but can't defend himself. He's glaring at me, trying to say my name.

'And there is harm done, actually, Abigail,' Deirdre says. 'My journal's gone missing.'

'It'll turn up,' I tell her.

'How do you know?'

'Either it will or it won't, but there's not much we can do about it.'

'But someone's been in my room, going through my things. It gives me the creeps.'

'Who – who's been in your room?'

She gives me a withering look. 'Well obviously I don't know who.'

Simon hasn't given up yet. He's shaking with fury. He points through the curtain, and I see it's not *Jason* he's trying for, but the other *J*.

'Was it Django?' I ask him. 'Did Django tell you to do it?'

He nods emphatically.

Deirdre snorts with annoyance. 'Oh for God's sake, Jason, if you've got nothing useful to contribute...'

'Look, everybody,' Aleksy says, 'I understand this. Deedee's journal. It's personal. We can respect that, Jason, yes? We can promise, each one of us, if it comes into our hands, not to look, not to read. OK?'

He's looking at me, so I make a submissive gesture and say, 'Yes, obviously.'

He turns to make eye contact with Abigail.

She says, 'Of course. We're not to read it. What is it, a newspaper?'

There's a pause while this sinks in, that Abigail doesn't know what a journal is. I hear the monkey clambering on the roof. Beyond the curtain the clarinet is still bleating and bubbling.

Abigail looks self-conscious. 'An old one, I thought, maybe, that Deirdre likes. Is it something else?'

'It's just a kind of notebook,' I tell her. Then I ask Aleksy, 'What about Django?'

'Here we go,' Deirdre says. 'It's always the same with you.'

'I only said...'

'You just can't stand that Django's happy and you're not. That he's full of life and you're... the opposite.'

'I only meant...'

'*What about Django?* Like a child who thinks he got the smaller piece of cake.'

'I meant, what about asking him...'

'Django would never take something of mine without

permission. He'd never take anything. I've never met anyone less interested in things.'

'What about asking him not to read it if it turns up, like Aleksy said – that's all I meant – the same as he asked all of us. Jesus Christ.'

There's more I want to tell her, if I can get my thoughts in order, but suddenly she's crying. Abigail gathers her up, one hand around her shoulder, the other smoothing her hair. She catches my eye and I decide to say nothing.

Between sobs, Deirdre says, 'It's not about that. There's nothing for anyone to read. I haven't *written* anything yet. Not *anything*. That's what I can't bear – that my whole life is just a blank.' For a while she weeps against Abigail's bosom. Then she pulls away and starts talking more clearly. 'It was a present to myself for my birthday. I went on a course called Writing the Spirit, and the teacher said write every day, keep a journal. So I bought it and it was so beautiful and I wanted something really significant to happen – not just, you know, went for a lovely ride, Pedro lost a shoe, blah, blah. I wanted to have a significant thought. Then people started getting sick and I didn't want to write someone died in our village today – not on the first page, like the first ever thing I wrote. And we were all scared. I was so scared it made me sick. People said you have to eat. They said eat fresh fruit. My mother phoned to tell me they were saying on Facebook to eat ginger. And I didn't want to just write that, about eating ginger. It was meant to be about my life, and my life had been suspended while these horrible things happened. Then my mother died, and that evening I opened the book and was about to write, my mother's dead, but I stopped and wondered who am I writing this for? Because suddenly everyone was dying, and I didn't know who'd be left to read it, who'd be left who knew or cared anything about me.'

It's quiet for a while. The clarinet's stopped. The light is going. If there's birdsong still it doesn't reach us through the walls. We stand in the heavy indoor silence thinking or not thinking. And it's not like silence used to be. It has no meaning. It's like the silence of cattle. We're just waiting for the next thing, whatever the next thing might be. And I'm back at Abbeymill Farm, the dead with their sunken faces and the flies drunk and reeling. I've no patience with Deirdre and her journal. The smallest loss is a window on catastrophe – by now we all know this – it's everybody's story but she claims it as her own.

Abigail touches Deirdre's face. 'I know, love,' she says, 'I know. There's nothing left but work. At least we still have that. Animals to feed, water to carry. That's all there is. It's what will save us – doing it, and having it to do.'

Deirdre hugs Abigail and kisses her and rests against her for a minute. She makes to leave through the curtains into the body of the church, then turns and puts her finger to her lips. Django is lying on his back on the altar, apparently asleep. Abigail smiles and I see that Django is to be endlessly indulged and I am forever to be thought mean-spirited and envious for not falling in love with him. Even Abigail, in the end, will take his side, and my anger will turn inward until there's nothing in my head but the stink of death and flies swarming because there'll be no one else who sees what I see.

The horse has pulled the cart a few steps and is munching the grass on the roadside. The monkey is jumping on the roof of the goose house, setting the geese scratching and hissing.

'You found geese,' Aleksy says. 'I'll ride with Jason. We'll set them down in the top field. Come, Rasputin, leave the birds alone.'

I lift Simon on to the cart and we move off. The women cross the lawn towards the house – no longer a lawn, with no reason to keep the grass down. The shadows of the orchard trees reach out towards them. Maud, crossing with buckets from the spring, waits for them by the front door. As we turn in through the gate, I hear the reassuring murmur of Abigail's voice and I see the gentle way she and Maud touch each other's arms and hands. I want to be soothed by the sight of it but I'm too angry to be soothed.

Agnes

I think I will become mad. I am already mad. They were right to put me here. I hear sounds. I am afraid to write what I hear. More than sounds – women whispering, breathing. I lie in bed and can't tell if the voices are outside me. I touch my mouth to see if it's me talking. I put the pillow over my head but the voices are louder. They are inside the walls or under the floor. What I took for a dream is no dream, or I'm asleep and can't wake up, or I'm dead and this room is the Book of Death.

Sometimes the voices make no sense. When they make sense it's worse because I know then it can't be the wind in the chimney or water leaking behind the parapet. And it can't be rats nesting, though I can hear their squeaks and the scratching of their little feet.

A voice says, 'My baby had a twist in its face and all its mouth gaping so I strangled it and said it came out dead.' A voice says, 'It was Milly stole Esther's bantam but she told them it was the scroungers and I agreed for fear of Milly's sharp nails.' A voice says, 'Back again dearie, where've you been?'

The voices say things about the Mistress. That she eats nothing but gorse and blackthorn. That she rocks in her chair alone in the schoolroom and rubs herself for pleasure with the Book of Moon.

I hear nothing of this during the day, only the shouts of the children coming to the schoolroom or the knocking of feet on the stairs. When the boards creak outside my door I know someone is listening for me or come with food for Brendan. They come with food for me too, the old women in their green veils. They unlock the door and put a bowl of stew on the floor and wait while I bring them my pot for emptying, but say nothing. I hear the horses, their hard hooves in the yard, and the cartwheels rattling.

It's only at night the voices come.

'It was me stole Esther's bantam because Esther had my husband in the barn.'

'I have scissors from the endtime that I use in secret to cut my hair.'

'A scrounger came to me in my dream and had me, and I liked it.'

I walk up and down and hum and hold my hands to my ears, but then I stand still and listen because I can't stop myself.

'I love Samuel so hard I ache to think of him, why won't Samuel love me back?'

When they brought me to the red room they took my shoes from me and my scarf, so I wouldn't hurt myself they said. Now my feet are all splinters from pacing in the dark and my hair falls around my face.

'They said I hid the gin jug after Annie's wedding and was drunk for two days but it was a lie, I was sick with the earache and fell on the stairs. And the Mistress means to flog me, don't let her flog me, I'll come every night with candles and sage if you'll stop her.'

They speak to me as though I can help them, as though I have power that they don't have, but I'm locked up here and can do nothing, not even for myself, not even to get food when I'm hungry or water to wash in.

'Clay comes to me at night in dreams and tells me he loves me, but by day he stares at the ground and scratches at his leg when I pass. If Milly fell sick of a cancer or slipped on the bank when the brook was in flood or ate poisoned toadstools would Clay love me best?'

My room has one window looking towards the moor. At first I could see nothing through it but a dim green light, the way a newt or a tadpole must see the sky when the pond is all weeds. But in the corner of one of the low panes was a hole big enough to put my arm through and I pulled away all the strands of ivy I could reach. I scratched myself on the glass and might have done worse if I'd taken less care. I might have killed myself like mother, without the pig to help me.

107

I might still.

Perhaps this is what they mean me to do, and taking my shoes and scarf was just to make me suffer.

I can see now down over the stable roof into the yard. And I can see the moorland road. And if I push myself against the wall on one side I can see the top of the vegetable field and on the other side the trees of the High Wood. But none of this clearly because of the dirt on the glass. And I can see that the walls are the colour of drying blood. I think of all the women who have been here before me since the endtime.

They speak to me as if they can guess my worst thoughts even before I've thought them.

'Janet had a child before she was married and smothered it for shame.'

It's not much of a room for pacing, though bigger than the rooms in our cottage. You can see where the roof leaks by the lines of moss growing down the walls. There's a basin from the endtime, full of dry leaves and mulch from the ivy that straggles over it, and a bed with a straw mattress and a straw pillow and a wool blanket. There's a mirror on the wall above the basin, but cracked and stained so it shows only pieces of my face. Between the pieces there's the wall and the mildew trapped behind the glass in patches of green and yellow.

In one corner of the room is a walled space like its own little room, and the walls inside covered in flat brown stones cut square like the stones on the kitchen floor. I sit here at night to quiet the voices, and pace here sometimes, though one big stride this way and then that way is all it takes. A carved ridge runs round the walls at the height of my waist, showing like a half buried tree root. Such delicate patterns only the endtimers could make. I rub my hand along it for comfort. And there's a shelf carved into the wall that I have made my secret place.

I don't know what I mean by this. In the red room there are no secrets. Or else everything is secret. I have become a secret. Do they talk about me in the village? I think they are afraid to think of me. There is a whisper of Agnes, daughter of Janet, and heads turn about to see who listens. The Reeds could see my secret place if they took a step from the door and looked. But I have put a green beetle shell there, and a white feather that might be from a dove's wing, and a round bottle stopper of glass that catches the light when I hold it to the window and draws lines of colour on the floor.

Was there a dove here to drop a feather? How did it get in? And did it die? Or did the feather catch in my hair as they dragged me down the moorland road?

Sometimes they seem to talk between themselves but know I'm listening.

'That Sarah had a child by Brendan when she wasn't much more than a child herself. Kept to her room for months while her belly swelled, studying the Book of Air. And Janet helped her have it in secret at the Hall. Then she and Brendan gave it to the scroungers. Janet told me this herself when she had a fever and thought it was her own dead mother mopping her face.'

My real secrets – my ink bottle, my pen, my book – I keep under my skirt where no one looks. The bottle is almost dry, but the empty pages still stare up at me, hungry for words. I will become mad if there is no more ink. If I don't bleed.

If they forgot to feed me, if I knew no one would come, if they were all dead of some disease and only me left alive, locked in this room, and one piece of bread only, I would take one bite each day and try to live. And so with my ink. I should make myself not write until I must.

'My father died when I was a child, and Roger came at night to our cottage and hurt me, and I thought if my mother died too I would be an orphan and live at the Hall, so I put hawthorn berries in her stew and she was sick until her skin turned yellow. For twenty years I've nursed her, but kept the cause hidden. I should be flogged to a rag.'

Sometimes at night the smell of sage rises from the herb garden all the way to my window to mingle with the honeysuckle blooming on the wall.

'Poor Janet had a child born tiny, before it showed, and

dead as a box. She buried it in secret, they said, and for weeks after lay staring at the wall. Then she took her brother Morton's leather belt and put it tight round her neck. So they locked her in the red room to bleed four times – once for each book, till she should be brought to a right understanding.'

'The Mistress goes to the Ruin every new moon and meets there with the Monk. They say you can see the teeth marks on her teats.'

'Janet was locked up once and was never the same after. Old Jack her father died clutching his heart to lose her.'

'It's nice to have you back, lovey, it's been too long.'

I'll go mad if the voices don't stop. If I don't bleed. If I have no ink.

Jason

Voices and visions were all in a day's work for Derek. He'd hear the word of God in the roar of the traffic. One day he told us he'd had a vision of a field bathed in golden light, a barn for worship, a river. 'Almost a week ago now,' he said. 'Last Thursday it must have been because it was the day Lester found a crack in the cylinder head, and we prayed over the bonnet.'

Lester had been a machinist, but had mashed his hand and taken early retirement. Then his wife left him for a trombone player who used to busk on the embankment, and Lester caught the Jesus bus.

'I took a walk along the canal,' Derek said, 'and asked for guidance. I saw the field floating on the water. I didn't think to mention it. Not until this showed up.' He held out the envelope, crumpled from sweaty hands and trouser pockets and smelling faintly of dung. 'It's been chasing us around the country. See all these addresses.'

It had come from a farmer called Lloyd Morgan. We'd met Lloyd at a revival meeting near Brecon. The date of the letter was the day of Derek's vision. It had been written, Derek assured us, at the very hour of his walk along the canal. Lloyd Morgan was offering the Jesus bus and its weary occupants a place of rest.

It was a few days later, on that last trip, that they sent us kids off up the road in search of blackberries and we found the orchard and I saw this place for the first time, and I swore I'd have it, with Penny as a witness, and little Tiffany, whose mother was on the game. We stayed that night on the side of the road, near the church. From the top deck where us kids slept you could see the chimney stacks through the trees. 'I'll have it,' I told myself as I went to sleep. 'I will, though.' If

Derek could have visions, so could I.

I woke from a dream of apples. I was still getting dressed when the bus started up. We only had forty miles to go, Derek said. We'd be at the farm in time for breakfast. Before we'd picked up any speed we passed the gateway to my house and I saw it had a name – Talgarth Hall. And there was the lawn sweeping up to the front door, and there were the apple trees. We turned into a lane that ran along the side of the orchard. I had a glimpse of the stables and a last look at the back of the house, as we rose between fields to a moor where sheep grazed, then down into another valley. Settling into a seat near the front I watched the roads narrowing, the villages getting meaner and more sparse. Crossing a bridge, we joined a river and followed it upstream.

Lloyd was at the entrance to the farm, filling potholes. He gave Derek a sideways nod and led us on foot through the yard and up a track. We followed at a perilous tilt, the old panels creaking, Derek wrenching the gear lever into first as the gradient steepened.

The field Lloyd had in mind for us sloped down towards the river. He had us park at the top end, next to a stone barn with an iron roof. When Derek cut the engine, it coughed a few times and sighed and the silence closed in. You felt the bus and everything in it come to rest. A butterfly settled on the windscreen. You could hear birdsong and the water washing the bank where the river curved around the bottom of the field. For a moment no one moved. I felt their contentment crowding in on me. I knew things would never be the same. I'd lived through changes, Dad dying, then Derek saving our souls, and I had a premonition that this was next – a change we'd never recover from.

Derek called a meeting. He showed us the cold water tap by the gate post, told us where we'd be digging the latrines, outlined his plans for the barn, including a couple of sleeping rooms and a gathering place with a log-burning stove. He led us in prayer. To mark this new beginning, he said, he was going to baptise us all in the river. Not all in one go, but over the next few days, because it would take time for the Lord to make known to him what new names we should take. Each of us in turn would renew our commitment to Jesus, opening our hearts to his love. First, though, Derek himself would have to be baptised. He asked Walter if he'd mind doing the honours. 'The oldest among us,' Derek called him 'our John the Baptist, if you will.' Was I the only one who felt, following that thought to its logical conclusion, that Derek was getting above himself? They did it after breakfast, both of them fully dressed, standing with the water up to their waists. We gathered under the trees to watch.

'From henceforth,' Derek said, 'I shall be called Caleb and this our field shall be known as Hebron.' He held his nose and dipped down into the water and up again.

While the water was still cascading from his hair, Walter began. 'I baptise thee, Caleb, in the name of the Father, Son and Holy Ghost. We thank you, Heavenly Father, that by water you have bestowed upon this thy servant the forgiveness of sin and have raised him to the new life of grace, for the sword outwears its sheath and the soul outwears the breast and the heart must pause to breathe and love itself have rest. Though the night was made for loving and the day returns too soon, yet we'll go no more a roving by the light of the moon...' He stopped and we heard the water tumbling over the rocks and watched the sand martins swooping in and out of their nests. Walter looked lost and cold.

After a moment, Derek said, 'Amen,' and helped him back to the bank where the women were ready with towels. Walter couldn't stop shivering, so they piled him with bedding and sat him by the stove.

Next morning Derek had his breakfast alone. He appeared while the girls were washing up. I'd thought about who would be next. Walter, obviously, then Lester, then the women. The kids would be done in order of age, probably. I wasn't looking forward to it. I could still remember the first time I'd been done – a humiliating experience at the age of ten to have to lower my head over the same pink bowl that Penny had been bathed in as a baby, and in our own front room with our new friends in Christ looking on, whoever they were.

anything to do with J's

childhood?

'I have prayed and fasted,' Derek said. 'I have sought guidance from the Good Book. I have looked in my heart where Jesus resides, my Lord and saviour.' His eyes had settled. I turned to see who he was looking at. It was my mother. 'Flo,' he said, 'the Lord who directs me in all my doings has removed the scales from my eyes. You are to take the name of Azubah.' And my mother did something I'd never seen her do before. She blushed.

In the Book of Daniel, Caro, Azubah was Caleb's wife. But if you'd been there you wouldn't have needed to know that. I knew it, but I didn't need to. Derek was coming on to my mother. In front of everyone. In front of me. There weren't any couples on the Jesus bus. I'd never noticed before. There was no reason why I should have. It was the way things were. The kids were too young. As far as I knew, the grown-ups were too old. None of them were married – not to each other, anyway. There'd been a kind of equality in that.

I saw Derek's game all right. He wanted my mother in a way that it had never occurred to me that anyone might want her. For this, the least of his crimes, I hated him.

I'd always been good – cheerful, eager to get stuck in and do my bit. Now I went on strike. Latrines were dug, the barn was kitted out for sleeping, an old sink was positioned under the water tap. Caleb was directing the construction of Hebron, and I wanted nothing to do with any of it. I slunk out of sight. I went up over the hill towards the woods, or sat by the river. Penny brought me scraps from the kitchen.

Walter was in the farmhouse, in bed with a chill. I climbed in the window and sat with him. I'd hear them calling for me. When someone came with food or a fresh hot water bottle, I'd hide in the wardrobe. Getting off the road was where we'd gone wrong, I was sure of that, and I sensed that Walter felt the same. I'd never thought much about Walter. Now he seemed like a frail lifeline, our only connection with the world beyond Lloyd Morgan's field. I hung around his room for days. I tried to get him to talk, but he was rambling.

'What did you mean, Walter, in the river, when you said we'll go no more a roving?'

'So late into the night,' he said.

'Yes, what did you mean?'

'Though the heart be still as loving and the moon be still as bright.'

'Do you think we should keep roving, keep travelling on the Jesus bus?'

'BJ Chaudhry loved that one. The Isles of Greece – that one too – where burning Sappho loved and sung, where grew the arts of war and peace, where Delos rose and Phoebus sprung. Eternal summer gilds them yet.' His eyes were moist with tears. 'But all... except their sun... is set.'

I could only just catch the last of it. After that he stopped talking. Everything slowed down. I don't know how long I sat there – an hour maybe. I thought he was asleep. For a while he made a noise in his throat like snoring. The intervals between the breaths stretched out, and out, and then he was quiet.

Next day I sat with the others for breakfast. My mother brought me bacon and eggs and some black pudding, which she knew I liked. She gave me a pleading look. 'Be a good boy, Jason. This is our future now.'

Derek stood up and said that everyone had been baptised except me, and today it was my turn. 'From now on,' he said, 'you shall be called Tarshish.'

I knew he meant to humble me. I said, 'Who's Tarshish when he's at home?'

And Derek said, 'You know, Tarshish son of Javan son of Gomer son of Japheth son of Noah who built the ark and lived for nine hundred and fifty years.'

And I said, 'Bugger that, I'm not changing my name to Tarshish.'

And Derek got in a strop. 'You wanna watch it son,' he said. 'I've had my eye on you, and I reckon you been pitching your tent towards Sodom.'

'That's a lie,' I said, 'a fucking lie and you know it.'

For a moment I thought he was going to hit me. But he closed his eyes and started praying. 'Dear Lord Jesus Christ, if it be thy will, cleanse this child of his foul words and foul thoughts and whatever else he's been getting up to.' He took a deep breath, while the wind touched the leaves with a dry sound. Then he opened his eyes and said, 'Come on Lester. Lloyd. Let's get on with it.'

I turned to run, but Lloyd was standing in my way. I felt his meaty hands on me. Then my legs were lifted off the ground. I saw faces swing past – Granny Cheryl with one hand over her mouth, little Tiffany squirming on her lap, Penny frowning. I saw my mother's eyes, large and sorrowful, before her head dropped. They carried me into the river and held me upright while I kicked about to find my footing.

'I baptise thee, Tarshish,' Derek said. And the rest of it. Then he pushed my head under the water and held it there and, swear to God, Caro, I thought I was done for.

That night I stole an old bike out of Lloyd's tractor shed. Penny was waiting for me by the farm gates at the end of the track.

She said, 'I knew you was gunna leave.'

I didn't say anything – just scowled and shrugged.

'Why didn't you tell me?'

'I didn't need to if you knew already.'

'Take me with you, then.'

'There's only one bike. You'd go too slow anyway. And the police would stop us.'

She started to cry. 'If you go, what'll I do?'

'You'll be all right, Pen.'

'I won't though.'

I left her crying on the edge of the road. The wheels had stopped turning and the Jesus bus was sinking into madness – I knew that. But I left her anyway.

Agnes

I know what women they are that speak to me at night. I know how I hear their voices. I have waited for the sun to rise so I could write this.

I was so frightened in the night that I crawled under the bed, though there was hardly space for me. The dust had gathered undisturbed and I must push my face against it, fearing the touch of mice and spiders.

Before, lying in bed, I was almost used to the talking if it was only stories of the next door children stealing from the garden or questions about how to please a man with kissing. But someone had started again about mother's dead baby, which I can't bear to think of. I clamped my teeth and said shut up shut up shut up until my voice was sore and the words lost their meaning. I battered my head on the mattress, afraid it would be the wall next and my skull would be mashed like a turnip.

And so I rolled on to the floor and went sliding headfirst on the splintery boards until even the greenish glint of moonlight was blocked out and I took more dust in at my nose than air.

But the voice came even closer than before. My hand found a hole in the floor the size of a saucer, and when I put my face to it, it was like a whispering at my ear.

I knew then that if I went to the window and looked down towards the yard and waited long enough I would see movement in the shadows and it would be a woman slipping from the end of the yard out into the field, or a woman crossing from the field into the yard. They might see each other in passing and say nothing but goodnight. Or nothing at all, each keeping the other's secret even to herself, a secret for the women of the village to keep from men and children and from the Mistress and all those who lived at the Hall.

It was the voices from the Grace Pool I could hear, coming up through the hidden pipe.

I put my mouth to the hole and caught the smell of smoke and sage.

I said, 'I'm thirsty, they don't bring enough water.' I said, 'Open the door. The key is in the lock, which I know because no light comes through the keyhole, and I hear only the key turning not the scraping of it in or out.' I said, 'I'm not mad but this room will make me mad.'

I think I slept for a while down there in the darkness.

I said, 'Hang pans on your fence that will clang when the children climb over.' I said, 'Peel a carrot for the baby to gnaw on, small enough for its little mouth, but not so small that it will choke.' I said, 'He will love you but only when you have stopped wanting him and then it will be his turn to blush and stammer, and the sight of his staring will make you think of nothing more interesting than field work that must be done and what you must cook for tea.'

There was light that came and went so quickly I thought I'd dreamt it. Then a low rumble of thunder. So it was lightning I'd seen, but too far off to bring rain.

I said, 'Your father is dead and there is nothing to be thought about it except now it is you that must plant the potatoes.'

I said, 'Sarah taught me to read the Book of Air and every utterance in it four times each time different, and was kind to me at my mother's burial, and I would kiss her hands if she was here.'

I said, 'There are four books but what if there were five?'

I said, 'We contain air and are contained by air, but the air in the red room was breathed in and in and out a thousand times before I was born and in all these years no one has taken a broom to its dust.'

I said, 'Bring me water. Or turn the key and let me fetch my own water.' I said, 'This room is memory and I am lost in it.' I said, 'This room is mad and I am its only thought.'

Jason

The goat has begun squealing again and jerking its legs. A final desperate struggle. When Aleksy carried it into the yard, it seemed to have no strength left for squealing, but made an odd snoring noise, staring white-eyed at nothing. He'd wrapped the broken leg with strips torn from his own shirt. You could see the bent shape of it even so, and the angle where the shattered bone had broken the skin, and the seeping blood.

'Deedee mustn't see,' Aleksy said. 'You know how she is. She loves her animals.'

But Deirdre, standing at the kitchen door, held herself together, though the colour drained from her face. 'Poor Esther. What happened? Did she wander on to the road? Stupid question. Sorry. No traffic.'

'Bring a bucket,' Aleksy said, 'and a sharp knife.'

'Funny word, traffic. So many words with nothing left to attach them to.'

'And a bowl or saucepan. To catch blood.'

'Yes, sorry. Knife, bowl. And you'll want a needle and thread.'

'Needle and thread?'

'For afterwards. For stitching her up.'

'Deedee...' Aleksy faced her with the goat twitching in his arms. 'Jason and I must kill the goat.'

'Oh.'

'For food. And all the goats one time or other. You know this. And pigs, and chickens.'

'Just a knife then.'

'And a bucket. And a bowl for blood.'

'How did you say it happened?'

'There was a trap in the wood.'

119

'And you don't think they're out there?' All her feeling for the goat has risen suddenly and spilled out in this question. 'You still don't think they're coming for us?'

'An old trap, Deedee. For rabbits. Rusted and forgotten.'

She turns in the doorway and retreats into the shadows.

Aleksy shouts after her, 'Make sure it's sharp, this knife.'

It knows it's done for. When Aleksy lays it down, the legs flail, scrabbling for purchase on the flagstones, and the squealing starts. I kneel on its chest, the way Aleksy tells me, and feel it heaving against me and put more weight on it to stop its bastard noise. It's Abigail who brings the knife and hands it to Aleksy. She sets down the bucket, while Aleksy squats, and she hands him a plastic ice cream tub. He puts it to one side of him and then to the other, and his face goes through its routine of involuntary grimaces. He's feeling the neck with his free hand. The knife shakes and then seems to jump forward, pulling his arm behind it. Aleksy's grunt is lost in the grunting of the goat. And the blood is on his trousers and on the stones and spirting at last into the ice cream tub. He takes the front leg and works it as if he's pumping water. The back legs kick and the whole body struggles under me and lies still. I'm panting as though I've run a mile, and when I stand up my legs shake.

Aleksy kneels in closer with the knife and saws an opening from the neck to the groin.

'Take hind legs,' he says. 'Hold her up, like this.'

I lift until only the head lies sideways on the stones. Abigail comes forward with the bucket, and the stomach and the intestines and all the neatly packed organs flop into it and rearrange themselves.

'Now water.'

Abigail goes to the corner of the yard, where a wheelie bin, fed by a truncated downpipe, brims from the recent rain.

Aleksy, still on one knee, looks up at me, his shoulders rising and falling. 'Next time easier,' he says.

'You've done it before though.'

'I watched my uncle maybe five, six times. Summers I helped on the farm.'

He helps me tie the goat by its hind legs to the stable door for the blood to drain, and I'm stirred suddenly with love for this short-legged bull of a man who knows things I don't know. I ask him, 'Was there fresh meat where you were... during the end times?' The phrase comes to me from my childhood, to name a time for which there is no name.

'Not so much.'

He isn't ready to talk about it, and I'm glad because neither am I.

Abigail is back with an aluminium bucket trailing a wet rope. Aleksy washes his hands and arms to the elbow, then slops water into the cavity and over the skin, sluicing the stones at our feet.

Later I help Abigail prepare a stew with onions, tinned carrots and tomatoes. We gather round the kitchen table. Aleksy raises a glass to Esther whose life was cut short to give us strength and pleasure, and we drink to her in water cold from the spring. We eat the stew with boiled turnip. It tastes good. Deirdre eats hungrily and takes the scrapings from the pot. Simon pushes the pieces of meat to the edge.

I say to him, 'Simon, eat what's on your plate.'

Django says, 'Simon's a vegetarian.'

'Simon will eat what the rest of us eat.'

'Yes, but only the vegetables.'

'There's little enough food, God knows. He needs protein.'

'Today is a new heaven, a new earth. Simon knows that better than any of us.'

'Don't speak for Simon. He can speak for himself. Simon, eat everything. You'll get sick if you don't eat.'

Abigail rests her hand on mine. 'Jason's right,' she says, looking at no one in particular. 'Simon must eat and grow strong. And when he's hungry, that's what he'll do.'

We don't stay long after the sun's gone down. Our life together has narrowed to these basic forms. Only Aleksy lingers in the kitchen, slumped in an armchair by the stove. Abigail has given him the biggest bedroom, but I don't know if he ever sleeps there. The monkey, who sat on his lap for a while searching his hair and beard for insects and morsels of food, has wandered off around the house. Abandoned, Aleksy would share a bed with any one of us, I suspect, or have us move all our beds together. Meanwhile he hugs himself in the glow of the fire, while footsteps creak overhead and the old timbers settle around him.

I'm woken by a sound that could be water singing in a loose pipe, but the plumbing's drained and the taps are stiffening with disuse. I'm reminded of mating cats but can't dispel the thought that the noise is human. It floats up from a lower room and pulls the hairs upright on my scalp. I put on a shirt and trousers and follow it down the half flight of stairs, along the passage, past the empty second floor bedrooms. I tread quietly, bare-footed on the oak steps, sliding my hand down the spiralling rail. It's a kind of keening I can hear, a quavering song of panic. It comes from Abigail's room, the room she shares with Maud, but there's nothing of Abigail's voice in the sound.

It was a kids' room before, remember Caro, and we'd left it the way it was.

I stand in the open doorway while my eyes adjust to the darkness. Maud is in the pink bed in the corner and Aleksy stands over her with his back to me, talking. I cross the room, passing Abigail in the blue bed under the window, and she's suddenly alert.

'Jason, what is it?'

'I don't know.'

We listen to the murmur of Aleksy's words and Maud's response, a high note, fragile and unsteady.

'Maud, it's all right.' Abigail gets up and stands beside me in her flannel nightie. 'Aleksy walks in his sleep,' she tells me. 'It's all right Maud, it's only Aleksy.'

Together we approach the foot of Maud's bed. She shivers under the quilt, eyes wide with fear. Aleksy holds the ice cream tub in one hand. He dips his thumb into the goat's blood and smears a dark stain on her forehead. Her mouth stays open but there's no sound.

Abigail leans her head towards me. 'What's he saying, Jason?'

'Washed... something. Washed in blood... I don't know that last word. Lamb, presumably. Washed in the blood of the lamb.'

'Is that Greek he's talking, then, or Hebrew?'

'It's Polish.'

'You know Polish? I've never heard it spoken.'

'A bit. Building site Polish.'

'It's all right Maud,' she says. 'We won't let him hurt you.' She touches Aleksy gently, just above the elbow. 'Come on, Aleksy, it's done now, washed and sorted. Everything's all right. Time for bed.'

He turns an ear towards her. Then he breathes in sharply and makes a sudden movement, both arms flying. The ice cream tub rises and tilts, slopping a dark stain across the quilt. Maud starts making noise again – a kind of pulsing hum. Aleksy's jabbering. So I give him a slap and he wakes up. 'Christ, Aleksy, look at this mess.'

There's terror on his face. He blasphemes in his own language. Abigail lifts the tub gently from his hands and he lets her, watching it go. Then he hugs me so I can hardly breath.

'Aleksy, go to bed.' Abigail's voice is quiet but commanding. 'Take him to his room, Jason, then help me with this. It's all right, Maud. It's all over.'

I put my arm round Aleksy's shoulder and steer him through the door and across the landing. The sky clears as we enter his room and the bed is flooded with cold light.

'I was dreaming, Jason.' It's an apology.

'I guessed.'

'I was dreaming that we stood in this garden and there was such food and we stood in the eyes of God, my five brothers and I, and my father home from prison and the twins still alive in their cot.'

'And the words?'

'Words?'

'Washed in the blood...'

I watch him search his memory, draw the vision back

from the darkness. 'We were all priests. All my brothers, all humanity.' He's sorry to be awake. 'And so here we are. And why here? Why us?'

'No reason.'

'You got it and survived? No one survived.'

Hear that, Caroline? He speaks like it's over. It's time to draw a line between what was and what is.

'Later maybe, Aleksy, as it went on, people... some of us... built up some kind of immunity. There'll be others out there somewhere.'

'But you got it for sure – sweats, staggers, blessing...?'

'I got it.'

'You painted? Constructed some beautiful thing?'

'I sang.'

Aleksy whistles through his teeth. 'I don't hear you sing now. And yet you sang. And the rest of us untouched.'

'We always knew there'd be some.'

'The immunes, sure. Rumours. But who believed them?'

'Everyone.'

'We needed someone to hate. Not so many left to choose from. Russians, Muslims, bankers... dying like the rest.'

'We had the soldiers to hate. The militias. We had every murdering bastard waiting in the shadows to steal what we'd stolen for ourselves.'

'Not big enough, not...' – he makes an expansive gesture – '... grand enough. The soul in pain demands an enemy worthy of hatred.'

I find I don't have much to say about the soul.

'And so it was us, after all – me, Deedee and Django, Abigail and poor dumb Maud – all immune. We carried the infection of life and we never knew.'

I leave Aleksy's room. Across the passage, Deirdre's door is ajar. She sits up in the four-poster bed, pulling the hair from her face. The monkey squats above on the canopy, tasting its own fleas. Just inside the room, a hand reaches up from the shadows and pushes the door shut – Django's hand.

By the time I get back, Abigail has settled Maud to sleep in the blue bed and pulled the blood-soaked bedding on to the floor. I bundle it up and carry it down to the yard. The shapes of the buildings are beginning to show against the grey sky. I walk into the top field to calm myself, picking my way between the neat rows of Aleksy's planting.

Agnes

Days pass, so many that I lose count. I am terribly afraid.

There is something I haven't written. Something that happened with Brendan when we visited the scroungers. This book, that pulls all my secrets out of me and tells them back to me in my own words, had no words for this. And what words will it find, even now?

When the pictures stopped, when the dream faded and all the light was gone from the wall, I couldn't wake but must sit with the silence churning. Brendan's voice was quieter than the pulsing of blood. I felt his breath warm on my neck and his arm around me. He felt huge to me then, like the man dark as an eggplant who sang a kiss is still a kiss. If I had thought of Jane. If I had made a space in my mind for her, as Sarah had taught me. But Sarah was far away. And I was somewhere deep inside myself where I could see nothing and think nothing, but could feel every hair on my skin, and the weight of him shifting in his fever and my own chair pushing sharp against me. And I knew only the strength of his hands and his kisses passing down into me like breath into a reed. Was it pain or pleasure I felt? There was pain, certainly. For him as well I think. I heard the suffering in his voice. But sweetness too at last – to hold him, to hush him into stillness. And a time between, when I was no longer Agnes but a field at seed time and all the horses of the village breaking in to trample me and scatter the starlings, and I was the pressed earth and the stones brittle from the winter frosts and the wings rising and wheeling.

Afterwards we walked in silence to the O, and Dell took me by the arm and showed me where she sleeps. I was glad to be in her company for that time, and away from Brendan. I longed to be with him, but I found myself afraid, because I felt there was a river inside me that might rise and burst out in a flood. It calmed me to talk to Dell, though she has such a strange way of talking that I understood only part of what she said.

There was a litter of kittens in a box by her bed. She told me they would live at the O and their mother would teach them to kill mice and rats. We played with the kittens, hugging and stroking them, and Dell hugged me too and stroked me. And I saw that living with Trevor and no one else she knew even less of mothering than I do. I liked to feel her hair, which was beautiful and dark with tiny curls so you could rest your face against it like a pillow. She asked what it was like to live among the planters and I said it was the only life I knew, and that we lived the way we had been taught to live by Jane, our first Governess, and Maud and Mother Abgale who gathered at the Hall at the endtime with those I have heard called the Moons. And she asked why this name, Moons, and I said it was because they came through the blessing and lived until it was their proper time to die, when their page had turned, as set down in the Book of Moon.

For a while we lay together in Dell's bed. And it soothed me to hold her and be held. I had envied her a little, though I am ashamed now to write this, because Bernard attended to her so closely. But I had quickly come to love her and take comfort in her company. How I long now to feel such warmth. Even to talk to another person. Even to breathe the air outside this room. I can wait and wait but I won't bleed. Another life stirs in my belly, feeding off the little food I get. There are plums in the orchard, but I'm not there to pick them. Who now lets the geese out in the morning and shuts them up at night against the fox?

Jason

The house creaks and murmurs in its sleep but I'm too agitated to rest. I go down to fetch some tools from the cupboard in the hall – pliers, an adjustable spanner – and climb the stairs again to the bathroom. Your bath floats, sleek and pale against the crimson walls. It reminds me of candles and scented oils, Caro, and your delicate breasts showing above the foam. But it'll have to go. We need it in the yard for the cattle to drink from. It's no use here, three flights up with no running water. It won't take me long to disconnect it – hot and cold, waste and overflow. Aleksy can help me shift it in the morning. No point being sentimental about plumbing. But I hesitate anyway.

The virus got you early, Caroline. People said the best were taken first and I believed them. The average sinners would muddle along behind. And who'd be left? Aleksy was right about the immunes. We began to hate them without knowing who they were, without having any reason to believe they existed. After the first wave of deaths, we sensed the scale of the disaster, and the rumours began. It was impossible to tell who out of all those so far untouched might be actually immune, but people were accused anyway. A doctor on his way home after a sixteen-hour shift on a fever ward was attacked by a mob in a hospital car park. His death was applauded in chatrooms. *Ha ha, not so untouchable now you smug fucker!*

I feel the distance between me and the others – Aleksy, Deirdre, Django – Abigail even, and Maud. It comes to me with sudden force. Who are they to squat in my house? They've never been touched by the blessing, not one of them, never felt its power and sweetness. I'd go through it all again – I would, Caroline – to feel that exultation. I travelled on the Jesus bus, I spread the word of grace abounding to all sinners, but I was a creature of sullen clay until I lost control of my limbs, here in my own hall, and felt the first stirrings of divinity. And now they come snivelling round my house like the end of time is their loss. I'll take Abigail's gun to the lot of them. Ha ha not so untouchable now!

I'm raving, Caro. Jesus Christ, I've resisted worshipping this sickness long enough. Resisted the other as well – the frenetic scramble for safety. Who never dreamt of his own mountain, ice cold air at three thousand feet, an endless uncontaminated food supply and a flame thrower to keep the sweating scroungers at bay?

And there were enough in such a panic to survive they didn't care what it took. *Breathe in my direction, dickwit, and you're dead.*

But more went the other way, elevated the condition, deferred to the priesthood of suffering.

We learnt the stages to watch for. We knew their names almost before we knew that we knew them. The sweats, the staggers, the blessing, the burn, the pit. Only the virus itself resisted naming, until it didn't need a name, because it had become the only topic of news or conversation.

It was the third stage that held our attention, the stage we were all induced to call the blessing, whether we used the word with awe or with irony, whether we whispered it or spat it out quotation marks and all. However we viewed it, the sight of it took us by the throat – always the same unmistakable thing and always unique. A moment of grace descending at last, too late, on every sufferer. Some talent previously unexpressed leaping towards consummation. People who had never drawn drew on pavements in whatever they could lay their hands on – mud, ketchup, plaster dust. The impulse held them sometimes for minutes only, sometimes for an aching half-hour of absorbed effort before the body rebelled. Often the impulse was to sing or pull music out of some instrument, intended or improvised. They might be thwarted by lack of materials, or by the collapse of the nervous system as the staggers merged into the burn. But the urge was always there.

It terrified us, as the thought of the Last Judgment or the Rapture terrifies true believers, with a terror that stops the breath and makes the hairs rise and the mind go blank. It was the only counterweight to the mundane labour of death. Because it wasn't long before mass graves became necessary. Bodies were loaded on to trucks, carted in skips, lugged or wheeled to collection points. Soldiers and armed police patrolled with megaphones and automatic weapons, commandeering vehicles and food. Self-appointed militias cohered and fragmented. There was no shortage of guns. The dead became landfill, were stacked on abandoned construction sites, loaded into stadiums for burning, were left where they lay in empty houses or dumped like bin bags on the pavement.

People became obsessed with the science of it. They'd stumble hollow-eyed from their computers sounding off about processes of synaptic transmission. Or they got religion. Theological disputes sprang up among people who'd been godless all their lives. The blessing had a divine origin, they said, that was obvious. But were we witnessing a rent in the veil between our illusory world and the eternal? Or were the sufferers clinging ever more ferociously to the wheel, their egos clamouring on the shore of oblivion?

Others sneered at these squabbles. It was never about us. No carbon-based life form could hope to grasp the complexity of the event. To the invading race, the victims of the blessing were nothing more than an instrument, a keyboard. Minds greater than ours comprehended these individual acts of creation as notes – not even notes – harmonics within notes within melodies within symphonies of meaning, and in this way communicated with each other through our dying gestures.

And some said fuck you to all this talk, ready with chisels and bread saws to slash any throat that stood between them and their next meal.

So I steered clear of other people and locked Simon indoors. For a while there was TV. The statements from successive health ministers and secretaries of defence were incoherent, but some kind of explanation emerged. Government-sponsored research had gone spectacularly wrong, or exceeded even the most crackbrained expectations. Either way, the resulting microbe was never meant to leave the lab. The details were murky – something about a caprine pituitary gland, something about synapses harvested from a cloned ape. The spokesman who revealed its codename, the Othello Project, was forced to resign hours before the virus got him.

The web was seizing up. News sites crashed or froze on cataclysmic headlines. Links took you nowhere, or wandered randomly, the whole thing kept going by emergency generators and a scattering of servers whispering to each other in the dark.

One day the power went off in our flat and didn't come on again. One day there was no more water. If I saw the last plane ever to curve over London towards Heathrow, the last bus to cross Blackfriars Bridge, I didn't know it was the last until the absence made it so.

We skulked as long as we could, me and Simon, nine flights up with no lift. A hundred and eight steps. It discouraged visitors. There was the fear of contagion. And I was afraid more particularly for Simon, that people would remember who he was. I think maybe I went a bit mad, Caro, when you were gone. After a while it was only us still living on the top three floors, so I barricaded the staircase. We scuttled like mice through the empty apartments, living on handfuls of rice and pasta, the odd shrivelled potato sprouting new growth, tins gathered from the kitchens of our dead neighbours, melted water sucked from their freezers. Out on the balcony scraps of furniture smouldered in the barbecue. But all the mechanisms of input and output had broken down. How much of my life I'd devoted to this. Pumping water indoors to be softened, heated, distributed. Expelling it, filtered of hair and food scraps, shitladen and frothing with detergent. Creating temperate, odourless environments. Marking off territories, the indoor world of people from the outdoor world of weather, vegetation, sewage, maggots, dung beetles.

We experimented as our diet changed. We dropped little news-wrapped turds to explode softly out of sight. We squatted in the furthest bath tub and left the watery discharge to drain. We craved vegetables and fresh meat. But water was our biggest problem. It was thirst that drove me down to ground level, to weave through backstreets, dodging the soldiers and the psychos. Nine flights down with the shit bucket. Nine flights up with as much water as I could carry.

During those weeks, I walked past Waterloo Station at dusk and heard the soft footfall of foxes on the IMAX roundabout. I saw a man shot on Hungerford Bridge for a bag of oranges. I watched a group of women roasting pigeons on a spit by Stamford Wharf, bartered a bar of chocolate for a couple of birds and took one back to Simon, hot and greasy in my pocket.

We were all back on the streets by then, whoever was left, scrabbling for food and fuel, dragging our water from the river, making contact. We watched rolling news wherever it still rolled, read crudely printed missives from self-appointed officials and agitators. Gatherings were forbidden but people gathered anyway – to protest, to heal, to riot, to rage at God or at science for abandoning us.

You were well out of it, Caroline, you and our baby that we'd both been so anxious to meet. Well out of it. But I'd have you back if I could.

When your time came – when I'd read through your first fever and we'd fought each other to a state of spitting rage – your limbs began wandering and your eyes turned inward and you lost interest in the argument. Somehow you got yourself to the hall cupboard and pulled everything out, ironing board, vacuum cleaner, mop, all in a clatter with a snowdrift of plastic bags, to uncover the leftover tins of emulsion.

The blessing was so focused always – we were beginning to learn that – so knowing.

You used the blank wall above the couch and a four-inch brush. The colours were russet and sage green – maybe it was this that put the orchard in your mind. The figure running among the trees had something of you about her. As you worked, the corner of a building appeared behind her, far off among the branches, a gable and an open window, and I got the story – the loose dress, the naked feet, the hair tangled with leaves. There was fear in the girl's eyes, but a kind of joy as well. It was an escape.

And I saw that what you'd painted might have been Jane running from Rochester, or Rochester's mad wife escaping from Rochester's attic, or your own child liberated from death in the womb to run in our orchard. Or perhaps you'd painted yourself in all of them, untouched, in a world before or after or beyond the virus.

I might have asked you, and you might have told me, but the burn was tightening your throat, pressuring your mind into strange channels.

It was a quick way to go, you can say that for it. You were gone, and soon enough it was all gone, centuries of technology, thousands of years of social order. The scope of our lives has narrowed intolerably. Six months ago I was hooked up to an intricate global network. Now I'm like this bath, stranded and useless. I'll drag it down the stairs myself and dump it in the yard. Then I'll walk barefoot on the lawn and see with the naked eye by moonlight the outer limits of life's possibilities. I'll take the Merc down to the road and drive as far as it'll go. And what will I find? Nothing but desolation and danger.

Unless I drive westward to the sea and accelerate from the top of a cliff.

But I find myself still troubled by the urge to live.

Agnes

I heard the key scraping in the lock and thought it was him. The Reeds come always two together, but I heard only one person on the stairs and the key turning, and I thought he had come to let me out, to take me to his room. Or better, to take me with him on Gideon's back to the towers to see Trevor and Dell.

I thought it was Brendan come to say he loves me, that he has sat in the turret in a sweat of pain for my pain, panting for my want of air, dry for my thirst, but it was Roland, awkward and sheepish, frightened to open the door more than a crack. I ran to him and asked if he had come to let me out, but he hushed me and slipped inside, pushing the door behind him. 'If they knew I'd come,' he said. 'If the Mistress knew.'

'What, then, if they knew?'

'I don't know what.'

'Then let me out.'

He stood against the door and held something out to me. 'I came to bring you these.'

I stood close and saw they were cherries.

'You must eat them though, and they mustn't find the stones.'

'How lovely to walk in the orchard.'

'I must take the stones with me.'

'Why won't you let me out?'

'Where would you go?'

'Maybe to the moor. I'd rather starve than stay here to scratch and shrivel.' I thought then of the text from the Book of Air that the Reeds had spoken when they left me on the moor: Better that crows and ravens should pick your flesh from your bones than they should be imprisoned in a workhouse coffin and moulder in a pauper's grave. I know now what it is to be imprisoned in a coffin, what it is to moulder. I took the cherries, but held off eating them, though I longed for them, they looked so round and sweet.

Roland was looking at the floor, all sullen. 'And me? Where would I go once they'd found I'd let you out?'

'Maybe there are other places than the Hall or the village.'

He gave me an odd look. 'I would have waited for you if you'd only stayed more like yourself.'

'How am I not like myself?'

'I'd have waited, but you were always traipsing to the turret, and then nowhere to be found, and now here. And Megan comes every day to the study.'

'Every day to the study, where I'd be if they'd let me. I went to the turret only when I was sent for.'

'And Annie is put to field work until she has her baby. So it's just the two of us, Megan and me.'

'And you'd rather sit in the murk than study and Megan cares less for book learning than for her own reflection.'

'I would have waited.'

I cried then, though I wanted not to, to think of our friendship and our game of kissing. I hadn't thought myself called by Roland but it hurt me to think of him and Megan, plump smiling Megan. The two of them writing in the study and Sarah humming with pleasure at their work.

'You must be quiet, Agnes, or they'll hear us.'

'Do you think they come every time I cry out or knock against the walls or kick the door? Every time I talk to people who only whisper back because they aren't really here?'

I saw he was frightened, not just of them but of me. Frightened of my stained face, my stinking clothes, my ungathered hair, of what I might do or say which could be anything because even I don't know any more.

I took a step towards him, but he turned his back on me. He must have had the key in his pocket because I heard it grinding in its hole. A murmur reached me from the Grace Pool so I went and sat between the tiled walls and started on the cherries, chewing to shut the noise out. I had my eyes shut tight, but I heard him come towards me, felt him sit beside me in the narrow space.

'My calling must be soon,' he said. 'A few days maybe if the rain holds off. While the moon still shines. You know I must be taken to the woods.'

I opened my eyes and saw his dark shape slumped against the wall, his head in his hands.

'So you and Megan have talked.'

'Yes.'

'And it's what you want.'

'It's what must happen.'

We said nothing else for a while. From where I sat the voice from the Grace Pool was no more than the hum of the river heard from the top field. The barn owl was busy in the yard. I ate until all the cherries were gone.

'You'll breathe untainted air though,' I said at last, 'and eat what food you choose and open your own casement, and drink from the spring and wash in it, and though you need never labour like a cottager you'll dig and plant, and feel the sun on your back, and the rain when the rain comes.'

He made a noise in his throat and I felt him move and straighten. Then he said, 'Do you know why I go so often to the murk?'

'Because your father sat there the day before he died reaching for hazelnuts.'

'No. Perhaps at first. But not anymore.'

'Why then?'

I waited for his answer and thought he had sunk again into his dark mood. But when he spoke his voice was full of life. It reminded me of our games on the stairs and along the passageways of the Hall.

'You know that thing you have in the kitchen to grind meat for a pie.'

'Yes.'

'The way the wheels turn against each other. Somebody thought of that.'

'The endtimers.'

'No. Somebody. And if meat, why not apples for cider?

Why not anything?'

'Not everything needs grinding.'

'But grinding's just one kind of work. Everything takes work. Do you see, Agnes? And you turning that handle is just a way of getting the work done.'

'It's me that turns the handle, not you.'

The Grace Pool was silent. The birds had begun their fierce urgent calling. It was light enough that I could see Roland's eyes. For that moment he wasn't looking at me but at the stone wall beside me. Or at something that no one else would see.

He said, 'I spend time in the murk so I can understand how it worked.'

'And do you?'

'Partly. There are notched wheels that turn against each other, like in your meat grinder. But more of them and they're knotted together and covered up, but I poke holes in the rust and I can see more of the hidden parts. It's like this, Agnes. There are two kinds of movement. There's turning like the movement of the grinder or the machine they used for opening tins – like the movement of a cartwheel along a track. And there's a forward and back movement like when you cut a piece of wood with a saw, or bread with a knife. Whoever made the murk knew how to turn sawing into wheeling, and now I do too.'

'And why would that be such a trick?' I had no patience with his dreaming. The new day would soon be here and all I wanted was to make the kitchen fire and bring in more logs and put the porridge on to cook, to be a person again and not a dried out thought rattling in the red room.

'Because that's part of the secret, Agnes.'

'What secret?'

'Of what made the murk move without a horse to pull it, without men to turn its wheels.'

'So what's the other part?'

'The harder part. I don't know what made the back and forward movement. Not a man's arm, but something like the punch of a fist over and over, but not a fist either. I think

137

something like a green log bursting in the fire. A blow to send the air rushing.'

'And all this so you can ride without a horse?' All I wanted was for Brendan to take me by the hand to the Mistress and to say he had called me and I had answered.

'Riding doesn't matter. What matters is finding something to push and push where there's no man to push.'

'Like when I boil the porridge in the clay pot,' I said. 'The lid is heavy but the steam doesn't mind.'

'Yes. Of course. I hadn't thought of that.'

'So maybe you should build a fire and blow the murk across the lawn with boiling porridge.'

'Maybe I should.'

I heard the eagerness in his voice and it made me angry. 'Except someone would have to carry the logs to feed the fire so the same person might as well push the murk.'

'It's not about the murk. I keep telling you. It's about what the endtimers knew. It's about how they lived and how we live. It's about work.'

'You talk about work but you don't even know what work is.' I was in a rage that the sun was rising, that he would soon be gone and I would be here still. 'Every day while she lived my mother carried water from the brook. And every day before they locked me in here I carried water from the well into the kitchen at the Hall. And a pot of water is as heavy as a stone and slops about like a squalling baby that won't lie still to be carried. You can sit in the murk and dream because you don't know what it is to live like a cottager.'

'Listen, Agnes. I have to go soon, or be caught here with you. I can't let you out, because they'd lock you away forever and send me to the forest to fight with wolves and scroungers.' He was looking at me now and his eyes were full of fire. 'I can tell Megan I don't love her. That I thought I did but it was a mistake. I'd take a beating from her father and suffer all their dark looks if I knew you wanted me and only me. If I knew you'd be good and let them let you go.'

His eyes were too fierce. I pulled my hair over my face to shut them out, and to cover my tears. But I couldn't hide my sobbing. I wanted to say what he wanted me to say, but I didn't know if it was true. Or if it was truly Brendan I wanted. Or if I wanted neither of them, but only to be myself.

And how could I promise to be good when I couldn't even promise to bleed when it was already past my time to bleed. Long before I'd stopped my noise he'd gone, locking the door again.

The cherry stones were on the floor beside me. He'd forgotten them in talking of the murk. Or in asking things of me I couldn't give. I picked them up because Roland didn't want them found, but thinking: who minds what moulders in this room? I took them to the window to push them through the broken pane, but kept hold of them because Roland had brought them. It was a kind thing he did to bring me cherries. So I hid them under the bed.

I looked in the mirror to see who this Agnes was that Roland had come to visit, to ask her what she had done with the Agnes everybody wanted her to be. If I turned my head I could see my eyes in one piece of the glass, my mouth in another, the dirt around it streaked with tears, such an ugly unwashed face for Roland to look at. It made me angry that any other villager could go to the river and I must stay uselessly here. I would ask the Reeds for water. I would hammer at the door and shout and no one should rest until I had water enough to wash in. Then I was sad again that mother was dead and Roland to marry Megan and there was no one to care about my face or any other part of me.

Down in the yard I heard the hollow sound of a dry log pulled from the pile, and another, and the horses whinnying. I felt the warmth of the sun on me and watched the stain on my mouth turn to blood. I thought I was hurt in some new way. Then I understood. Not dirt, and not blood either, but cherry juice. And I had wasted it. If I had kept the cherries, if I had waited for Roland to go, I might have squashed them between my legs, letting the juice run on my skin and stain my skirt. I would have shown the Reeds when they came for my pot.

But now I have nothing to show, and must hide even what I have, rubbing at my face with spit.

Jason

There's a noise of knocking and creaking and I think I'm listening to the rocking chair. But the rocking chair is down in the TV room – the snug, you called it, a better name for it now the TV is dead. It's the bedroom door I can hear. The draught from the window has set it off. It would be an easy job to fix the catch, but it's low on my list.

I think I was dreaming of the rocking chair – because of the door creaking, probably, and maybe because of what happened with Simon earlier this evening.

I was in the kitchen and heard a racket from the snug. When I went in, the monkey was clinging to the side of the rocking chair, throwing himself one way and then the other and making those high humming notes that sound like laughter. Simon was sitting on the floor in front of the chair, watching the TV screen solemnly, absorbed by its blankness.

'All right, Si?' I said.

He didn't look at me. He just said, 'My head hurts.'

'Too much telly.'

When he raised his eyes to meet mine, I thought at first he was annoyed at my stupid joke. Then I saw his puzzlement.

'Uncle Jason.'

'Yes, Si.'

'Where are all the...' He sniffed and hummed and his neck tightened, so I squatted to his level and waited for the word to pop out. '... people?'

'They died, Simon, remember. They caught the virus and died.'

'No they didn't.'

'It's sad, I know.' I put a hand on his arm. 'I'd bring them back if I could.'

'No, I mean on TV. Where are they all?'

'Oh. They were just people too.'

Aleksy came into the room. 'Come, Rasputin. I've a treat for you.'

The monkey clambered from the rocking chair to his shoulder.

'Not the cartoons,' Simon said. 'They weren't people. Sponge Bob, Dora the Ex... plorer.'

'No they weren't people. But people had to draw them and do their voices. People had to send them whizzing through space to our TV and make the electricity so you could switch it on.'

He thought about that for a bit. Then he said, 'My head hurts a lot.'

Aleksy stopped in the doorway. 'You have headache? I get you aspirin. How about that?'

Simon looked up at him with a blank expression.

'Didn't no one ever give you aspirin?'

Simon shrugged.

'A pill to make your headache better?'

Simon thought about this, and said, 'Baby cetamol.'

'Baby seat moll?'

'Zackly.'

'I get you this, then. Baby seat moll. I mix it in water.'

'And Urs'la...' He paused. It wasn't the sound he was struggling with but the memory. 'Urs'la gave me rescue remedy.'

'How many drops?'

Simon held up three fingers.

'So one baby seat moll mixed up in water with three drops Urs'la's special remedy.'

I followed Aleksy into the passage. 'Aleksy, what are doing? We haven't got any of that stuff.'

'You know, Jason,' he said, 'you are not always so clever.'

Simon was saying my name, so I went back into the den and sat in the rocking chair.

'When someone died, Urs'la mmm-planted a tree.'

'That was nice of her.'

'Can we, then?'

'Can we what?'

'Mmm-plant trees.'

'I suppose.'

'How many?'

'I don't know.'

'Count up how many.'

'I can't do that, Si, no one can do that.'

'Count up.' He was glaring at me now. 'On your fingers. One for each person.'

'Christ, Si, there aren't enough fingers.'

Django came in. 'What's happening, Simon? Aleksy says you're in pain.'

'Calm down, Django. It's just a headache.'

'Don't speak for him. He has his own voice.'

Aleksy reappeared, holding a glass with an inch of cloudy water in it. 'Here you are, Simon. Drink up like good boy.'

Django put a hand between them. 'What's that you're giving him?'

'Nothing. Something for his head.'

'So is it nothing, or is it something?' Django gave an ambiguous smile. 'You see, Simon, how they'd pull you along with cords of deceit.'

'Take it, Simon,' Aleksy said. 'Will make you feel better.'

'Cords of deceit like cart ropes. But you're not a horse, are you Simon. You're not an ox.'

'For God's sake, Django,' I said, 'let him drink it or not drink it, what difference does it make?'

Abigail stood in the doorway, drawn by our raised voices. I was conscious of how she must see us, confronting each other, ready to fight for control of Simon's headache.

'Simon,' she said, 'go and fetch some logs for the stove. Fill two baskets. Then you should go to bed.'

When Simon was gone, Aleksy raised his arms in a gesture of surrender, drank the cloudy water, and followed Simon to the door, swinging the empty glass. Django relaxed, as though the sight of this placebo had really unnerved him. He flashed me a smile that expressed either conciliation or triumph – I couldn't tell which – and went out into the yard.

I was alone with Abigail. She hesitated then asked me what the argument was about.

'Django's got this obsession with controlling Simon, what he eats and drinks even. And Simon seems to think he's got to along with it. It really gets to me.'

She put a hand on my arm. 'Don't let it, though, Jason. I want you not to be angry.'

'It's not just about food. He's filling him with weird ideas.'

'We can cope with all that. But we have to be the grown-ups, you and me. That's what we have to do now.'

I was conscious then, being close to her, that I'd sweated all day and hadn't been to the spring yet to wash. She didn't seem to mind and I was glad of that. I had a mad impulse to kiss her, but I didn't. I'm glad of that too. Her stillness calmed me, as it always does.

After a moment she said, 'I should help Maud with the milking,' and I was alone with the rocking chair and the television.

The wind's getting stronger, and the sound of the door comes louder and more frequent. I get out of bed and look around for something the right thickness to wedge under it. There are your old books, Caroline, in the alcoves on either side of the chimney breast, novels mainly. Even after you started reading on a tablet and declared yourself corrupted, you hung on to them. I hesitate to use anything you once loved.

It occurs to me that I should teach Simon to read. And I should teach him to count and do sums. We should get the TV out of the snug and put the room to better use. Except there's nothing useful to be learnt now by sitting in a classroom.

On the top shelf, there's an old computer manual, impenetrably useless even when computers still worked. I reach it down. I'm on my knees with the door shut and I hesitate, thinking of Simon and his headache. Remember how he used to climb into our bed, Caro, when he first came to live with us.

After you'd gone we always slept together until we left London. One of these nights, I reckon he'll need me again, and I don't want my door shut against him. So I open the door as wide as its hinges will allow and jam the manual between its lower edge and the floorboards.

For a while I stand at the window. There's a clear sky full of stars and the sound of the wind pushing through the trees and the house breathing.

Agnes

I have done what I could. For part of the night I smelt the air in the woods. But they tricked me and things are worse than ever. I have heard words harder than any text in the Book of Air.

I knew if I cut my arm on the glass they would see where the blood came from. If I called them to see the blood while it was fresh, the wound in my wrist would show and they would bind it up and slap me for my insolence. But with the cherries eaten only blood would do. I had the pen and nothing else and must use it somewhere they wouldn't see.

I was afraid to at first and sat with the pen, not sure how to begin. Then the Reeds came with food and left, and came again having emptied my pot, and I knew I must wait another day to be set free. At dusk I made myself do it, sitting in the narrow space where the walls are tiled in stone. There was more blood than I meant. I cried out, but no one came.

Even if they hear me, they know not to come.

After a time I reached up and took my white feather from the shelf and soaked its tip. I crawled on my knees to the door and pushed the feather under it. Then I crouched low to the floor with my mouth to the crack and blew, watching with one eye while the feather lifted, scurried and settled. I slept then, just I where I lay.

Footsteps woke me and the creaking of boards on the landing. Then silence. Then the scrape of the key – not turned but pulled from the lock – and the sound of breathing, with a faint roughness in the throat that told me who this was that looked for me through the keyhole. The room was full of greenish moonlight. If I had lain in the bed, Brendan would have seen me there. If I had been asleep how long would he have watched?

I got to my knees, steadying myself on the door, and whispered that I was ready, that it was time. My eye searched for his and saw movement, then light, then darkness as the key slid in.

'You see the blood,' I said. 'It's time. You can let me out.'

I heard his tread on the staircase and shouted, 'Tell them it's time.'

I thought I might wait until morning, but it was still dark when the Reeds came. They led me down the backstairs, through the stables, and out into the High Wood, careless of my weakness and my bare feet. I asked them were they taking me home, told them this wasn't the way, asked if the Mistress had seen my blood. They said nothing, but I felt the hardness of their hands.

There was a fire burning in the clearing among the birches and a pot steaming over the flames. I was dizzy with hunger and the summer air and the smell of the broth. They knelt me on the ground and let me sink back on my heels. One of the women took a ladle and filled a cup. I raised my hands to take it, but they kept hold, pouring faster than I could swallow and I coughed some of it back. Sweet and sharp it was with a taste of earth. They poured more and my mouth was all peat water and fungus. They threw a blanket round me and for a while I watched the flames rise and weave and spit sparks as big as fireflies.

Then I was pulled up again and led stumbling in among the trees to another clearing, where ancient oaks towered above me. They sat me on a chair facing a dark figure, thickly veiled, and behind her, like blossom on a bush, a blaze of candles to blind me. She made a movement with her hand and we were alone. Everything moved oddly. I saw all the blades of grass where the light caught them, the different ways they curled and twisted, and the caterpillars climbing.

Her eyes were covered but I felt her looking.

I asked her, 'Why have you brought me here? What is this place?'

Her answer was no more than a whisper. 'The dialogue box.'

'What is the dialogue box?'

'My domain.'

'What happens here?'

'A window opens.'

'I want to go home.'

'Your home is the red room.'

'I was to stay until I bled. The Mistress promised.' I felt the tears coming, I felt so sorry for myself. 'I am Agnes daughter of Janet. Agnes daughter of Walt who died when I had seen only eight summers. My home is Walt's cottage – my cottage. I want my own bed.'

'You are a cry from the red room, a knocking on floorboards, a scrape at the door.'

'I am Agnes.'

She leant towards me and murmured at my ear, 'Pass a word and use a name.'

'Agnes, daughter of Janet. I work at the Hall, chopping wood, lighting fires, sweeping staircases and passageways, studying the Book of Air.'

'Figuring the task bar.'

'I feel strange. Am I dreaming you?'

'They've put you in a sleep state.'

'Where is Brendan?'

'Lost in the Book of Windows.'

'Where is my mother?'

'Your mother is dead. Why did you speak like that at her burial?'

'She lived all those years. She wasn't nothing. If Jane why not Janet? Where is Janet's book?'

'There are four books. Everybody knows this.'

'Cooking and scrubbing, sweeping the ash from the fire grate, feeding the pig.'

'Four books with the Book of Death.'

'Food for the pig is all she is now. No more talking in her sleep. No more pain. No more sighing. No more stinking of piss.'

'Can you be trusted with a secret, Agnes?'

'Yes, anything.'

'I don't think so. You spoke at your mother's burial about the Reader.'

'Where is he? Where is Brendan? It was wrong of him to let them take me.'

There was a sound then and a movement of the head and I knew who this was. Not a Reed at all, not a woman even, but Brendan himself. I would have known him at once if they hadn't fed me mushrooms.

'Can you be trusted to be good,' he said, 'if the Mistress lets you out? Will you stop your mouth at burials? Will you keep these wild thoughts to yourself?'

'Will she let me out?'

'If she does.'

'This is blood on my skirt, look. You can tell her. And tell her I'm sick. My throat is sore. It's too cruel to lock me up. My feet are bruised from pacing.'

'Show me, Agnes.'

I raised one foot towards him and he took it on his lap. So soothing it was to be held, to feel his hands on my ankle and on the aching sinews of my calf. He reached for the other foot. There was such steadiness in his touch, and so firmly he held and stroked me, drawing my skirt above my knee and pulling me towards him, that I felt my whole body grow slack and the tears come freely to wet my face.

Then such sorrow and compassion in his sighing. 'And this will be our secret, Agnes?'

'Oh yes,' I said, 'our secret.' And I was so lost to myself that there was only pleasure as the hands strayed higher, opening me to the cool night air, so content I was to know nothing and to think nothing and to let my body become servant to another's will. I had no sense of danger, until I remembered my book held tight against my back by the belt at my waist.

I moved suddenly to straighten myself and to hold his hands from reaching around and underneath me.

I said, 'I have a bigger secret, anyway, bigger than this. Bigger than riding to see the scroungers.'

He stopped and looked at me, 'What secret?'

I wouldn't have said these things. I would have kept everything hidden. But the broth the women fed me had moved me sideways from myself.

'What secret, Agnes?'

'I have a baby.'

'But you bled.' He made no more effort to soften his voice.

So I cried to him directly in his own person. 'Why have you done this to me, sir? Locked me away to hear voices and go mad?'

'Not me. The Mistress. The women.'

'Why did you let them?'

'It's been cruel for me too, to lie so close to you, night after night, and think I only had to unlock your door and have you. I've fought myself to leave you alone. And all the time thinking it wouldn't be so long. You'd bleed and they'd let you out.'

'I wanted to bleed. I wanted to so badly.'

'And you did. I saw the feather. I see the stain on your skirt.'

'I knew I wouldn't, so I cut myself.'

I heard him breathing noisily in the dark and felt him pull away. He said, 'This is worse.' Then he asked me, 'What will you say about this baby?'

'Whatever you want me to say.'

'Promise then.'

'And you'll make them let me out?'

'Promise first.'

'I promise.'

'To say what I tell you to say.'

'I've promised. What then?'

'That you were made to. By a scrounger.'

'Oh. But I can't.' I knew all in a rush that there would be a child, a child to grow up in the village and be scorned because she was a scrounger's litter. I couldn't let them think that. Her life must be more than mine, even if I must make mine nothing. 'Please sir,' I said, 'something else.'

'What something?'

'That it was my fault. That I came to you while you were asleep. Or drunk on gin. That I milked you while you snored. Because your soul cried out to mine in your dreams. Because I am without shame like a sow in heat. Because I want… Because I want my child to be your child, to know all the secrets of the Book of Windows.'

'There are no secrets.' He pulled the veil from his head and I could see the dark outline of his face. For a moment he tugged at the neck of his shirt as if he couldn't breathe. 'The Book of Windows,' he said, 'has no secrets because it has no meaning. It was left to us to make us howl and gibber.' He spoke so urgently, so angrily that I felt the warmth of his spit.

'But all the highest wisdom.'

'Listen to me Agnes. I have read it every way it can be read. Yes, they told us it was the highest wisdom of the endtime, strained and simmered to its essence, that it was the moment of blessing, the breath of all the dying endtimers brought together into one living breath. But I can find in it only the fever that killed them. They were raving who wrote it, parched with the heat of their own blood. What has been boiled and burned away is any touch of thought and all that's left is ash. I know all the words. I have them in my heart. I say them over, slow and solemn. I bring them here to the darkness of the wood hoping for their wings to open like moths rising into brightness. I speak them to you, Agnes, calling to the spirit of Jane in you, watching for any answering spark, but nothing comes.' He stared at the ground and I listened to the noise of his breathing. 'You saw the pictures, Agnes, as I saw them. The scroungers sit and stare and in the time it takes a villager to plough a field or roast a pig they know more about calling than I've learned from all my years with the Book of Windows.'

'But they can't do it.'

'No, they can't do it, they can't call and be heard, but they can hear the calling. They can see how the endtimers lived and what they looked like.'

'But they can't go when they're called.'

He looked at me then and said 'No' and made such a hollow sound of it that for the moment my own sadness was swept away by his.

'And now here's one more thing you've tricked out of me,' he said, 'one more thing for you to babble about – that Brendan has searched his book to its bottom and found nothing.'

'What trick? And what if you have found nothing? Why are you afraid? There's no one to lock the door on you, to hurt you and starve you of water.'

'You don't know.'

'You're the Reader. You live in the turret at the Hall. The backstairs are yours, and the stables. You come and go as you like.'

'Because, Agnes. Because of what I know. But what if I know nothing? Less even than the villagers think everyone knows?'

The shadows deepened around him and he seemed hunched under their weight. Tiny creatures crept and scurried between us, voles and stag beetles and ants, every one making its own sound. The air shifted and the slender boughs dipped and straightened. I seemed to hear a single twig and the soft fibres of a single leaf snagging on it. Then the wood was a heaving din as if a door had swung open and let the noise out, every forest creature rooting and nestling.

'If I say, sir, that I crept naked into your bed when you were sleeping.'

'No Agnes.'

'If I say that I made you. That I held a kitchen knife at your neck and said either tell me all the secrets of the Book of Windows or give me a child that can learn them or I'll slice you like a boiled chicken. And you said one of those I can't do. And I said which. And you said the secrets are for those who give their lives to book learning. And I said, of the other two then, choose.'

'No Agnes.' And he whistled as you would whistle a dog.

'If I say I put the knife to my own neck and made you do it.'

'No.'

'What then?'

But the women were coming out of the shadows. I hadn't thought that the Reeds answered to the Reader's whistle.

'Then you are nothing but a coward, afraid to stand up to the Mistress, afraid to do what even poor stammering Daniel found the courage to do when he claimed Annie, though the child wasn't his.'

It was only then that I saw Uncle Morton's limp and the solid shape of Peter under the straggle of leaves. And I felt their hands on me again, hands strong enough to wrestle a ram, to fell a tree with three blows of the axe.

'You must go back to the red room, Agnes.'

'Then I shall keep no secrets, not yours nor mine, but shout every secret from my window.'

'And the villagers will bend to their digging and cover their heads to shut out your noise.'

'They come to me at night.'

'Who comes to you?'

'I know I'm not the first. There was a child you sent to live with the scroungers.'

'No one comes to you, Agnes.'

'The child you had with Sarah that my mother helped her have, when your child with my mother was already buried in secret.'

I felt the sting of his hand on my cheek and against my ear, and would have fallen if the men hadn't held me.

He spoke quietly, spitting the words. 'There was no child, not with Sarah, not with Janet.'

Whatever I shouted then was caught in the scarf pulled across my face.

They hurt my feet dragging them through the woods. I am bruised with kicking and the force of their hands on me, my nails broken on branches, on doorframes and banisters.

I shall be here now until the baby is born. If the baby lives to be born. If I live to see it. I shall dwindle and sicken until my thoughts wander. When my baby is dead, they'll let me out. When I'm broken. Like a sparrow searching for the air, hitting the walls until it's too weak to fly. The daylight will hurt my eyes and every sound will scare me and I shall cower in the cottage like my mother, scratching a pig for company. They know my secrets now. Brendan knows all my secrets. I've given them up to him for nothing. Brendan doesn't love me and never loved me.

All except my book. My book is what Brendan doesn't know. The book is what no one knows because it's beyond their guessing.

The ink pot is dry. I'm down to the last scratching. Without ink the book is nothing. If I don't write and if no one reads, it's nothing. A dream I must wake up from. Agnes daughter of Janet. This is how I write. This is not a text. What is it then?

Jason

Abigail finds me digging. I'm deep in my hole, puddling in murky water, levering up shards of blue-green shale. My life is no bigger than this hole. My mind is as dark.

'Surely that's enough.'

Her features are blurred in the bright air. I step sideways, lose my balance and stagger. My shoulder settles softly against the clay wall.

'Rest, Jason. Drink some water.'

'I want to get this done.'

'And you will, but you must take care of yourself. Let me help you up.'

I rub my eyes. Her hand reaches down out of a rainbow of shifting light and I raise a hand to meet it. She steadies herself. Cradling a piece of rock, I hoist myself on to the ladder. Three steps up and I'm able to dump the rock at ground level and pull myself out. I stand clumsily. My boots are heavy with mud.

'I have to get my strength back.'

'But you push yourself too hard.' Letting go of my hand, she pulls a cloth from her belt and wipes my face.

'Is that blood on your skirt?'

'I've been making jam. Now sit there and don't move. I'm getting you water.'

I settle on the pile of rock and picture what has to be done – the stone lining, the brick flu, the timber structure – door towards the house, window facing the hills for privacy. Some jackdaws are squabbling outside the kitchen. Then Abigail is back with two cups and a jug of water, cold from the spring.

She asks me when I last saw Simon.

'I don't know. Breakfast I suppose.'

We sat around the kitchen table with mugs of nettle tea.

Abigail poached eggs, dropping them one at a time loose in a pan of boiling water, while I sliced up a bowl of apples. And we talked about the day. Maud and Deirdre had milked the cows already and let the hens and geese out to scratch and peck on the lawn. I'd done an hour's digging. Aleksy had been in the top field, hacking weeds. Django? It was anyone's guess what Django had been up to, but here he was anyway, ready to eat. Abigail had given Simon a wash and dressed him in his long trousers and a woolly jumper and he sat for a bit, kicking the legs of his chair and humming between bites of egg before drifting out to play in the yard.

'We have blades,' Aleksy said, 'knives, scythes, axes. But what about... you know, stones to sharpen them?'

'Whetstones.'

'Exactly, Jason. What about whetstones? Scythes you must sharpen all the time or the grasses don't get cut, just...' He made a whistling noise, dropping his arm from the vertical to the horizontal.

'You want to go out this morning,' Abigail asked him, 'to find whetstones?'

'Whetstones, yes, and whatever else. To take another look round the farms out on the English Road. I take the cart, if Deedee comes. I don't handle the horse so good.'

Deirdre was distracted. I thought perhaps she hadn't slept, or was concentrating on not losing her breakfast. She looked around the table at the rest of us, opened her mouth to speak, shrugged and said nothing. She was reluctant to go – that was obvious – but perhaps just as reluctant to lose her status as horse expert. Maybe being alone with Aleksy was a factor, but I couldn't tell whether it was a draw or a deterrent.

'So if you two go,' Abigail said, 'and Jason digs, Maud can wash clothes and bedding while it's fine.'

Everyone seemed OK with that.

'And Django, you could help me get more wood in.'

An ordinary morning. The kind of morning we've come to think of as ordinary. Except that Simon's missing, and Abigail has pulled me from my digging to enquire about him.

'So that's the last time you saw him – at breakfast?'

'What about Django? Has Django got him?'

'Django went off by himself about an hour ago – to gather nuts, he said – and left me boiling the jam. Simon wanders but he likes to know where the grown-ups are.'

'I heard him playing in the shed when I was crossing the yard. Since then I've had my head in this hole.'

Not quite true, now I think about it. I looked out later when Aleksy and Deirdre were pulling the cart from the shed, still with its awning advertising Deirdre's shop and loaded with empty boxes – the big horse so quiet, stepping back neatly for Deirdre to hitch it up, and the canvas flapping. Abigail and Django had paused in their work, Django resting on his axe, Abigail looking up from the woodpile. For a moment then I wondered who was watching Simon, but the dark trench claimed my attention.

'Have you looked upstairs?'

'I've been up and down, calling.'

'He sometimes won't answer if he's busy with something. What goes on in his head, Abigail? Does he think about everything that's happened?'

'Children have ways of coping.'

'What kind of a life is he going to have?'

'Easier than ours. He'll grow up into it. It'll be what he's used to. We're still adjusting. He'll know what his life is from the start.'

It calms me to hear her talk like this. 'And he'll be all right when we're all gone?'

'There'll be others, surely. Other children.' She blushes and looks away towards the moor.

'Deirdre's, to start with. You know she's pregnant.'

'She told you then.' She faces me, with a puzzled look that says, *why you, I wonder?* 'She asked me to keep it to myself for now.'

'It's sort of obvious I suppose. If you know what to look for.'

'And you know?'

'Caroline was pregnant. My wife. We were expecting a child.'

'Oh.' She takes my hand, calloused and flaked with mud and holds it in her lap. 'I'm sorry, Jason. That's hard.'

'Not as things go.'

I'm conscious of what I'm not saying, not owning up to, while I'm accepting Abigail's sympathy – that I didn't discover Deirdre's secret by looking. 'I'm sorry, I'm muddying your skirt.'

'That's all right.'

The geese come waddling round the side of the house. They push their necks forward and run hissing at the jackdaws, who heave themselves into the air.

'Can I ask you something, Jason?'

'Of course you can.'

'How come Simon's skin is so dark?'

The question takes me by surprise. I mean, Caro, if someone had asked me something like that in normal times, before the virus, I've had said, *how come you've got shit for brains?* But Abigail so obviously means no harm by it that I try to give her a serious answer. 'Random – that was what Simon's dad called himself... Random was West Indian. I mean that's where his parents were from.'

'From India.'

'Not *Indian* Indian. From Jamaica or Trinidad or somewhere. You know – Afro-Caribbean.'

'You mean they were from Africa?'

'Originally, I suppose. Their ancestors were. Would have been taken to the West Indies as slaves. But Random was from Peckham.'

She looks blank.

'That's in south London. You don't know what I'm talking about, do you?'

'Sorry. You must find me very stupid. I've seen Indians. There was an Indian family in the village near our farm. But I've never seen an African.'

'What kind of a life have you had, Abigail?'

'A simple enough life, I suppose. Simpler than yours. We had a tractor and running water and hot water for washing and cleaning. But we kept to ourselves and ate mainly what we grew.'

'Did you watch telly? Use the internet?'

'No, nothing like that.'

'But you went to school?'

'We weren't to talk to strangers. But the grown-ups taught us things. And when I grew up I taught the younger ones.'

'Like Maud.'

'I did what I could for Maud.'

It's like watching a bird settle on a branch, hearing her talk. You don't move. You hold your breath almost. Challenge or probe, show too much curiosity, and the wings flap, the branch dips and rises, and she's gone.

But I ask anyway. 'Did you have children?'

'No.' She looks at her hands. 'Not yet.'

'And did Maud never speak?'

'She was chatty enough at one time.'

'And what happened?'

She hesitates, drinks from her mug. 'It's not my story to tell.'

'I'll wait for Maud's version, then, shall I?'

She looks at me to see that I'm joking and she laughs. She's inclined to cover her face – I feel the impulse in her hand – but instead she turns away, and I see how the laughter lightens her and how young she is.

I'm wondering which of us will be first to let go of the other's hand and get on with what needs doing. Then we hear the cart on the drive. It's moving faster than it should. We're halfway across the yard when the horse comes round the side of the house, dragging the cart at a speed that tilts it on to its outer wheels at the turn. The geese scatter. The jackdaws flap from the stable roof, making their harsh noise. Deirdre pulls sharply on the reins and the horse rears up.

Aleksy is slumped beside her. Deirdre's shouting, 'He's hit, they shot him, he's losing blood.' We're all over him, trying to help him down – Deirdre above him on the cart, Abigail lifting his legs, me pulling at him, taking the weight. And Aleksy's thumping me, pummelling my shoulder. 'Not me. The boy. See to the boy.' I pull away and he stumbles to the ground, cursing in Polish.

I get on the cart and fling the cardboard boxes aside.

And there's Simon in a foetal crouch. He rocks from side to side, humming to himself.

'What is it, Si? Where'd they get you?'

Abigail is beside me, straightening Simon's legs, feeling for damage, touching his arms and fingers.

I lift his hand gently from the side of his head. There's a gash above the ear, muddied and bleeding – not a bullet wound.

'Is it your head, Si? Does it hurt anywhere else?'

He's crammed with words that won't come out.

I carry him into the kitchen, following the trail of Aleksy's blood. Aleksy is sideways on a kitchen chair, his good arm clinging to the back. Deirdre has cut the shirt sleeve from the injured arm. For a moment the wound is bright and open like a mouth, blood pulsing out of it. She's knotted a tea towel above and winds it tight with a spoon. Abigail has pushed aside jars of jam to make space on the table for her sewing box. She pulls out pin cushions and reels of thread. She has a sheet over her shoulder. Maud comes up from the cellar with a bottle of brandy. They've got stuff stored away I don't even know about. The kettle's already rattling on the stove.

I sit Simon on a chair and crouch to look at him. There's no colour in his face. The external bleeding isn't much but I'm worried about the knock to his skull. Behind him, Aleksy's doing a lot of grunting. Maud and Abigail hold him still while Deirdre sews him up. Simon keeps twisting round to look, so I give up and turn his chair the other way.

When I start cleaning the wound Simon says, 'Ow' and puts his hand up but he doesn't take his eyes off the main attraction. 'I said Ow.'

'I heard you, but I've got to make sure it's clean before I put a bandage on.'

Aleksy asks Deirdre if she's done this before.

'With a horse, once, I did,' she says.

'Well remember, please, that I am not a horse.'

I explode at them. 'Christ, you two, what were you thinking, taking Simon?'

'He was on the cart,' Deirdre says. 'He was playing in the boxes. We were a mile away before we knew.'

Aleksy grunts. 'Stop talking and sew, you psycho bitch horse doctor.'

Simon giggles.

I ask him what's funny and he shrugs. 'He called her a cycle horse witch doctor.'

'Tell me what happened today. Who attacked you?'

'Yellow people,' he says.

Yellow people? And they threw stones at you?'

'Sticks and stones will break your bones.'

'And fired a gun?'

'It was loud.'

'Were you scared?'

'I hid in my house.'

'You would have been safer back here, you know, in a real house with stone walls. You can build your house in the dining room if you like. Do you want to do that?'

'OK.'

'Did the stones hit your house and knock it down?'

'I looked out the door.'

'Why did you do that?'

'When Aleksy...'

'When Aleksy was shot?'

He nods. 'And...'

'He started making all that noise.'

'Yes.'

Abigail comes with the brandy and a strip torn from her sheet for a bandage and leaves them beside me on the table.

'I'm going to put some alcohol on this, Simon,' I tell him. 'It might sting.'

He pulls away, shaking his head.

'I've got to. It's so it won't get infected.'

He looks at me now. 'But Jangle says...'

'What? What does he say?'

'Jangle says I'm inf... inf...'

'You're *not* infected, Simon. I got sick and now I'm better. But you're fine.'

'Not that.' He's annoyed with me for getting it wrong. 'Jangle says I'm inf...isible.'

'Invisible? How does he make that out?' I'm laughing and I can see he doesn't like it. I reach for the brandy bottle. 'Is it a game,' I ask him, 'some game you and Django play?'

This doesn't help. He's struggling to say no, or not a game, or to call me naughty for laughing.

'Just hold still,' I tell him. I put a corner of the bandage to the mouth of the brandy bottle, up-end it, stand it back on the table and dab the wound.

'Ow ow, I said ow.'

'Are you invisible all the time, or only some of the time?'

'All the time, Jangle says.'

'And are you invisible to everyone? Can I see you? Can Django see you? What about Abigail?'

I can tell these are annoyingly stupid questions.

'You can't mmm....'

There's a b word buzzing in his throat. His eyes bulge and he does his vomit face. I take Abigail's bandage and begin winding it about his head.

'...mmmbeat me.'

I stop what I'm doing, hold his head and look into his face. 'No one's going to beat you, Simon. Did someone say they would? Did Django?'

'No. You...'

'I can't, I get it. And I won't beat you. Whatever you do. No one will. I promise.'

'No one. Ever. Jangle says.'

I split the end of the bandage to tie it round his head. It bothers me that he's talking like this. No one's ever hit him, as far as I know.

Deirdre has finished with Aleksy, so I take Simon by the hand to join them. Aleksy's still clinging to his chair. He's pale and sweaty and breathing hard. Maud comes from the stove with a warm flannel and wipes his face.

'You all right?' I ask him.

'Better than ever.'

'Simon says you were attacked by yellow people.'

Aleksy nods. 'Fluorescent jackets.'

'Like a uniform,' Deirdre says. 'An army.'

'What if they're just people,' Abigail says, 'like us, and these jackets are just what they had?'

'That's what I tell her. Listen to Abigail, Deedee. These people find a warehouse somewhere. Nice waterproof jackets hanging on hooks. Who cares what they look like?'

'Dozens of them? All the same?'

'Dozens! Who says dozens?'

'I saw at least a dozen.'

'Not so many. I saw maybe five.'

'They were among the trees.'

'Exactly. Trees, shadows, patches of sunlight enough to blind you. You see someone here and then here. Same few people, scurrying about.'

'Scurrying! These men had guns, Aleksy.'

'Maybe men. Maybe women and children. Maybe just children.'

'An army of men. I'm telling you, Abigail. Jason, listen. Armed with guns. They nearly killed you, Aleksy. You're not thinking straight. He isn't thinking. They're organised. They were waiting for us.'

'Kill me? With this scratch?'

'It was a warning shot.'

'It was a pop gun. A small handgun maybe in the hands of a child. Bang, bang, bang. Couldn't hit me once. Just this graze. Couldn't hit any of us. Some soldier wanted to kill us, Deedee, we'd be dead.'

'And we will be. They'll come for us, now they know where we are.'

'And how they know this?'

'If they followed us.'

'If. If.'

'It's not the same for you, Aleksy. Listen to me, Abigail. Aleksy thinks this is the worst that can happen – a bullet in the arm. Even a bullet in the head isn't the worst. Getting shot isn't the worst, Jason.' She turns back to Abigail. 'They're men. They don't know what we know.'

'Forget men and women, Deedee. It's land, OK? Our land. Their land. We don't go past the woods no more, then they don't come for us. Live, let live.'

Abigail puts her arms round Deirdre. 'We're safe here, love. They won't hurt us here. You did a good job. See how we take care of each other.' She stoops to gather up the bloody scraps of sheeting. She gives the floor around Aleksy's chair a rough wipe and stands up with her bundle. 'Maud, make a pot of tea. Real tea. Use three bags and let it sit. We all need tea. And then we'll clean this place up.' She goes out the back door into the yard.

Aleksy and Simon are comparing bandages and I'm asking Deirdre about the time she sewed up a horse and Maud's warming the teapot, when Django comes in from the yard with Abigail behind him. 'Where is he?' He drops his shoulder bag on the floor and hazelnuts spill out. 'Is he OK?'

'I'll be fine,' Aleksy says. 'Strong as an ox.'

Django doesn't respond. He crosses to where Simon is standing and drops to his knees. 'Who did this to you?'

'Yellow people.'

'Butter and honey shall he eat.' Django is talking to himself, then louder to all of us. 'Butter and honey shall he eat that he may know to refuse evil, and choose the good.' He's impatient, exasperated. He stands and turns to Abigail. 'Do we have butter and honey?'

'There is no butter, Django. There's cream...'

'Why aren't we making butter?'

'You want butter,' Aleksy says, 'build a churn. Here's a project for you. We'll all be happy. Even happier if you help with wheat so next year we'll have bread to spread it on. You see Abigail's made jam already.'

'And honey?'

'We'll have honey,' Abigail says, 'in the spring. There are hives in one of the cottage gardens.'

'Not till the spring?'

'Maud's kept bees before. She knows what she's doing.'

'We talked about this, Django,' Deirdre says. 'Weren't you here? We'll be able to make candles from the wax.'

'Cream then, and jam, stirred together in a cup.' It's meant as an order. No one moves but Django doesn't notice. 'For butter and honey shall everyone eat that is left in the land.' He's looking at Simon again. He lifts him under the arms and stands him on a chair. He's fiddling with the knot of the bandage. When he begins to unwind it, I step in to stop him. 'What d'you think you're up to?'

'Don't touch him.' He speaks fiercely. 'You smell of the earth.'

'I've been digging a toilet. What have you been doing?'

'Your pomp is brought down to the grave with the noise of your viols. The worms are spread under you, and the worms cover you.'

I don't know how to answer this. The bandage slips off and I move in to take Simon in my arms, to hold him from danger. I watch in silence as Django puts a finger gently to the graze. Slender musician's hands he has. Simon closes his eyes but doesn't wince or complain.

Django speaks in a murmur. 'Shot, and nothing to show for it.'

'He wasn't shot,' I tell him.

'You'd think so, to look at it now. It's hardly a scrape. You see, Simon, no one can beat you.'

'What did you say?'

'Invincible, that's what you are.'

'Why do you tell him these things?'

'You built towers, Jason.' He turns on me, eyes blazing. 'You raised up palaces and they're brought to ruin. For you said in your heart, I will exalt my throne above the stars of heaven, I will ascend above the heights of the clouds, I will be like the most high. But thorns shall come up in your palaces. They will become a habitation of jackals and a haunt for owls. The high ones of stature shall be cut down, the haughty shall be humbled, and a little child shall lead them.'

'Hey, Django,' Aleksy says, 'you eat too many of your own nuts, I think.'

'Stop this, Django,' I tell him. 'Stop filling his head with this nonsense.'

Abigail says, 'Maud's made tea, Django. Real tea. I think you should have some. We've all had a bit of a shock.' She fills a cup and hands it to him on a saucer. 'There's milk, look, in the jug on the table.'

When he takes hold of the saucer, the cup rattles. 'Yes, all right,' he says. He looks at the tea and then at Abigail. 'Tea. What a treat. It smells good. Thanks, Abigail. Thank you, Maud. Thank you.'

Maud steps forward and rests the palm of her hand on his forehead.

'Is he hot?' Deirdre asks her. 'Is it the sweats? It can't be the sweats. It doesn't make sense. Not after all this time. Who would he catch it from?'

Abigail tells him to sit down and to drink some tea, and he does as he's told, but when she asks him how he feels, he looks at her vaguely as if he'd forgotten she was there.

Deirdre's asking him where he's been. Did he meet anyone while he was gathering nuts?

'Let him be,' Aleksy says. 'Just his brain overheating. He thinks too much.'

'I'm fine, thanks, Abigail,' Django says at last. 'Just need to lie down for a bit.' He gets up and puts his tea cup on the table. 'No offence, this room is stifling.' We watch him go out into the hall and hear his footsteps on the stairs.

Agnes

Something has happened that I couldn't have guessed or hoped for. Better than a pot full of ink, though I have that too. I am out of the red room, away from the Hall and the village. Somewhere among the ruins of the endtimers – more than that I can't say. Somewhere on the road is all I know.

The day after they fuddled my brain in the woods – that was the worst day. Worse than when my father died, because I felt it was my own death. They might have wrapped me then and laid me in a pit. I put my face to the broken window to catch what air I could. I tasted the edge with my tongue. I put my wrist to the glass to test its sharpness. I cut myself enough to drag the pain out of my head. I sat in the space between the tiled walls with my arm aching sweetly and heard myself called by the broken glass. I had eaten nothing since their filthy broth and nothing much before that. Moths gathered in my stomach. My head rose up in the narrow space, away from the rest of me and I felt I had at last learnt the secret of calling that the endtimers had mastered, that Jane knew and teaches us to long for. The cracked glass called me from its tangle of ivy, aching to be washed of its dust and mildew, washed in fresh blood, and I rose up in answer like smoke from a candle.

That night I crawled under the bed when the voices came, and answered each one with a cherry stone dropped into the hole. Each time I heard the clatter and the echo and the distant plop as the Grace Pool received it.

And then a voice came that I knew better than the others. 'Agnes, is it really you? Do you hear me when I speak?'

I opened my mouth to answer but breathed in dust and all that came was coughing and noise. My throat hurt and there was no sound left in it.

'Bessie whispered it was you, but I don't know if I can believe her... My baby is kicking, I lie gently on my side so as not to hurt it... I hope you're there and can hear me... I'm half afraid of what kind of a creature it will be when it's born at last... I hope they let you out... I can't stay long, Daniel will wonder where I am... Think of me sometimes...'

Maybe she said more, I don't know. I slept and was woken by steps outside the door. I thought it might be Roland come again, or Brendan to hold me, to fall on his knees and hold his head against my belly and plead with me to love him in spite of everything, so I could tell him it was too late and he should suffer for all he had made me suffer.

The door opened a crack and a voice whispered my name. It was a woman's voice. I held still, afraid it was the Reeds come to beat me, the Reeds who weren't Reeds, being men under their leafy veils. The door opened and closed and again I heard my name. I crawled from my hiding place, rose to my knees and to my feet. I stumbled a little but put out a hand to the wall. Even in the darkness I was ashamed of my condition, ashamed of my hair loose on my face and the dirt and the blood and my dress torn and unwashed, ashamed of the tears that came too easily, of the snot thick and salty on my tongue, of my own sour smell.

'Agnes,' she said, and again, 'Agnes, child.'

I tried to speak but my throat filled up and the breath was snatched from me.

'What happened to you?'

I said, 'If I had remembered Jane. If I had held myself ready, a pen balanced for writing.'

'You can't stay here.'

'They'll make me stay.'

'Are you strong enough to ride?'

'If Gideon's back is strong enough to take me.'

'Agnes, Agnes, they've starved you almost to nothing.'

'If I'd remembered. That the temple is not a room but a mind ready for learning.'

'You have somewhere to go.'

I didn't feel safe to answer, but I saw it wasn't a question. Or if it was a question, Sarah took my silence for an answer.

'You'd know how to find them again?'

'You know about the scroungers?'

'About them, yes. Some things I once heard.'

'From Brendan?'

'Was there a child among them? Not a child any more. A girl of your age.'

'There's a girl who lives with Trevor. Brendan took her something, a gift from the Hall.'

'Tell me about her. What do they call her?'

'Dell.'

'Of course. Dell for Adele, orphan child.' Her eyes shone with tears. 'Does he take care of her, this Trevor? Is she safe from harm? Is she happy?'

'They take care of each other.'

'And you could find your way back to them?'

'Maybe I could.'

'Tell me about her. What does she look like? Is she healthy? What colour is her hair?'

'It springs out from her head like a sheep's wool before shearing. Not pale like a sheep but dark and lovely. She smiles and laughs and sometimes looks solemn. She helps Trevor feed the Jane Writer and cooks for all the scroungers who come.'

I stopped, afraid that Sarah could no longer hear me for her sobbing. I saw then that her own hair is as dark as Dell's, with a glow in it like the night sky. Too little of it shows, she wears her scarf so neatly.

When she was quiet again and we had stood together for a moment, she said I should take food from the kitchen and some clean clothes and a blanket to sleep in and leave while it was still dark. She led me out on to the landing.

Seeing Brendan's door, I wondered if he was studying or asleep or away in the forest. I felt such bitterness that he had left me to answer for our wrongdoing, when he was surely more to blame than I, to be locked away, and now to be banished from

169

everything I had ever known, every place that had comforted me. I thought I might tell Sarah that I was carrying a child and whose child it was. I thought even of telling her about this book, but was too afraid. I asked instead if I could be alone for a minute in the study to remember the times I had been happiest at the Hall. So she left me there and said I should be quick and meet her in the stable. I felt bad but the red room has made me cunning. I feel bad still, thinking about how Sarah saved me and was my true friend, but I'm glad I have the ink.

Sarah had brought a bucket of water to the stable and a towel, so I could wash my face. She stroked my hair and said she would miss me. She has some new book learners, she said – Megan's sister, Peg and Rachel's boy, Ralph – but none as quick as me. She held me close and I felt her tears. She spoke soothingly to Gideon as I saddled him, saying that he must take a good look at the stable that he might not see again for a while. I thought she might have said forever but would not, either for my sake or for her own.

Then I led him quietly out into the yard, climbed on his back, turned once to see Sarah standing in the shadow of the Hall, then rode up into the High Wood to skirt the village. The sky was clear. There was a sweet smell of garlic as I reached the trees, and moonlight enough to wash the colour from the bluebells. I heard a noise of laughter and running and wondered who would be out so late. I slid to the ground, ducked in between low branches, until I could hear nothing but Gideon grazing and the sounds of the wood.

Then something else, close by. A twig cracking and an intake of breath. I was ready to run, to climb on Gideon's back and kick him to a gallop. I wouldn't be locked away again. But someone spoke my name and I knew at once who it was.

'Annie,' I said, 'why are you here. Isn't it late?'

I heard the branches moving as she stepped towards me. 'The men have tied Roland in the wood. We have to know where, so we can help Megan find him in the morning. And then we can prepare for the wedding day. Oh Agnes, I'm so glad they let you out. What a fool Roland is. He should have waited.'

'Roland and Megan. So that's settled then.'

'I must go to Megan's cottage to sleep with the others outside her window. Will you come?' She turned her face towards me in the moonlight and rested her hand gently on my neck. I could see she had more to say and was afraid. 'I spoke tonight at the Grace Pool. '

'Yes, I heard you.'

'So it's true what Bessie said.'

'They didn't let me out, Annie. I tricked them and took their key.'

'I don't understand. It was only for a month.'

'I was to stay until I bleed, but I won't bleed until my baby is born.

'A baby? Oh Agnes.' She pulled me against her and I felt how firm and round her belly was. 'Is it Roland's?'

'No. Of course not.'

I thought her next question would be about Brendan. I wouldn't tell but I didn't want to lie. So before she could ask, I said, 'Tell me about Daniel. Is he kind to you, Annie?'

'He loves me.'

'And do you love him?'

'I love not sleeping under my father's roof. I must cook and clean for him still, as I have done since my mother died, and see him at work in the fields, but I go home to my own cottage with Daniel who has never once hurt me.'

I didn't want to think about Uncle Morton. So I asked instead about the geese. 'Do they grow?' I said. 'Are they fat and happy?

That made her smile. 'They're fierce. They strain their necks when anyone comes in the yard, and run towards them screaming and flapping. When you let them out tomorrow, they'll be sweet and calm, and you'll see how they love you.'

'I'll never see the geese again, Annie. Someone else will have to feed them, and wring their necks and pluck them for the pot. I can't go with you to Megan's cottage. I have to be miles from here before the sun rises.'

She didn't say anything but stood silently in the mottled shadows, with her arms hanging. Then I heard her sobbing, tight little bleats of grief high in her throat. I took her in my arms and she let herself be held. Her sadness was more than I could bear. So I left her there, stiff and shaking. I climbed on Gideon's back and set off along through the wood.

I was not far along the track when I saw Roland. I pulled again on Gideon's rope and held still. Roland sat on the ground, bound to the trunk of a tree with sacking and bindweed. I watched him from a distance of forty steps, as a cottager might stand in her doorway to watch her neighbour across the street. And I saw that he saw me too. He was there for his calling, tied by the young men of the village to sit out the night, and at first dawn to call to Megan – his soul calling to hers. And from her bedroom she would hear him. She would know, anyway, that it was time, having sat awake all night. And her friends would be there already outside her window to help her down from the sill, and to run with her through the wood. Not finding him, not at first, for all the men whistling and barking from other trees, but moving at last to where they knew he waited, so that Megan might be drawn to claim him, and everyone could start in wonder, and laugh and tell whoever would listen that she had come to his calling. And then such kissing. And the pair of them to be left to make their promises and enjoy each other and watched only later in sleep, and not to be flogged for it either since a wedding was sure to follow.

What children we are, I thought, to play these games. Running in the woods like children. The endtimers knew how to call to each other, but the knowledge is lost to us. We should do what we know how to do, feed and clothe ourselves, and leave these longings. This reaching for what we will never grasp makes us pine uselessly. We are all of us in the red room and the housework neglected.

Gideon flicked his tale and ducked from the flies that settled on him. Then he stooped his head to eat, stirring his flanks, content to have grass to pull on. If I were a horse, I thought, I would graze and nothing more. But always I've longed for what I can't have. Since my father died I've lived half in a dream.

I watched Roland and he watched me, both thinking our own thoughts. I felt sorry for him that he must wait for Megan and would rather wait for me. Sorrier for myself, sent away forever from everything I've ever known. I feared he might shout my name and so draw others to find me whether he meant to or not, so I put my finger to my lip and watched him fiercely, while I roused the horse. As I passed, his eyes widened to see me so brazen, but he made no sound. And so I left the village.

It hurts me now to think of what I've left and might never see again. I think of the geese trailing from the stable yard and over the lawn. I think of the trees – the gnarly orchard branches that will soon bend under the weight of plums and apples, the aspens and the willows by the river, the ancient oaks in the High Wood. And I think of the words I might have spoken to Roland. 'Forget Megan. Come with me and live among the scroungers. I'll make you happier than she ever could.' I should have dropped to the ground, crawled on my knees to kiss his feet. 'I'm bad and I don't deserve you, but if Daniel can love Annie's baby you can learn to love mine. Everything will be all right if you'll only come.' Words I couldn't speak because I was too proud. And too angry. And because I don't believe them and wouldn't have meant them. Because they aren't true. Too good for me? What has Roland done to earn my love? To make himself worthy of me? I should have spat in his face and called him a weakling to be snared by Megan's sly smiles and straying fingers.

And yet I might have said those things, and I might have meant them, true or not.

I make slower progress than when I sat behind with Brendan. Though I am no weight on his back, I let Gideon stop more often and haven't Brendan's skill at driving him on. The night is warm still and he breathes heavily.

I wait now while he rests by a stream. Or he waits for me to write these sad things in my book.

Jason

Django's lurking in his room. Abigail says he might be sick but she doesn't think it's serious. So he'll be back to his old self again soon enough, worse luck. Meanwhile he gets to lie around in my house without even pretending to contribute.

There was a time when I would have known how to put a stop to it. Dealing with squatters could be ugly but someone had to do it. You bought some property. It stood empty while you were putting a deal together, fixing someone on the planning committee, waiting the last neighbour to see sense and sell up – all that. Some squatters were sneaky about it – broke in the back way and kept a low profile. Others were on a mission, championing the cause of the underclass, going on as though you were the criminal for having shelled out good money for the place. Either way the police were wary of getting involved. You could apply for a court order and wait until it got messy. Quicker and easier to get round there yourself and sort it. You needed to know where to apply pressure, how hard to lean. A couple of apes and a crowbar would usually do it. No harm done except to the door, which the squatters had usually nailed up anyway or otherwise brutalised. The apes were mainly for show.

There was this stub of a backstreet near the Elephant. It was a run-down terrace – a lot of student bedsits and short term lets, and the odd old timer watching telly behind threadbare curtains and shuffling out once a week for the pension and some cat food from Tesco's. But someone had opened a creperie on the corner. At the other end was a tapas bar with seats on the pavement and a glazed frontage that opened up on warm summer evenings. The street had gentrification written all over it. It didn't take me long to acquire vacant possession of three adjacent houses and I was ready to make my mark. And then came the padlock on the door and the posters in the windows announcing the death of capitalism and advertising cooperative vegetables.

When I broke in I wasn't expecting to surprise my kid sister in her underwear. In all the empty houses in all the towns in all the world she had to squat in mine. She was high on something and there was a boy beside her on the mattress so out of it he could hardly stand. The place stank of skunk, stale pizza and piss.

I never told you, Caroline. You were my new life. You didn't need to know any of this. I'd put it behind me, mostly, by the time we met. I was going legit. This was the fag end of an old way of doing business. I was moving into luxury new build. There were grants for transforming brown field sites. I was getting into steel and glass with balconies and river views, 24-hour concierge services, underground parking, onsite gym facilities. London was booming and I was going to be part of it. People would be a problem I'd leave to estate agents. This wasn't the moment to come face to face with my past.

It wasn't just the Jesus bus I'd left behind. I was fourteen when I cycled away from Lloyd's farm. I thought I'd get odd jobs like Derek but no one hires a kid to fix their plumbing. I scrounged my way to London and lived rough with the piss-artists and glue-sniffers. On the street, everyone's got a story, and most of the stories are bullshit. You could drown in the steady drip of self-pity. I was moving up and didn't much care how. I did my share of begging, scrounging the fare for the last bus home to nowhere. And there are things men will pay you to do in cars and doorways that aren't easy to forget. But I had my eye on the future. Finally I talked my way on to a building site and started earning regular money. Some people are proud of the rags to riches thing. I just wanted the stink of rags out of my nostrils.

The last thing I needed was Penny showing up as my long-lost family, drug-addled and high on Jesus. You were my life now, Caro. I wasn't ready to introduce you to the memory of Flo and Derek. Penny reminded me of myself and I didn't want to look. She wept and clung to me and I thought of her at the mouth of Lloyd's farm, pleading not to be left behind. I peeled her off and the boy got up off the mattress to take a swing at me. Jack, she called him, or Zak. He called me a Tory cunt. I told him how I voted was none of his fucking business and gave him a smack. It wasn't for calling me a name. It was for dragging Penny down to his level. And it was for all the crap I'd taken over the years from crackheads.

Penny swore at me and called me a bully. She was dressing herself, pulling her clothes on as if she had to be somewhere in a hurry. 'All those years in Hebron,' she said, 'I stood up for you. And everyone said forget him, he's no good. And they were right.'

I said I was sorry. Jack or Zak was crouched at her feet, bleeding from his nose. I told the guys I could handle it from here and they should wait outside.

'We weren't supposed to talk about you,' Penny said, 'me and mum. Caleb would go mental if he heard your name.'

'Caleb?'

'He'd have me stand in the field for everyone to pray over.'

'Derek, you mean.'

'Then he'd have Lloyd give me an extra job – mucking out the pigs or weeding the vegetables.'

'But you got away. I'm glad, Pen. Really I am. How long have you been in London?'

'I left when Mum died. Sorry, I don't suppose anyone told you.'

It was a shock. I was upset and I knew I had no right to be. I suppose I'd thought there'd always be time to think about all that later. 'What did she die of?'

'I don't know.' Penny was busy gathering things from around the room, stuffing them into a bag. 'Cancer maybe. She stopped eating. Lost a lot of weight. She was in pain but pretended not to be. It took months.'

'Christ. You don't even know? What did the doctors say? Was she in hospital?'

'They examined her afterwards, I think. I'm not sure. Caleb dealt with all that.'

'She wasn't seeing a doctor? No one was treating her?'

'She was dying, Jason. What good's a doctor when you're dying?'

'I don't know! What kind of a question is that? Someone should've been taking care of her.'

'Well *you* weren't. You were long gone.'

'Because Derek was a lunatic. He would have done me in if I'd stayed.'

'You can't talk about him like that. Not to me.'

'Why the hell not?'

'Because he chose me.' She looked surprised as she said it, like someone remembering the weird part of a dream. She stopped packing and just stared at the floor. 'Caleb chose me as his wife.'

I was stunned. It was something I hadn't thought of, a whole other dimension of madness. 'And that's why you left.'

'I married him. Mum died and we gathered next day in the lower corner of Hebron under the willows and Lloyd said the words from the book. That's the way Caleb said it had to be done – life flowing on like the river.'

'And you didn't mind?'

'I thought it'd be better, anyway, than mucking out the pigs.'

'Jesus Christ, Penny. What did they do to you?'

'It wasn't their fault. It wasn't anyone's fault but mine.' She was on the move again. She'd found her boots and was busy putting them on, tugging at the laces. 'I should have been stronger. I didn't know what it would be like. I was prepared for pain. I thought I'd just lie there and it and would be over with, and then the others would treat me with respect. I didn't know it would be worse than that. When it came to it, it was more than I could handle.'

'So how did you get away?'

'I went to the village with Lloyd and left him in the shop. There was a delivery van outside and I hid in the back. When the driver found me I waved down a car.'

'I wish...'

'What do you wish, Jase?'

'I wish I'd come for you. As soon as I could drive. As soon as I was earning.'

'Well I wish you'd never left and mum had never died and everything had stayed just the way it was, that's what I wish.'

I very nearly said, *come home with me then – we can't have mum back, but you don't have to live like this*. I've thought since that that's what I should have said.

Jack or Zak was on this knees in the corner, retching. Penny went over and rubbed his shoulders and told him he'd be all right.

'Does he have to do that there?' I said. 'There's a bathroom.'

'Yeah,' the boy said, 'but you've turned the water off, haven't you, you Tory wanker.'

'There's a stopcock in the street – or didn't that occur to you?' It made me angry. And not just because it was my house. It wasn't about ownership. That's what people like him never understood. It was about making things better. It was about preserving something of value. A house like this that had been constructed by skilled working men, bricklayers and plasterers and carpenters, and had stood for a hundred and fifty years, shifting and breathing like a living thing.

I gave Penny a few hundred quid, which was everything I had on me. She said she didn't want my money but she took it anyway. And I gave her my number and told her to phone if she needed anything. I was ready to find her a job and somewhere to live, but she never called. I think I hoped she wouldn't. Either she lost my number or she didn't need any help or she knew me better than I knew myself.

I didn't see her again for five years. A lot had happened, including a recession that left us all staring into the abyss. With most of my money in London property I'd come out of it OK. Some sales had fallen through and I was stretched on a couple of projects, but I wasn't hurting like some. I was doing up that house in Kensington. Big beautiful windows opening on to a square full of trees. The painters had covered the glass with newspapers and masking tape. It was a cold day but the afternoon sun came in low and bright, lifting the headlines and making silhouettes of the faces. I was in and out checking the work. The sky darkened and there were only the naked bulbs where the light fittings would be. And I saw Penny on the arm of this bloke. There were other faces behind them, all smiles, and another picture next to it of the same bloke with some other woman having a set-to. RANDOMESTIC the headline said. Meant nothing to me. But Penny's face was unmistakable even with short hair.

The boys were cleaning their brushes and hammering the lids on the paint tins. There was that sharp clean smell of fresh paint that always reminded me of my dad.

'Hey, Kevin. What paper's this?'

Kevin shrugged.

'Where d'you get it? Is it today's, I mean, or what?'

Kevin was ready to defend himself, as if I'd accused him of something. I was up the stepladder peeling the page off the glass.

'Christ, boss, it's only a paper.'

It was the *Evening Standard*, two days old.

'Who is this bloke then?' I asked.

'I dunno. Some twat?'

His name was Random, a South London boy, a singer. He'd made a big splash the year before with an album called Randometrix. Now he was in trouble with his live-in girlfriend because he'd been celebrating the release of Randomocracy and had been photographed coming out of a nightclub with some other bird. Band member Penny Farthing, the paper called her.

They offered a sample of his lyrics. Put them in a box in bigger print. *Don't care if she black or white, long as she right in the head, not dead from the neck up. Don't want no girl who don't know jack. Don't care if she beige or pink, long as she got no smalltime rinky dink dream in her eye, no chink of a cash machine.*

I read it out and asked the boys what it meant.

'It don't mean nothing, boss,' Kevin said. 'It's a song.'

I googled Random later. Somebody called him a leading exponent of anarcho rap. There was a link to the title track of his new album. *The party's over. Get off your well-fed arses and on your feet. We've burst your pretty balloons. Randomocracy is in the street.*

He looked like the enemy – it was the end of *my* party he was celebrating, the bursting of *my* balloon – but as a class warrior I didn't take him seriously. We were both riding the same wave.

I was always good at pushing things out of my mind and dealing with what was in front of me. But I'd never really shaken the thought of Penny in that squat. I felt bad about her. And my life had changed since then. I was feeling more sure of you, Caro. The recession had slowed me down, but it had also given me Talgarth Hall on a plate. I had a sense that I'd arrived somewhere. And Penny was family. So I tracked down Random's agent and emailed a message for Penny with my new number telling her I'd like her to call.

We met for a drink. I almost didn't recognise her, walked right past her table looking for the same rat's nest hair and refugee dress I remembered from her squatting days. She'd dyed her hair silver blond with a pink forelock. She was bubbling with excitement. I asked her where she was living and she said Random was renting a flat with a recording studio in the basement and for now she was living there with other members of the band, and Random sometimes, though he had his own place. But they had plans, her and Random. He just had to finish with his girlfriend.

'And you're a singer now?'

'I've always been a singer, Jase. It's just no one ever noticed before. We weren't supposed to sing in Hebron, remember. Random's about the music but about so much more than the music. Random's got something really important to say.'

What I'd never noticed was how good-looking she was, my kid sister. And there was something fierce about her that made you pay attention even when she was talking crap.

She wanted us to get together, the four of us. I said OK, on condition that she didn't talk about the Jesus bus. I explained that as far as you were concerned I'd lived in Southwark until my Dad died and my mum had taken up with Derek. Penny said she'd finished with all that anyway, never thought about it. She was making her own life. Sod Caleb and sod Jesus.

So we met in that pub in Borough Market. Random was a performer and I saw how you took against him, Caro. You were kind to Penny because she was my sister and because you were a kind person. But Random pressed all the wrong buttons. 'You so fine, Caro-line' wasn't the kind of flattery you were susceptible to. I watched your eyes roll and glaze over. Me he called the Argonaut, which I didn't mind. It was a step up from Tory cunt anyway. He had a nickname for Penny too. You thought he was calling her Masha, and asked if it was Russian. He laughed. 'Russian, that's good. She might be Russian. She might be from Paraguay. That's why I call her Mash-up because she come from all over, you know, bit of this, bit of that. She my mongrel queen, my riverside penthouse life-on-the-street scene, my going-some-place has-been. She a champagne and caviar backroom piss-up. Gotta get real, gotta fess up, she my hard living, feather bed, down and dirty, pristine mash-up.' He'd do that, without asking anyone's permission – break into words. And then he'd laugh enough for everyone. His accent was hard to place – two parts Peckham, one part Caribbean, with a dash of something more exotic – Tonbridge, maybe. I had him pegged as a fraud from the start. I couldn't help liking him though. He was just making his way in the world. No different from me. It was just that I sold property, while he sold himself, or some version of himself. That's what we did back then, when there was a world to make your way in. We lived on our wits. And he was being nice enough to Penny, so I liked him for that. I'd run out on her twice, which so far he hadn't. I was happy for him to put on whatever face worked for him.

Afterwards we walked through the market to the station. You led the way, eager to get home. Random kept pace with you, knowing he'd failed to charm you, not ready to give up on an audience. Penny and I trailed behind, wandering among the iron pillars.

'Remember,' I said, 'you can always come to me if you need help.'

'Why would I need help? Random loves me. He's excited about our baby.'

'Jesus, Pen, you're not pregnant are you?'

'Why shouldn't I be? I'm old enough.'

'And Random's the father?'

'Obviously.'

'And you think he's going to stick around?'

She stopped walking. 'You're a real shit, you know that?'

'I'm just looking out for you.'

'I don't see you for years and then you crap on my life, on everything I've got.'

'What you've got is great. It's what you're going to have when this baby is born that worries me.'

'He loves me, Jase. He's my family now. He's done more for me than you ever did.'

'And what about his career?'

'Our career, you mean – his and mine and the band's. You see, we don't think the way you do. The whole money system's on the way out, by the way, the whole property thing. Then you'll be the one needing help.'

'Yeah, come the revolution. Meanwhile family values aren't exactly an asset in his line of work, are they. It's not like he's a vicar or an MP. His life isn't meant to be tidy. He doesn't call himself Random for nothing.'

She called me a bastard and a mean-minded capitalist fuckhead and some other things I couldn't hear for the train screeching overhead.

Later I put a cheque in the mail with a note telling her to buy something nice for the baby. I got a text saying 'ta bro'. After that she blipped off my radar.

Agnes

What have I done? I heard his bones break. Unless it was the branches breaking under him to slow his fall. There was a cracking anyway that held my heart from beating until it must race to catch up. It was a long fall and I'd never have had the strength to do it, but he stood on the edge of the road where it rises on stalks above the forest.

There are walls in perfect lines on either side, and places where the road has crumbled and the wall has fallen away, or the wall arches through the air and nothing under it.

It was a long fall. How long I don't know with the trees in leaf, the green roof sagging under him to sway up again once he was gone.

I think he's dead. Or I wish him dead but think the branches saved him. He may be dead whether I wish him dead or not. I hope he doesn't lie broken for wolves and crows to find.

It was night still when I heard him on his horse come after me. I was on the high part of the road and nowhere to hide, no shadow to stand in and a staring moon. I was walking, leading Gideon by the reins. He shouted to me and said he'd ridden hard to fetch me back.

'Ride all you want,' I told him, 'I won't come.'

He dropped from his horse and came closer. I thought even then he would beg me to claim him from himself, to lead him by the hand to my father's cottage, as if I had come that night to his calling and we'd slept, and just then woken dew-stained in the woods, blushing at muffled footsteps and laughter and the primrose petals falling from our hair.

But he said only that he'd find a cottage boy to take me, to call my child his and care for it.

I wouldn't let myself answer I felt such bitterness, but turned my back and walked on, pulling Gideon after.

He shouted that I'd never find my way. 'The scroungers will kill you, or worse,' he said. He caught up with me and spoke in a softer voice. 'Don't judge me harshly, Agnes. I can't choose for myself as you can.' I turned and saw tears on his face and his arm rising roughly to smudge them.

'You dare to cry? I was friendless and far from home and knew nothing and you took what you had no right to take. And then you stood by and let them punish me. I'll never trust you again or like you or think you wise.'

He looked at the ground then, and let the tears come, which made me more angry.

'And you can't call it love, or say you didn't know what you were doing. Because I wasn't the first. There was Sarah before me.'

'I did my best for Sarah.' He wiped his face with his sleeve and lifted his eyes to meet mine. 'If you've found out her secret it wasn't me who told it.'

'Half the village knows how you took her child from her and gave it to the scroungers.'

'To save her from shame.'

'To save yourself. Everything, always, for yourself. Even my poor mother.' I'd meant never to breathe a word of what I'd learnt about Janet's baby, born dead or smothered soon after, of the belt she'd tied around her neck, and the punishment that followed. I didn't even want to think of it. But seeing Brendan so mawkishly sorry for himself, I found I had to speak.

He was staring at me in surprise.

'You see,' I said, 'I know about that too, and I wasn't yet born.'

'What harm did I ever do to Janet?'

'She was driven mad, I know that, by the death of her baby, and suffered as I did in the red room, and she was only half alive when my father married her and there was nothing left for him but your leavings.'

I watched him labouring to take this in. 'You don't know, Agnes.' He shook his head bitterly and looked away over the canopy of trees. 'There's so much you don't know.'

'What, though? What don't I know?'

'I was a boy when Janet came to my bed.' He met my eye, daring me to say otherwise. 'A boy without parents to watch out for me. And Janet was the girl who'd held my hand and led me to the spring to wash and to the kitchen to pour me a cup of milk, and had settled me to sleep before walking home from the Hall each evening. I understood nothing, except that it was daybreak and she was doing what she had never done before, getting into bed beside me.'

'Liar.'

'She meant me to be the father of her child but her child already had a father.'

'How could you know that? How could you be sure?'

'Because when she made to kiss me I could tell she didn't mean it, and she left off soon enough and turned away and I heard her sobbing. I understood none of this till later.'

'Liar, liar.'

'I never harmed her.'

'Who then, if not you?'

'Oh, Agnes.' He looked at me fiercely. 'Only your Uncle Morton is left alive to say what went on in that cottage.'

I hit him then, letting go of Gideon's rope to swing at him with both fists as I would have swung an axe at a tree. He stepped backwards, caught his foot on a vine branch. He frowned at me as if I was a puzzling sentence in the Book of Windows. The branches swung apart to let him in and closed again behind him. If he had fallen dead in the pond, the green water would have closed over him just so, settling again as if it thought nothing of him and couldn't tell the Reader from a dropped corn sack. I heard branches breaking and the movement of startled birds, and a grunt like the last breath pushed out of him. Then more cracking that might have been his neck or his limbs or the limbs of trees. I waited for the noises to stop. I forgot to breathe while I waited to see if he would cry in pain from the ground. But I heard nothing so I let out my own gasp of pain and went on my way.

Day has come and thunder with it and now rain enough to drown me and make a muddy river of the track. I take shelter under a sagging iron roof while I eat and write.

I would never have hit him if he hadn't told such lies about my mother. If he hadn't come so close to the edge of the road he would have come to no harm.

Soon I must ride again, drenched as I am. Ruins lie all around me in the forest. I start at every sound, thinking it's the Monk, swinging by his tail to catch me, though I don't believe in the Monk and have worse things to fear. There is nothing for me here but sadness and danger.

Jason

From up here on the roof I can see the world – the woods and fields our world has shrunk to. It was hairy getting up this high. Aleksy helped me lay some boards on the stable roof and we raised an extension ladder from there, roping it to a downpipe to give it some stability. I found a couple of claw hammers in the shed and a bag of roofing nails and we hauled up a stack of slates reclaimed from the old outhouse. The trees in the High Wood are our nearest neighbours and their branches wave at us and sing. The wind is strong up here, but the rain has held off and for now we're safe inside the parapet.

When I helped Aleksy on to the roof, I asked him if it reminded him of his circus days.

He wasn't amused. 'I work with animals. Sometimes a strongman act with elephants. For one season, when I was fourteen, shot from a cannon. But the tightrope and trapeze I left to others. These are different skills, you understand Jason, like bricklayer or plasterer.'

He's careless of his bandaged arm, but I can see it hurts him to use it. We've made a late start, after clearing a patch of thistles and digging it over to plant cabbages, but we've still got an hour or so of daylight. We've brought up a broom and a stiff brush. I set Aleksy sweeping up whatever's blown into the valleys, checking to see where the lead might have buckled or split. There's spleenwort sprouting from the brickwork round one of the chimneystacks and moss on some of the lower slates where the water is slow to drain. I clean out the drainage holes in the parapet walls and lean over to pull an old nest from a cast iron hopper head. I see where some of the slates have slipped and a couple with long cracks in them, and I begin patching.

After a while we hear the cattle clattering into the yard for their second milking – the Friesians and the Jerseys. I have a better sense of them now that Abigail has walked me through their field at sunset. Deirdre shouts a question and falls silent while Maud, I suppose, shows her what to do. There are footsteps below in the house, a window slides open and shut again, and I picture Abigail dusting and cleaning, a few strands of hair escaping her headscarf to fall across her work-smudged face. There's a smell of smoke from the lawn and faintly in the distance a two-note call.

'Listen, Aleksy.'

'What is it?'

'Can't you hear the cuckoo?'

Aleksy laughs. 'Too late for the cuckoo, old man. It's September already, maybe October. Cuckoos all flew south three, four months ago.'

The smell of the bonfire gets sharper. They're burning the dry thistle stalks. I lean over the parapet and see the orange glow and the grey smoke rising from it. And there's Simon – the dark mop of his hair appearing from under the portico. He waddles towards the fire, his movement hampered by the weight of whatever he's got in his basket. Perhaps Abigail has recruited him to help her clean the house. Approaching the flames, he pauses and shifts into a slow orbit, staying as close as the heat will allow, throwing things from his basket, little patches of darkness to scatter sparks and sink into the flames.

'What do you think they're burning down there?'

Aleksy looks up from his sweeping. 'They're cooking our dinner. Hot dogs maybe. Remember sausages?'

'Remember bread rolls...' I hear the cuckoo again. Something isn't right. 'Have you seen Django?'

'Not since he took to his room.'

Simon's basket is empty. He looks towards the house, raising his face to an upstairs window. He puts the basket down and picks up something else – a jug or vase. Holding it in both hands he hurls the contents towards the fire. There's a belch of white flame which sends him staggering backwards. Then the sound reaches me – a whoop and a fluttering pressure in the gut.

'Jesus Christ. It's petrol.'

The noise has brought Aleksy to the edge of the roof. 'Who got petrol?'

'Help me down before that boy kills himself.'

Aleksy follows me around the edge of the roof. I stand for moment looking down into the yard where the cows are still penned. The first step over the parapet is the worst, turning your back on the drop and feeling with a foot for the first rung. The stonework seems to tilt and I have a strange feeling that I'm suspended under it looking up. A shadow crosses my vision and I think I'm going to black out. Then the world rights itself and I'm clinging to the parapet with my feet on the ladder. And I'm able to make the descent.

In the yard, Maud looks up from her milking. I see the question in her eyes but don't stop to answer.

When I reach the bonfire, Simon is sitting at its edge, rocking forward and back, muttering, the empty basket on one side of him, the jug on the other. Smoke and ash rise behind him and the trees at the lawn's edge shimmer in the heat. 'I won't burn mmm...' he says, and makes his carp face. 'I won't burn mmm...' – lips pursed, neck bulging.

'What is it, Si?'

He looks up and I see he's got his favourite book. He clutches it tight to his chest. 'I won't. You can't make me.'

'Burn Moon?'

'I won't, I won't, I won't.'

'Course not. Why would you?'

'Just the others.'

'What others?'

'The others. From the house.' And I see what's on the fire. The smouldering remains of books – your books, Caroline. Your favourite girls – George and Virginia, Margaret and Angela, Ali and Zadie. Books I'd never got round to and maybe never would, but important to you, part of who you were. Because

189

if my way of knowing the world was to feel its texture and to shape it under my hand, yours was to read. You once said you thought of characters in a story as leaves that show you the force and direction of the wind. The wind is too big, too unseeable, you said. But the leaf stirs and twists and makes the wind visible.

'Simon, Simon, what have you done?'

'What's happening?' Deirdre comes round from the yard with Aleksy.

Through the flames, I see Abigail pushing a wheelbarrow of windfall apples up through the grass from the orchard. 'Did we need a fire?' She rests the wheelbarrow, draws a sleeve across her forehead and tucks the stray hairs under her scarf.

'It's not your fire, then?' Aleksy asks her.

I'm listening to that two-note call again, faint above the spitting and cracking. 'It's too early for a fire,' I tell him, 'and it's too sodding late for a cuckoo.'

The cuckoo stops and there's a giggle. Then the same two clarinet notes, a little falling tune.

'That bastard, I should have known.' I look up at the house, at the open bedroom windows.

Aleksy steps in front of me. 'A fire, Jason. Not such a big deal. A bit of petrol, maybe, siphoned from your car.'

'He burned the books. Look.' The edges curl and shrivel. Black flakes drift up and scatter. The immensity of it catches in my throat.

'Books.' Aleksy shrugs and makes a puffing noise. 'Maybe these are not so important. You got penicillin on your bookcase? You got sausages? We got to eat, old man. We got to feed ourselves and stay warm. We don't got to read. Punish the boy if you like, but don't make a meal of it. He's five years old. He burns your books, so give him a slap, give him a hug. He don't do it no more. Now we get back to work.'

'This is nothing to do with Simon. It's Django's going to have to pay for this.'

'Pay, of course. Give Django a shovel. He can spread

the cowshit on the field. Hear that, Abigail. Django works tomorrow or he don't eat.'

I hear the sound of a sliding sash and see Django stepping through the landing window on to the roof of the portico, naked apart from his clarinet. 'The people that walked in darkness,' he says 'have seen a great light.'

'Come down here and say that, you fucker.'

'And a little child shall lead them.'

Maud, who has just appeared at the corner of the house, covers her face and walks to join us with her eyes on the ground.

'We grope like the blind along a wall,' Django says, 'feeling our way like blind people. The sun shines but we stumble about in the dark. The world is full of life, but *we're dead.'*

'You will be, you cunt.'

'Your graven images are all vanity. Your delectable things will do you no good.'

'Yes, but they were my graven images, fuckwit, not yours.' He turns his back on me, turns his skinny backside to climb in through the window. I shout after him, 'They were my delectable things.'

Aleksy puts his hand on my arm to calm me. 'Mine, yours. What does this matter?'

'It matters to *me. Mine*, not Django's. *My* house, *my* books.'

'By what law? A dead law for dead people.'

'I worked for this house.'

'And now we all work for it. Maud, look, with her milking. Abigail in the orchard. Me, I help you fix up the roof good. Django, even, making a fire. Maybe we cook on it.'

'We didn't need a fire. There's a stove in the kitchen. We needed books.'

'Why we need these books? Who said about books until now? The world is full of books and no one to read them. We need books, we write our own. The world is ours now. No one to tell us to read this or that.'

'See, Jason.' Django comes down the steps from the front door, easy in his nakedness. 'A new heaven and a new earth.'

Maud blushes and stares at the grass.

'No, Django. The same heaven, the same sodding earth. And everything we ever knew and ever remembered, where is it? Not on Wikipedia anymore.'

'No, Jason,' Aleksy says, 'you are right. Not on Wikipedia, but here – head and heart.' He puts his forefinger to his temple, then his hand to his chest. 'This is where we know things. Let's go help Maud with the cows.'

'No.'

'Then sleep. You work too hard.'

'I don't need sleep. I need to sort out that bastard.'

'It's done now, Jason,' Abigail says. 'Spilt milk.'

'See, Abigail agrees. We'll find more books later, my friend, when the planting's done and all the fruit is in.'

But I've already lunged at Django and knocked him to the ground. I hear him say, 'Mind my reed,' see the instrument fall in the grass. Then my hands are round his neck. I want to stop his mouth, fix him so he can't smile. His legs squirm and kick. I feel his fists on my shoulders and against my head. My mind goes blank. There are other hands on me and I'm rolling on the grass and there's blood coming from my nose.

'These books,' Aleksy says, angry and breathing hard, 'they tell us how to make power from wind?' His face hovers low over mine, not quite in focus.

I shake my head.

'How to make a machine to grind corn, maybe? How to irrigate in a dry season, how to kill greenfly or blight?'

'Probably not.'

'What then?'

'I don't know. They tell stories.'

'Stories? What stories?'

'I never read them. They were my wife's.'

'All your life, you never read them. And you're alive still and she's dead.'

I stand up, leaving Django coughing into the grass, shake myself free of Aleksy's hand. Maud stands apart, humming to herself. Abigail is holding Simon against her, stroking his head. She looks at me sadly and I'm stung to a new fury that she should blame me for Django's crime.

I walk rapidly towards the orchard where the sun is setting among the trees.

I hear Deirdre say, 'He's right though, Aleksy. He's right, Django. Look at all you've burned. What a waste. What are we going to do now on winter evenings?'

Aleksy laughs. 'Milk cows same as summer. Chop wood so we don't freeze. Save candles.'

'And when the cows are milked?'

'What you like, Deedee – play party games, make babies.'

I turn and stride back towards them, shaking with rage. Abigail is on her knees, tending to Django's bleeding lip. She's pulled her apron off and laid it on his lap. I'm glad to see them all shrink from me as I approach, to know they respect my anger if not my rights.

'That's it, Django,' I tell him, 'I want you out of here.'

No one argues. They can see I might do anything. Even I don't know what I might do. I'll take them all on, smash up the fragile order of things. I want Django gone. I'll give him five minutes to get dressed and pack some clothes, I'll let Deirdre and Abigail stuff food in his bag if they want, but I won't stop until he's off my land. Because of what he's done. Because the others can't grasp the horror of what he's done. Because I can't find the words to explain it to them.

And it happens, just that way, because I say it must. No one argues. I watch him walk off into the woods in his tight trousers and stripy blazer, stepping lightly like a boy on a camping trip, fearless of hunger or of having his throat cut for a decent pair of boots. The others watch too, keeping their thoughts to themselves. I turn from the front door and Abigail's behind me in the hall, studying my face. And I see that I'm being managed. We've lost your books, Caroline. Django, who I never trusted, has burned them. I should at least feel vindicated, but I find myself diminished.

I walk past Abigail and take the main staircase to the second floor, and the half-flight to our bedroom. The door's wide open, wedged to stop it banging, and to let Simon in. Whatever books were on the shelves are gone. I go to our bed, where I sleep alone, and pull all the pillows off. It's still here, your copy of *Jane Eyre*. This at least I've still got. It's nothing much to look at – a cardboard cover the colour of pondweed. But yours, loved by you since childhood, and all I've got left of you. Now I'm on the bed, I'm not sure I can get up, not sure I want to. My body shakes, gripped by the memory of sickness. I hear the murmur of voices and then nothing but the sound of my own breathing.

Django's out there somewhere, and others like him, skulking in the woods, hiding in ditches, scuttling through atriums and shopping malls, bedding down where the roof doesn't leak with their valuables held close and one eye open for snatchers.

Agnes

I was sick five days they say, sweating with fever. I rode hard in my dreams. At every turn of the road I met Brendan, his eyes puzzling over the strange tilt the world had taken and me rushing backwards from the sight of him to swing away through the trees, like the Monk, with my heart torn out of me.

And how many days before that, dragging through the forest, blinded by rain, all the time thinking I would never find the O. And I would have stayed lost, that's certain, if a woman leading a mule cart hadn't spoken to me kindly. What she said I couldn't tell, but when I said I was looking for the O, she smiled, showing me the few teeth she had left, and nodded for me to climb on her cart, a wild-looking woman with an unsteady walk, wrapped in rags. She let me nest among her vegetables, and I saw nothing until she shook me awake and we were here.

Trevor says I was lucky. There are some on the road, he says, who would have stripped me of everything, or roped me with the dogs and set me to work till I was all bone. But this pelting rain had likely driven them to shelter. Even a tracker would find the scent bleared and the trail washed from the road.

I understand more of what they say now than before, though there are still words I have to guess at. They asked me why I came without Brendan. I told them I am punished and sent away from the village for something I did. I haven't told them what. How would I say? I haven't told them I killed Brendan, if that's truly what I've done. He was their friend. More than that, I think he was Dell's father, though perhaps she doesn't know it.

I see more of how they live at the O. Every night there's eating and drinking. Singing often, too. So every night is like the village at the end of a wedding, except different people from one time to another, not always the same neighbours. I see that all this pleasure is work for Trevor and Dell. People come with animals for cooking and other things they call gear or tat and Dell gives them some of what's in the pot and fills their mugs. And later those who want are put somewhere to sleep.

Dell lets me help her in the kitchen, though I've hardly the strength to shell peas. I asked her today how many scroungers are there. She didn't understand. 'The villagers that you call planters come to forty,' I told her. 'Fifty maybe.' I showed with my fingers in case she didn't know her numbers. 'People die and there are babies so it changes, but maybe fifty. So how many scroungers?'

She shrugged. 'As many as there are people in the world. Because that's all we are, us you call scroungers.'

'So how many does that come to?'

'Cheese, Agnes, no one can tell that.' She put her hand on my forehead then to see if my fever was still up.

'But if you had to guess.'

'See, Ag,' she said, sitting by me, 'it's this way. There are some we know. More we don't and never will. Some live nearby, catching and cropping. Some live by dealing, moving on to find in one place what's wanted in another. Some we see regular when the weather changes. Some once and never again. Maybe they tell us their names and we remember. Or else we know them by something they brought one time – a strong pan or a sack of partridge eggs. They might tell us their racket. They might not. It doesn't matter. If they're hungry or need a bed they come to the O.'

I think of the O as a circle and always room inside. Like the letter. I tried to explain this to Dell, but she didn't understand. She told me O is short for O Tell Do, though not many call it that. 'But its real name,' she said, 'is O Tell Do Lucks, which no one calls it except Trevor. When he's drunk, or sad about Cat.'

'Who's Cat?' I asked her.

'Cat was Trevor's girl. Lovely she was, and sharp as a knife. She was born at the O and always lived here. It was her mother's, and then hers when her mother died. Cat raised me from a baby. Then she got knocked up. She'd carried before, Trevor says, but always lost them. She cried out all day long when it was her time, then all the night after, but not so much. By morning she was dead, and the tiddler dead inside her. Now it's just Trevor and me.'

Later Dell came to see I was warm in my bed. She asked who'd sent me away and why.

I told her the Mistress. 'But she didn't really send me away. She locked me in the red room, a room at the Hall. And I escaped.'

Dell looked me up and down and asked me, 'Have you had your minstrels?'

I told her I didn't understand.

'Your rag time,' she said. Then I wept and that was all the answer she needed. 'And for that you're sent out?'

I cried harder to see myself as Dell saw me, punished and rejected for what any woman might come to.

She shook her head and said, 'That isn't right.' She put her arms round me then and rocked me this way and that saying 'shush' and 'poor rabbit'.

It was cold so she got under the blanket with me and it was nice holding her close and being held.

After a while I asked her what would happen here to someone in my case.

She shrugged. 'Anything. Or nothing. There are some men who'll care for a child but more who talk big while you're giving them what they want, then first sign of trouble they're gone.' A shudder passed through her. I looked in her face and her eyes were wet.

'Oh Dell,' I said, 'sweet Dell, you've had a baby.'

'If you call it that. A tiddler the size of a carrot.'

'And it died?'

'A trader came wanting breakfast and I'd puked up in the meat pot and I had nothing to feed him. Trevor made out it was dogs broke into the kitchen, but the trader guessed it was me.

197

He slapped me up, kneed me in the belly.'

'And did Trevor know? I mean, about the baby?'

'Not until after, when he had to mop me up.'

I thought how much easier than hers my life had been, everything neat and ordered.

I asked her if she ever thought about how she might have lived if Cat and Trevor hadn't raised her.

She said, 'All I know is what Trevor told me. I was brought here as a baby by Brendan and a planter girl, a sad-eyed wisp called Janet, who maybe was my mother but didn't say.'

'Not your mother, Dell. My mother.'

'Janet was your mother? Then I'm sorry she wasn't mine too, so we could have been sisters.'

I knew then I must tell her what I could about her parents. That the man she called Brendan was truly her father – she wept at that and said she'd always felt it – and that her mother was the best and most beautiful woman.'

'Still alive, then,' she said. 'So why did she ditch me?'

'Oh, she would have kept you and loved you, I'm sure of it, if they'd let her.'

After a while Dell slept and so did I. When I woke she was gone. The morning light was thin through the trees and I heard them outside, Dell and Trevor, talking and chopping logs for the cooking.

I hear them now, and last night's sleepers stumbling down the stairs, laughing or cursing and calling for food. And I feel so sorry for myself. Once I had a cottage and my own little room in it that I kept neat and clean. And I had a mother who loved me in her way. I had Sarah to read me texts from the Book or Air. I had Roland, who knew almost everything about me. In time we would have married. I would have led him to his bed at the Hall and it would have been our bed. But he chose Megan because I let this book fill me with wrong thoughts, and I let Brendan trick me into thinking I loved him, and because I lost my way. I miss my father. I think of his treasures hidden in the cottage – the knife with the sliding blades, the wren he carved for me, the silver chain – and think I shall never see them again.

Jason

I didn't see Penny for three or four years – not until I was about to start work on the old maternity hospital in Bermondsey. I loved that project – beautiful Victorian brickwork and one spectacular wall of smoked glass spanning the gap between the north and south wings. High-ceilinged, big-windowed spaces, accessed directly from a glazed atrium, the old dark corridors carved up into en suite bathrooms. It was going to be perfect. Never happened, of course. What happened was the virus. And people lost interest in luxury apartments, along with the whole money system, the whole property thing. But we weren't there yet. We had no idea what was about to hit. We were all still scrabbling to get ahead. I thought the worst thing we had to deal with was Brexit, starting with a lot of jumpy foreign investors scared that London was dropping off the map. And I figured I could ride that wave.

The atrium was going to be built on what had been the hospital garden, a patch of ground bounded on three sides by the walls of the building and open to the west to catch the afternoon sun. We were ready to start on the foundations when the protestors moved in. They called themselves the Urban Diggers. Their literature said that they were planting for a sustainable future. They reckoned my proposed extension would bury one of the last green spaces in the borough and they were asserting their right as citizens of the planet to grow vegetables. Bivouacs sprouted overnight. The Diggers walked between them with watering cans.

I ventured on to my own property, introduced myself, and asked to speak to their leader. They said they didn't have a leader but would delegate some people to meet me. I invited their delegation to my office. They countered with the One

World Cafe on the corner – breakfast at seven. I suppose they thought I'd be a walkover at that hour of the morning, seeing I was a member of the idle rich.

I was tempted to tell them to go fuck themselves, but I wanted to work something out so I could get on with the job.

I made sure to get there early. I watched them through the window dodging the morning traffic, three of them and a kid. When they pushed open the door, I realised their secret weapon wasn't vegan omelette and camomile tea at the crack of dawn, but Penny. There she was in a headscarf, cotton dress and rubber boots, reinvented as an Urban Digger, chin forward, ready for a fight. The kid was Random's, I could see that. A white-haired woman held him by the hand and waited while he raised his foot over the threshold. Trailing after them was a beautiful Asian girl.

I introduced myself.

Penny said, 'They know who you are, Jason.'

'So they know you're my sister? I hope they don't hold it against you?'

'We don't believe in genetics, Jason. We're environmentalists.'

It was the kind of thing Penny said and you weren't sure if it was a joke or not. She was bright but had these gaps, like someone who hasn't been speaking the language very long.

Only the older woman, Ursula, gave a smile, but she was looking down at Simon and might have been smiling at him or might just have been smiling out of general contentment. The Asian girl, who was called Aisha, looked at me solemnly and rubbed Penny's back.

I made my arguments. I was preserving a piece of historic London. It was a cutting edge development in terms of energy use. It fulfilled all the requirements for social inclusion. I wasn't Satan. I wasn't even one of Satan's lesser minions. So the economy was in the crapper – people still needed somewhere to live. I'd make a donation in their name to an environmental cause, the World Wildlife Fund or some tree-planting outfit. I'd find them another plot in the borough, a piece of land the same the size, give them free use of it for a year to grow their vegetables.

But they weren't there to negotiate. They'd come to convert me. Couldn't I see there were too many buildings already and not enough land? That we were choking the planet with our emissions, stoking the flames of our own destruction? Aisha and Penny did most of the talking, Aisha reacting to Penny's agitation by stroking her arm or touching her hair. The meeting went nowhere.

As we were leaving, Simon held something up to me. It was a plastic dog. It looked grubby, and I thought maybe one of the Diggers had found it buried in the hospital garden.

I squatted to his level, 'What's this?'

He held it up to one eye. 'This is Dumpy. Dumpy is mine dog. He's a brave dog.'

'He looks fierce.'

'He has ventures. If you're mean to me Dumpy will biten you. And if you're mean to Dumpy and make him cry I will biten you until you say sorry.'

'Now, Simon,' Ursula said gently, 'no biting. Little boys who bite must be sent to their room.'

With his eyes still on me, Simon nodded. 'Yes, withouten any ice cream.'

I asked if he'd mind being sent to his room.

He thought about this and said, 'No.'

'Why not?'

He gave a sly grin. 'Because I haven't gotten a room.'

'You haven't?'

'No.' He leant towards me as if to tell a secret. 'I got mine Dora Splorer snuggle bag.'

Outside on the pavement, while Aisha and Penny watched for a break in the traffic, Ursula said, 'We don't mean you any harm, you know.'

'You just want to stop me earning a living.'

'If it means more buildings, yes.'

'And what am I supposed to do about that?'

Her face wrinkled up in a smile. 'Take up gardening.'

The hospital project was stalled. But I wanted to make peace with Penny. If things were going to get messy with the Diggers, and it was heading that way, I wanted to give her and Simon a chance to get out of there. I also wanted to give her our news – your news, Caro. So I phoned and we arranged to meet in a pub by the river.

I got some drinks and we sat on a bench on the Embankment looking at the lights along the Thames. I asked about Simon and she said he was fine.

'How's he enjoying life in a tent?'

'Oh that. We're not doing that any more. The Diggers are irrelevant.'

'That's a relief.'

She seemed on edge. 'There's this book I've been reading. It puts it all in perspective.'

'Good. Perspective is good.'

'It makes the Diggers seem so trivial, so... marginal.'

'Great! I'll buy a dozen copies for Ursula and her friends. Maybe it'll persuade them to get off my case.'

'Forget the Diggers. Listen, Jason. I'm telling you something important.'

'Me first. Caroline's pregnant.'

'What?'

'I'm going to be a father.'

I didn't know she was going to cry until the tears spilled down her face. I put my arms round her and her body felt frail. She clung to my neck, shaking and sobbing.

'What's the matter?'

'It's not a good time.'

'It's now or never, Pen. I'm over forty. Caroline's thirty-four. If we're going to have a family we'd better get on with it.'

'But look at what's happening to the planet. Look at this weather. It's November, Jason, and we're sitting outside. Doesn't it freak you out?'

'Of course it does, if I stop to think about it. But what can

I do? What can any of us do by ourselves?'

She pulled back and looked into my face. 'Is that it then? We give up?'

'No, we elect governments and they create regulations. It's like speed limits. Everyone cheats a bit, we moan when we get caught, but we know they're right.'

'That's pathetic, Jason. I mean it's insane how utterly pathetic that is.' She turned away from me, felt around in her shoulder bag and pulled out a book. 'You should read this.'

'What is it?'

'Just read it, OK.'

It was *Kishar in Crisis*. I'd never seen it before, never heard of it. How could I know it would soon be notorious and Penny with it? It was just some book. The subtitle, *the seven paradoxes of human survival*, was just a bunch of words – the kind of words publishers put on the front of a million books to say this one's important, buy this one, the way an estate agent might describe any random block of flats as a prestigious development affording luxury accommodation and iconic views. It was sales talk. I saw nothing sinister in it. And I didn't feel threatened by the blurb that called it *a self-help manual for Planet Earth*. I completely missed the point, that there might be some kind of tension between the planet's survival and ours. If it was there to be seen, I didn't see it. All I saw was this garish black and yellow cover and a title I only half understood.

'What is it then, Kishar?'

'*She*, not *it*.'

'Who's *she* then, when she's at home?'

'She was babble-odeon.'

'You what?'

'You know, from babble-odea. She was a babble-odeon earth goddess.

'Babylonian, you mean,' I said, 'from Babylon. Like the Whore of Babylon.'

Penny shrugged. And in a way she was right to shrug. So what if she mispronounced a word? Why should it bother me if she mangled Babylon beyond recognition? It did, though. That kind of knowledge, what Dad called book-learning, might be overrated, but I saw how vulnerable Penny was without it.

'The thing is BK's a genius.'

'BK?'

'BK Compton who wrote it. She understands everything. This book is huge. It's...' she struggled for a word that could express her sense of it. 'It's got everything in it, everything that matters – that's what Troy says. Not because it's got all the answers but because it chucks out all the old questions and replaces them with the only important question.'

'Which is?'

'It's a big book, Jason. I didn't say I'd read it all.'

'And Troy's what... a sky god?'

'Troy's my boyfriend.'

'And what does he do, this Troy?'

'What's it matter what he does?'

'Which means he's unemployed and grows his own vegetables, I suppose.'

'He's a zoologist. With a real job. See, that took you by surprise. He does research in a lab. He's got a PhD and everything.'

'All right, you got me. Research into what?'

'I don't know exactly. The environment.'

'That'll keep him busy then – there's a lot of it about.'

'And he's big in the solutionists.'

'Who are they?'

'People who've read this book, mostly. People who are looking for the solution.'

I wanted to ask her – hadn't she been here before? They give you a book. They say, it's all in here, this is all you need. But I said nothing.

She phoned me next morning and told me to forget about the solutionists. I was late for a meeting and snarled up in traffic on Tower Bridge.

'How do you mean, forget about them?'

'Forget I mentioned them.'

'I had forgotten them until you just mentioned them again.'

'It's just that they're not important. I made it sound like they're important but they're not.'

'You didn't make them sound important. You just said they were looking for a solution.'

'So you hadn't forgotten. You remembered everything I said.'

'I remember it now you've reminded me.'

She didn't respond and I thought maybe we'd been cut off. The weather had broken and rain was hammering the roof of the car and falling in fat drops on the windscreen.

'It's just that Troy gets annoyed at me.'

'About what?'

'He says I shoot my mouth off.'

'He sounds like a charmer.'

'Please don't think badly of him.'

'Why shouldn't I?'

'Because we're moving in together.'

'Are you sure that's a good idea?'

'And because the thing is, Jason, something terrible happened to him when he was a kid. His dad murdered his mum. And he actually saw it happen. Can you imagine what that must have felt like? He was only eight. It must have felt like it was his fault.'

'Why must it?'

'It just must have felt like that, that's all I'm saying. Because I think it left him feeling he had to hold everything together, be responsible for everyone.'

'Your childhood was a hardly a picnic.'

'Exactly. Which is maybe why I understand him.'

She texted me a few weeks later. I gathered that Troy wanted to meet me or she wanted me to meet him or some combination of the two. I suggested a pub on Blackfriars Road. I might have taken you with me, Caro, but I reckoned you could do without the aggravation.

I got there late and they'd already found a table in the window. Penny went to the bar and left me with Troy. When I sat down he seemed to be waiting for me to speak.

'So you're a zoologist,' I said.

'Yeah, I work at the zoo. Hang out with the reptiles in the reptile house.'

'But I thought...'

'You thought what?'

'Penny said you work in a lab.'

'Oh, she told you that. I usually don't. I prefer to keep things in separate compartments. Work life, home life, pub life, whatever.'

'Sorry. She didn't say it was a secret.'

'It's not a secret. It's just that it's my business not your business.'

He wasn't good at eye contact. He could do it, look you in the eye – he'd fixed me a couple of times already – but it was always too much. And it was a relief when his stare shifted – to his phone, the door, the noisy table in the far corner. He seemed restless and distracted, but there was this stillness in him at the same time that unnerved me, some predatory quality.

He nodded towards the street. 'You drove here.'

'Yes, I did.'

'I know you did. Penny recognised your tank. We saw you go past twice looking for somewhere to park. It gets tedious I should think. You should get rid of it.'

'What?'

'The tank. Sell it for scrap. Get a bike.'

'Sorry, I'm confused. Is that *your* business or *my* business?'

'I'm just saying. It must be hard always looking for places to park.'

'Well it is, but I need a vehicle for the job.'

'Which is?'

'Penny didn't tell you?'

'I wanted to hear your version. She gets things wrong sometimes.'

'I build things.'

'Things?'

'Buildings.'

'You build buildings.'

'Yes, look, I know you'd rather I did something else, but that happens to be what I do. And I could tell you why it's a good thing, like nursing or teaching or growing vegetables, because people like living indoors with roofs to keep the rain out and running water and drains so that the streets aren't open sewers and everyone doesn't get dysentery, but that's my business not your business and I prefer to keep things in separate compartments.'

'No offence, Jason. You do whatever it is you do.' He smiled, just slightly – a thin sneer of a smile – and he seemed to relax. He'd got me wound up and it made him feel better.

'So, Troy, I hear you're interested in finding solutions.'

'How do you mean?'

'Penny said you're a solutionist or something.'

'I don't think so. I think you got that wrong.'

I wouldn't have mentioned the solutionists. I intended not to, but I wanted to throw him off balance. I assumed it was important to him, whatever it was, because Penny had phoned specifically to tell me it wasn't. It was either that or ask him how his dad was doing.

Troy was looking out the window, looking at me, looking out the window again. 'No, you've got me there. I don't even know what that is. You've gone off on some sort of tangent with that one.'

Penny came with the drinks on a tray – a lager for me, something short and fizzy for her, ginger ale maybe, and an obscene quantity of watered down orange juice for Troy. She put the tray down on the table and perched on the edge of a chair. 'I hope you two found something to talk about.' She looked at us, each of us in turn.

Troy was staring at the tray. 'That's not enough change.' There was a tenner and a scattering of coins. 'I gave you a twenty.'

'That's all the change I got, Troy, honest.'

'And you didn't count it?'

'There's hundreds of people up there. Look. It took me ages just to get served.'

'So you're saying you weren't paying attention?'

'Are you sure it's not enough?'

Without warning, Troy reached across the table and put a hand to Penny's face. I thought he meant to take her by the ear like a schoolteacher in an old film. But just as abruptly he pulled back. His hand hovered for a moment above the table and opened with the index and middle fingers pointing upwards. The pound coin between them caught the light, glinting as it turned. He smiled, put the coin in his pocket and gathered up the rest of the money.

Penny had gone pale and her breathing was shallow. She said, 'What was that about?'

'You've been talking to Jason about our hobby.'

She looked puzzled.

'You know – our little magic circle – the illusionists.' He articulated the word, the wrong word, with exaggerated care. 'I hope you haven't given away any tricks.'

'I don't know what you mean. I don't know any tricks.'

'That's what you do with the reptiles, then, is it?' I said, 'in the reptile house – teach them magic tricks?'

'Yeah. The snakes are the worst. Hard doing magic if you don't have hands.'

We sat for a while, listening to other people's laughter and the sirens on Blackfriars Road.

Then Troy said, 'We're going to have to go now, aren't we, Pen.'

'But we just got here.'

'I think you must have left the gas on. I can smell it from here. Can't you smell something, Jason? You must have left something cooking, Pen. One of these days, you'll burn the place down.'

I told Penny to call me. If she needed anything, she had my number. I meant if he hit her, or scared her to the point that she just had to get out and needed somewhere to crash, somewhere to hide.

I googled Troy. I had that one name and I had zoology,

which turned out to be enough. He *did* have a PhD – from Imperial College. Something to do with mutations in zoonotic diseases, which I discovered were diseases that originate in animals – HIV, swine fever, avian flu, that sort of thing. For some reason I was reassured. He was more or less who Penny thought he was, even he was a mean fucker. I thought no more about it. I had my own problems.

Weeks passed, a month or more maybe and Penny phoned. 'Jason, I need to borrow your car. The SUV. We're moving, Simon and me, and we've got all this stuff.'

'I didn't know you could drive.'

'There's a lot about me you don't know.'

'I didn't know you *believed* in driving. Aren't cars part of the problem?'

'Are you going to lend me the car or not?'

'If you need a car I'll get you a car.'

'Is that a yes, then? I can't do it on the bus, can I?'

'Yes, you can have a car. And a driver to go with it, if you like. Is this for a day, a weekend, what?'

'A driver to go with it?'

'That's what I said.'

'Like the driver's just another commodity.'

'Not a commodity, no. A person who drives for a living and will be glad of the work.'

'And of course you'll pay for this car and this driver.'

'That's what I'm offering.'

'Money. That's what it always comes down to with you, isn't it.'

'That's the way things work, Pen, until the whole system breaks down and we go back to bartering.'

'But I didn't ask for your money, I just asked to borrow your car.'

I took a deep breath. 'And you've definitely got a licence.'

'I said, didn't I? Are you calling me a liar?'

'Penny, I'm just trying to help you out. Christ, when did I become the enemy?'

There was silence and I realised she was crying.

'Tell me what's going on.'

'We're moving out of London. There's this community. They want me. I feel at home there. I need to move some stuff – mainly clothes, a bit of furniture – you know.'

'So I should drive you.'

'Stop trying to organise my life, all right?' I heard exasperation, but something else as well, something I didn't expect – panic.

'Is everything OK, Penny?'

'We've got it worked out, see. We just drive down with our stuff, stay overnight and drive back. Then I get the train down at the weekend with Simon. That's it, that's the way we're doing it.'

'We – who's we?'

'Me and Troy.'

'Ah.'

I was listening to silence again. Then the sound of breathing, quick sharp breaths.

'Oh fuck off then Jason if that's the way you feel. Fucking fuck right off.'

A van pulled out from the kerb and I overreacted. For a moment I was straddling the centre line with a bus hurtling towards me. I jerked back to my own side of the road and slowed down while my heart rate settled.

Why was I even listening to Penny? Why was I willing to consider lending her a car? I wasn't even convinced she could drive. Probably Troy would end up driving, which would be better in the sense that he probably *could* drive and worse in the sense that he was more than slightly deranged.

The phone rang and it was Penny. She was crying again. Or still crying from the last call. 'Don't be angry with me Jason. Just lend me the car, OK? I promised you would, that's all, and I can't go back on it. I *can't*. This is the way we planned it.'

There was more like this. What's the point of going over it? I lent her the Nissan, that's all. I wasn't there when she picked it up. I'd remembered you had an appointment at the clinic,

Caroline, for your first scan, and I'd promised to come with you. So I filled it with petrol and left the keys with my secretary and set off with you in the Mercedes. I didn't hear until later that she'd shown up with Troy and that she'd looked sort of out of it.

That got me worried. I googled the solutionists without any luck. So I added the word *Kishar* and discovered I hadn't been paying attention. The *Kishar solution* in all its mutations was everywhere, bubbling just under the surface. BK Compton was revered and occasionally reviled. I found myself in chatrooms where people earnestly debated what kind of solution she had in mind. There were references to the book's conclusion. So I dug out the copy of *Kishar in Crisis* Penny had given me and turned to the end. There it was, the very last sentence – *Once we accept that we are the problem, it doesn't take much to imagine the solution.* But what did that *mean*? Even fans of the book couldn't agree. Was it advocating population control? Should people stop breeding altogether? Should governments put hormones in the water like fluoride? In interviews, BK herself had always refused to elaborate.

By next morning it was national news. The Elmbridge Farm suicide cult. Seven people found dead in a barn in Kent, the door sealed and a Nissan Pathfinder inside with its engine still running. Presumed cause of death – carbon monoxide poisoning. They'd left a cryptic note. *The solution starts here.*

Within hours everyone knew about the solutionists. Pundits analysed the features of cult behaviour. A few warned that this might be the start of a trend, but most treated it as the end rather than the beginning of something. BK Compton was not available for comment.

We'd seen our baby moving on a screen, but the deaths overshadowed our celebrations. I was sick with grief and guilt and unfocused dread. You tried to help, but had your own feelings to cope with – fury, mainly, that Penny had dragged me into this madness.

I look at your picture now in its silver frame. The beach front at Brighton. I have no right to mourn you with so many dead, so much irrevocably destroyed. I do though, Caro. And what if I could have you back and the rest gone, or have the rest back – the whole ruined world – and you dead. What if I had that choice? It wouldn't really be a choice, even if I was offered it. Death is OK. It's always been OK. People die. They die young. Even children die. That's nature. But what the solutionists did – that was something else.

Agnes

Dell has shown me such a treasure. Cat gave it her as a child, said it came from Janet who slipped it in her hand all those years ago while Brendan was seeing to his horse. Janet didn't say, but Cat knew it was from Dell's mother.

It's a picture of a woman, pale and faintly coloured but so beautiful and so skilfully made she might be alive, her hair loose and flying as though the wind is blowing right through the cracked glass. The frame is silver and carved with lilies. I've seen treasures like it at the Hall, some on the shelves in the turret.

'Is it my mother?'

'Not your mother, no. It's from the endtime. No villager could make such a thing.'

'I thought so.' She was disappointed, but not too much. I could tell she had more to show me. 'I loved it as a tot, kissed and snuggled it in my bed. Later, though, I found something else.' She turned it over and fiddled at the back of it. At last she lifted out a thin piece of wood and a sheet of paper, fine but rough down one edge, and with writing on both sides. It didn't make sense at first. I'd never seen paper like it that wasn't part of a book. Then I understood.

'Oh Dell.' I didn't know what else to say. It disturbed and excited me to see it, to know the Book of Air was spoiled and that Sarah had done this in secret for her baby daughter and known it all these years and told no one. 'Oh Dell. It's beautiful.'

And it was. It was the colour of milk, with tiny delicate letters, quite black and each one perfect. Stroking it I could feel where the letters lay, something like the scales on a fish. I thought at first this was the paper itself, but the margins were butter smooth, so it must be the ink made this small roughness. I saw then there was a line drawn in the margin against some of the words. I read them aloud, while Dell listened.

'The whole consciousness of my life lorn, my love lost, my hope quenched, my faith death-struck, swayed full and mighty above me in one sullen mass. That bitter hour cannot be described. In truth, the waters came into my soul, I sank in deep mire, I felt no standing, I came into deep waters, the floods overflowed me.'

Dell said, 'What does it mean?'

'It's a page from the Book of Air, and this text she's marked for you to study.'

'But all what you said about it, what does it mean?'

'I'm not sure what it means. I don't understand all of it, but it's about Jane's sadness.'

'And Jane's my mother?'

'No.'

'Who then? What's Jane to me?'

'Oh, Jane is everything. Our first Governess.' I saw there was a lot to explain. 'She wrote the Book of Air. This is a hard text, though, and must be read four ways like any text in the book, so Jane's sadness is only one part of it. This text is about water. Because water, like earth and fire, brings death as well as life. And even air, the most precious, can be poisoned with disease. And they must fight with each other, as fire boils water, and water quenches fire. And here, you see, Jane's hope is quenched – like a flame by water.'

'But what do I care about these four meanings? One meaning would be enough if it was meant for me. What did my mother mean by it?'

'Oh, but of course.' I saw it then, Sarah's purpose in pulling this page from the book. 'She meant her own sadness to be losing you, to be losing her love, her hope in life.'

'And all that's in this paper, among these marks? How can you know, from so long ago and her not here to tell you what she meant?'

I could see Dell didn't understand me – she has no sense of writing, of how powerful and beautiful it is. 'It's what the writing says,' I told her, 'and the meaning she found in the writing – a fifth meaning, you see, just for you.' I thought of how I might explain this. Of how I might understand it myself, what Sarah had done with a single stroke of her pen. 'Like a message,' I said, 'but written in ink.'

'I get it. It was her way of passing me the word.'

Dell smiled and I saw in her face for the first time her mother's loveliness. And I was filled suddenly with such longing that I couldn't sit with her, but walked out among the ruins. For want of the broad fields of my childhood rising up on to the moors where the sheep graze in summer, I looked up at the sky and imagined myself rising into its emptiness. There were faint clouds misting over the moon and I told myself that this was the same moon that shone right now over the village, and that however far you travelled it would be there just the same, but offering no comfort. I wept then for the sadness of things and thought myself a page torn from my own life, and my life like the Book of Air spoiled for ever.

Jason

Django's back. Abigail came to my room at dawn to let me know, while I was still in bed. She asked me not to be angry. I was too weak to argue with her. My temperature's been up these past few days. These fevers come and go like aftershocks and I pay them no attention, except they slow me down. She told me Django wants to apologise to me for burning the books. He acknowledges that he had no right to do it without my permission. He knows what he did was wrong. Perhaps he said these things. Abigail wants me to believe that he said them, anyway.

She sat on my bed and felt my forehead. 'You're warm.'

'Just a bit. I'll be all right.'

'You push yourself too hard.' Then she rested her hand against my chest. 'And there's so much sadness and trouble in you.'

'In all of us.'

'Yes. It's not just our bodies we need to take care of.'

It was nice to be touched by Abigail, to feel the tension ease in me and my resentment at Django loosen its grip.

He'd turned up with food apparently – mushrooms and blackberries – and asked if he could cook, to make things right between us, all of us eating together as a gesture of reconciliation. Those things he probably *did* say. They sound like Django.

He's laid the table in the dining room and got a big fire going and lit candles. I don't know what kind of sense this makes. Django's a pyromaniac. So as a punishment he gets to light candles – from a meagre supply that we can't begin to replenish until spring. But to please Abigail, and because I haven't the strength to fight, or the means to win, I sit with them, while Aleksy raises a glass of water to the cook and to peace in all our hearts and to the sown wheat.

While Django is serving dinner, Aleksy leans towards me. 'We all lost things,' he says. 'It makes us grip tight to what we got left. Your books. Deedee's wallet. I understand.' He pulls something out of his pocket. It's a pipe. 'This I carry with me always. Maybe I never see tobacco again.' He shrugs. 'Even so.'

Django's stew has an earthy smell. There are a few woody carrots chopped up in it and a small amount of rice and a lot of herbs and two kinds of mushrooms. The mushrooms have been delicately sliced and lie in cross section on the plate – pale flat ones and smaller darker ones with pointed caps and stringy stalks.

Their fibrous texture makes me long for meat. Deirdre sits beside me in a low-cut dress with flimsy straps to remind us all of a lost world.

We talk about the day's work and what must be done tomorrow. Aleksy has some news. One of the two sows, which he found rooting in the wood and enticed home with a bucket of milk and peelings, is definitely pregnant. There's a surge of optimism. I listen to the others talking and begin to feel better. With the first frost we'll slaughter one of the cows and roast joints of beef. Next year, if we survive the winter, we'll have potatoes and parsnips and we'll grow tomatoes in the greenhouse. And by the autumn there'll be bread if we live that long. And sooner than that we'll make a churn if the cows keep giving milk, and fry our mushrooms in butter, and our eggs too if the hens and geese keep laying, and we'll experiment with better ways to make cheese, hard nutty cheddar that will sit in the cellar with the apples and feed us like kings all through next winter. Our ambitions grow extravagant. I begin to talk as freely as the others. I eat Django's strange stew and feel my resistance slide away.

It's a warm evening and the fire is hot so Maud opens the windows and we watch the glow of the sun and the shadows drawing lines across the lawn. Our laughter blows out over the valley, is inhaled back into the room, drifts out again to settle in the undergrowth where the remains of human habitation are slowly rotting. Purple leaves stir at my elbow and I sense some creature scratching among the roots. A single leaf brushes the branches as it falls. Settling softly, it shrinks and dwindles into mulch. I wonder that I can hear so sharply and see so acutely into the shadows, bending my vision over the window sill, watching time accelerate, but I find it's not so surprising after all because my head has floated away from my body and time jumps randomly at every pulse.

Aleksy laughs with his mouth wide open, his head pushed forward, the lips drawn back from the teeth. Beside me, Deirdre makes high gasping noises that remind me of the monkey, and I wonder if it *is* the monkey, chattering somewhere among the trees, and Deirdre has opened her mouth not to laugh but to express astonishment at Aleksy's teeth, which are like the teeth of a horse. Sitting with her back to the fireplace, Maud laughs with her hands across her mouth because her head has imprisoned such monstrous secrets that no sound can be trusted not to let the cat out of the bag.

'Say it, Maud,' I tell her, loud in her face. 'Just blurt it out.' And she looks at me amazed as if I'm the one who's mute.

Time lurches forward. I know this because Django is sitting on the floor beside the fire, playing his clarinet. He blows into the flames and his notes scatter with the ash. Another lurch, and he's back at the head of the table with his bowler hat on and we're eating his blackberries. My spoon tilts and the berries scatter across the tablecloth. I hunt them down among the vegetation – the stalks and blooms that interweave in repeated patterns across the table to where Abigail sits watching me with open-mouthed surprise.

I'm drunk. I look at my glass, lift it to my nose and sip, but taste nothing but water.

'It's time you all knew about Simon.' Django says this, and I'm surprised because no one knows more about Simon than me. 'Look, everyone,' he says, 'there's something I want to show you.' He takes a scrap of paper from the pocket of his deckchair blazer and unfolds it. It's from a newspaper – a photo and a column of print. 'Someone left the paper on the bus. It was turned to that picture. I saw at once.'

The cutting passes around the table. It's from another time – an age of buses, an age of newspapers piled in their thousands at tube stations, commuters thronging the escalators, millions of words printed morning and night. The picture swims up at me in bright colour then settles back into shades of grey. It's Simon, my Simon, standing outside a pub, and a policewoman holding his hand. What's this new trick? Cleverer than a bunch of flowers – Django's pulling bits of our past out of his pocket.

Deirdre peers at it. 'But that's...'

'Yes.' Django nods eagerly as if it's the lesson for the day and she's the first to get it.

'That's... the boy. The Elmbridge boy.'

'Of course. Now look what's above his head.'

'In this house? The Elmbridge boy?'

'Yes. In this house. But look.'

Aleksy leans across to pull the paper from Deirdre's hand. 'What is it, Django?'

'It's a sign.' He's immensely pleased with himself.

'It's a pub sign, Django,' I tell him. 'We all remember pub signs.'

'It's the sundial.'

'Yes, that's the name of the pub – the Sundial.'

'There are no accidents.'

'There are accidents all the time.'

We're locked in this argument, Django and me, and it already feels as if lives depend on it – Simon's life and mine too, maybe. But so far no one else knows what we're talking about, and I'm not even sure *I* do. The ground is shifting under us and we're all scrabbling for a foothold. Except Django, who seems to have swallowed every candle in the room and to glow with the accumulated light.

'I will cause the sun's shadow to move ten degrees backward on the sundial.'

'Yes, Django, it's in the Bible. I could find the page in about thirty seconds. Listen, all of you – just because it's in the Bible doesn't mean it means anything. Anything's in the Bible if you look hard enough. So there's a sundial in Isaiah, and here's a sundial. So what? The shadow on this sundial isn't going anywhere. It's a picture somebody's painted of a sundial because that happens to be the name of the pub.'

'I didn't say it was a miracle, Jason.' Django gestures towards me for everyone's benefit, because my anger is a count against me, a warning that I might lose control of myself again and go for his throat. 'I said it was a sign. And why is it so important to you to deny it?'

'I'd like to know this, actually.' It's Aleksy grunting his way into the argument. 'Why is this so important to you that you get all excited – that this is a sign or not such a sign?'

'Not to me. It means nothing to me one way or the other. It's Django's cutting. I say we put it on the fire with the books.'

Deirdre has taken it back from Aleksy and is studying it. 'It *is* our Simon. Look Aleksy.' She holds it for Aleksy to see and looks at me bewildered. 'Our little Simon is the Elmbridge boy?'

'Yes.' I'm relieved that's he's *our little* Simon – that's two reasons not to lynch him.

'So his mother…'

'Yes.'

'She was your sister.'

'Yes.'

'And she was one of *them*?'

'One of who?' Abigail asks, looking at Deirdre, then at me. 'Who is the Elmbridge boy?'

Deirdre is amazed. 'You don't remember? Where *were* you?'

'It was the sundial I saw first.' Django is still telling his story. 'And he had this canvas bag over his shoulder, see. And what was in it? It says, here, in the fifth paragraph, look. A honey sandwich. And I saw that the prophecies were being fulfilled. Butter and honey shall he eat, that he may know to refuse evil.'

'But Abigail, you must know about the Elmbridge gang, surely. Everyone knows. It was all their fault. They released the virus.'

'No, Deirdre,' I say, 'that was never proved.'

'Only because all the people trying to prove it kept dying.'

'And you never knew this?' Aleksy is intrigued by this fresh evidence of Abigail's isolation. 'They kept this from you? You were in a Cistercian convent, or how?'

But Abigail is looking at me. 'They're saying Simon's mother did this?'

'No, not Simon's mother. She was as much a victim...'

'Oh come on, Jason,' Deirdre says, 'for God's sake.'

'As much a victim as anyone.'

'And there I was, on the top deck of the number 68 with this discarded newspaper in my hand, and I started sweating. I'd been given a glimpse of the light that would lead us out of this darkness even as the darkness fell.'

'So this boy,' Aleksy says, 'this boy who walked away unharmed from Elmbridge Farm. This boy is Simon? Your nephew?' He's looking at me and he's having difficulty focusing on my face, or I am on his. His eyes grow and shrink and are their own size again.

And Django is still talking. 'It just felt like flu to start with, nothing out of the ordinary. But as soon as I got home I wheeled my bike out from under the stairs in my building and hung it from the light in the stairwell. I put a broom through the spokes and hung more things from it, so it was like a mobile – round things, saucepan lids, a clock. Wheels within wheels, see, like in Ezekiel. And the wheels were angels, and I heard their wings like the noise of great waters. Then I couldn't stand up any more and Mrs Burgess from the ground floor flat put me to bed.'

'You've had it.' Deirdre stares at Django as if she's just seen one of Ezekiel's angels.

'No one knew what it was. By the time I'd come through Mrs Burgess was past help and it was everywhere.'

'You've had it, the blessing and everything, and you never said.'

'You never asked.'

'No one survived.'

Aleksy nods at me. 'Jason survived.'

'No one at the beginning, though.'

'Not many perhaps,' Django says. 'But not many saw the sundial. Saw it for what it was, I mean.'

We're looking at the newspaper cutting again, which shakes in Deirdre's hands. I have to shut my eyes and take another look to be sure the shadow on the sundial isn't moving.

'Wait though, Django.' Deirdre says. 'This means you knew Simon before we got here? You knew him already?'

'I'd never met him.'

'But you had this picture of the Elmbridge boy in your pocket. And now here we are. And here's the Elmbridge boy.'

'We were guided.'

'By you. You knew where to find him. You lied to us.'

'I never lied. You assumed….'

'I assumed you were telling the truth.'

'I was led, Deirdre. We all were.'

'You let me think you didn't know where we were going. That this road, and then this road just felt right. And then this road. Until, hey look, a big house. Let's see if anyone's there.'

'Your country is desolate, your cities are burned with fire.'

I ask him, 'How did you know where to find us?'

'It was all there for anyone who wanted to know – back then when the internet worked – where you lived, what properties you owned.'

For no reason I can see, Deirdre is weeping.

'And the daughter of Zion is left as a cottage in a vineyard, as a lodge in a garden of cucumbers.' Django rubs Deirdre's back, kneads her shoulders, rocks in sympathy with her. His voice is low. 'I never lied.'

'Well what would you call it?'

'Then flew one of the seraphim unto me, having a live coal in his hand, which he had taken with the tongs from off the altar and he laid it upon my mouth.'

'What does that *mean*?' She's still arguing but the fight has gone out of her. 'That's just words. You don't even make sense.'

'It's the only sense I can make. I saw Simon and I knew, and

222

I was burned up with the knowledge. My mouth was on fire. I said to the angel, here am I, send me.'

'Which means what, exactly?'

'Which means we're in the exact middle of a living miracle. I will give a child to be their prince, it says. And here he is, asleep upstairs in his bed. Which means this is written. Our *lives* are written. Doesn't that make a difference?' He laughs, and it's an infectious shout of laughter.

There's something wrong with Django's reasoning that I can't quite put my finger on, and I don't much want to anyway, because I find it's so much easier knowing it all has a purpose.

'They shall obtain joy and gladness, and sorrow and sighing shall flee away. That... *that* is what's written.' Django is leaning out at the window, shouting up at the sky. 'A new heaven,' he says, 'and a new earth.'

And it feels new. Everything lifts and pulses with a vividness I've never seen before. I find myself inclined to laugh. 'Look at this place, though,' I say, 'this house, that lawn, those trees. You can see why I wanted it.'

Somebody must have moved first or we must all have felt drawn by the evening air because here we are on the steps by the front door. House martins wheel restlessly above us and the shadows on the grass are merging into one shadow. We cross the lawn to the orchard and wander among the trees, dividing and dispersing and regrouping according to some logic that I think would be apparent to me if I was sitting on a branch looking down. Then one after another we fall and on our backs and watch the sky.

'Let's go for a spin.' It's Aleksy talking. I think he means *this* – what we're already doing – spinning through space while we cling with our backs to the ground. But he says, 'Let's go for a spin in Jason's beautiful car.'

It's a preposterous idea. But the car's still there, by the front door, where I abandoned it in my fever. And here we are, and none of us with a better idea. So we run from the orchard and across the gravel drive and through the grass. Abigail is ahead of me and I see how lovely she is, moving with a swaying ease that takes her no effort. So much of Deirdre's elegance is stitched together and slipped on like her dress. It's all coded messages, referring to something other than itself.

We reach the car and climb in, except Maud, who backs away shaking her head. Aleksy takes the driving seat with Deirdre beside him, her stockinged feet on the dashboard, Django and Abigail and me sprawled in the back, all of us laughing as the car jerks forward and we sink against the cushioned leather, breathing its luxurious smell. We curve round over the lawn and back to the drive, heading towards the house. The arch of the inner gateway passes over head and we're in the stable yard, vibrated by cobbles. The horses whinny in their stalls, setting up a din in the hen house.

Aleksy pulls us into a tight circle and just before we hit the stable door he brakes, throws us into reverse and forward again, and here we are back on the drive. The moon has risen to greet us. I think we might lift our weight off the ground and spin through wisps of cloud to join it. But instead we drift on to the lawn and down towards the corner where the grass breaks up into wilder growth and the brook runs among weeds and rushes. We bounce over the rough ground, and it seems nothing for such a vehicle to hop the brook, squeeze between saplings and flatten itself under the lowest railing of the fence to reach the road which is its home. But Aleksy hits the brakes. We tilt into the brook and the car stalls.

Deirdre stops laughing and Abigail is clutching my arm. We stare through the windscreen at the church tower and the dark space where the road disappears among trees towards everything we've lost and everything that threatens our existence. Then we climb out of the Merc in silence and wander back the way we came, spreading out now the car isn't here to hold us together, Deirdre with an arm round Aleksy's neck, Django going his own way. Abigail gathers up Maud and leads her towards the house. After a moment I find myself alone on the lawn and no reason to be here or anywhere in particular.

Agnes

I went with Dell this morning to fetch water from the river. I work with her every day now. When my limbs ache and my head is fogged from labour I find I can forget my troubles. Dell loads the bowls and bottles on a cart and wheels it through the forest paths. Their name for the river is the canal, and a strange looking river it is, as straight as a furrow and edged with bricks, except where its walls have tumbled in. We walked beside it for a while in search of blackberries, pulling the water cart among the ruined towers. Here and there the flow is held up by great walls where the endtimers built bridges and left no space underneath for the water, so it must find its way through cracks and crevices to spray down like piss buckets emptied from cottage windows.

When we'd filled our pans with blackberries, Dell said she had something to show me. She took me off the path towards a building that stands high as the Hall, though breached near the roof. She pulled aside a crumbling piece of iron that left its red stains on her, and there was a break in the wall, enough for us to crawl through on our bellies.

We stood up in a vast room. A staircase rose curving towards patches of sky. We walked among aspens, stepped over rusting roof beams and branches where woodlice lived. The air had the forest smell of dank earth and thick unweeded growth. The deep din of the woodland was dulled by the walls, but a startled jay rose up with a clamour and a pair of squirrels leapt away out of sight. Climbing things covered the walls and straggled above us from the galleries – ivy and bindweed and long flowered honeysuckle. Dell took a handful where she stood and pulled it aside. And I caught the stink of mildew. There were shelves tightly packed with what I took at first for narrow boxes, each a different colour, each with the faded marks of writing that I strained to read, turning my head to follow the run of letters. She reached out a hand, pulled a box from the shelf and gave it me. An edge of it split and broke into layers like onion skin. And I saw at last what it was, what they all were, what I think they had been all along to my eyes, while my mind had said this wasn't possible – a flood, a dizzying bee swarm of books, an orchard branch so laden you'd fear it would break.

Not four books only, then, with the Book of Death. Not five even with my own secret book. Not ten or twenty. As I pulled aside more strands of ivy, I saw enough for every person in the village each to have one. And more than that – more than I knew how to count.

I reached for another and opened it, stiff and cracking, to a page as ridged as a barley field when the wind blows. Another would hardly open, lying damp in my hands, its edges ripe with mould. I found pages on which the ink had faded almost to nothing, pages that were more hole than paper, and a nest of mice that fell squealing among the roots at our feet and scattered into corners.

But my eyes had found a text. And in another book a second text. And every text was a voice speaking through my voice.

'The world seemed getting larger round poor Gwendolen, and she more solitary and helpless in the midst.'

'Because what's the use of learning that I am one of a long row only – finding out that there is set down in some old book somebody just like me, and to know that I shall only act her part; making me sad, that's all.'

'I tried to breathe but my breath would not come and I felt myself rush bodily out of myself and out and out and out and all the time bodily in the wind. I went out swiftly, all of myself, and I knew I was dead and it had all been a mistake to think you just died.'

'You pierce my soul. I am half agony, half hope. Tell me not that I am too late, that such precious feelings are gone for ever. I offer myself to you again with a heart even more your own, than when you almost broke it eight and a half years ago.'

'And this also, said Marlow suddenly, has been one of the dark places of the earth.'

'As she unfastened her brooch at the mirror, she smiled faintly to see her face all smeared with the yellow dust of lilies.'

'Agnes. Please, Agnes. What is it? What are you mouthing on about?' Dell's voice came to me as if from another place, though she stood beside me, pulling at my arm.

'All these books,' I said. 'No one knows. They think. The Mistress says. Everyone says.'

'But what are they? Why do they matter?'

'These people, these thoughts. All this time they've been here waiting. This sadness and hoping, this darkness and dust of lilies, this rushing into the wind. And they'll go on waiting, and being found and being lost again. As if they don't mind – to be read, not to be read.' Truly, I didn't know what I meant.

And still my mind is a whirl of questions. What are these books? What is this book I write in now? Did everyone among the endtimers have her own book to tell her own story in, as I have mine? Who allowed them this? The child in my belly pushes up against my heart. I breathe fast and shallow but find no air. The world is not as I thought it was.

'Who says these words, though, Agnes?'

I couldn't answer.

Jason

I slept – perhaps just for a moment – and dreamt that Walter, wandering through the house, peered in at our bedroom and found me and Abigail having sex. He blessed us in the name of Our Lord BJ Choudhry. Then there was a child, a little girl. And it was our child, Caro, yours and mine.

I remember the print-outs from your scan – those shadowy images that told us we were going to have a girl. By the following morning we'd stopped looking, and could watch only the repeated footage of paramedics carrying the bodies from the outhouse at Elmbridge Farm, and interviews with the neighbours who'd observed suspicious comings and goings, and the mother of one of the dead, weeping for her baby girl who'd shown such promise as a gymnast. They'd found incongruous pictures of Penny in her Random days – party girl Penny Farthing – and one with a dead-eyed look that hinted at drug abuse. There was nothing of Troy but a blurred picture of a student in a mortar board with a sneer for whoever held the camera.

Meanwhile the Nissan had led the police to me and I was telling them everything I knew. The journalists were all over our building, pumping the staff and the other residents for gossip, crowding the gate to press their lenses to my windscreen. The only way I could protect you was to let you stay a prisoner in the flat, while I attended to business. At first it looked as if they meant to cast me as an accomplice – the one who'd supplied the weapon. But it didn't take them long to spot the ironies. A property developer with a gas-guzzling SUV in the middle of a stand-off with environmentalists – I looked less like an accessory than the prime target. So off they went to cosy up to the Urban Diggers and get the dirt on the crazies, the environmentals, the nutroast nutjobs. They were desperate for more on the family connection, but they never found the Jesus bus. The only thing Penny and I had in common was a mysterious past – we'd both popped up from nowhere.

For a couple of days Simon gave them a new angle – the Elmbridge boy found wandering with an uneaten sandwich in his satchel and a scrawled note pinned to his coat saying *taek care of mi boy its not his falt*. And I got the full measure of the state of education in Hebron, and a fresh stab of remorse for leaving my sister there. For me Simon's survival was a miracle. I'd waited for the call to identify the body of a child and here he was alive and unharmed. And you were heroic, Caroline. You hated Penny for what she'd done to me, but you took Simon in without a murmur.

Then the Elmbridge Cult was lost in a blizzard of fresh news – a mystery virus causing panic across the south east. The reporters knew it was a mystery. They could sense the panic. They could more or less count the dead. Beyond that they knew nothing. The virus had been brought into the country by migrant farm workers. It had been spread by asylum seekers released from a detention centre near Dover. It had mutated in the intestines of an ibex goat smuggled into the east end for religious purposes. A leaked document from the ministry of defence allowed some smart investigative journalist to make the link between the Elmbridge suicide cult, government zoologist Dr Troy Phelps and a top secret research project. But factions remained loyal to earlier theories, or cohered around later ones, however mystical or bizarre.

Meanwhile the view from our flat over Blackfriars Bridge was transformed from one day to the next like a film fast-forwarding through seasons of change. Like waking up to snow, we saw one morning the bus stops abandoned and the roads clogged with cyclists in surgical masks. Another day it was nothing but ambulances. When the roads emptied and even the cyclists were gone, who knew whether they were at home avoiding contagion, or sick already? But not everyone had caught it, because suddenly they were sitting in cars in furious gridlock responding to rumours of food to be found in the west, or safety in the Scottish Highlands. That's when the armoured vehicles appeared and the soldiers, to set up their checkpoint on the bridge. And we knew that the vans and trucks they waved through were loaded with the dead. Dogs prowled and congregated, indifferent to traffic lanes and military authority, but not to the marksmen sent to shoot them and to shoot the shoppers who looked too much like looters, until the shoppers who survived were all looters, any system of retail having broken down. And the streets were left to scavengers, and unsupervised children, and people wheeling corpses on supermarket trolleys, and to snarling clusters of survivalists dressed in ill-sorted uniforms and body armour, and to strange eruptions of emptiness and silence – and, distinct from all of these, the sudden gatherings of awestruck onlookers, little pockets of order, as one after another succumbed to the condition's strangest symptom.

'The blessing,' I said, holding your hand at the window when the news first began to break. 'They're calling it the blessing.'

'Yes.'

'Why this singing, though, this drawing, this construction of strange objects?'

'I don't know. Maybe because it's our deepest instinct – to make meaning.'

'Even when there *is* no meaning?'

'Especially then.' And I felt the terror in your grip.

And who was I in all this? An onlooker from a high window, a nurse, a reader of *Jane Eyre*. A scavenger when it became necessary. A looter and barterer. A dodger of military bullets and a street fighter when I couldn't avoid it. A shit-dumper and a grunting water carrier.

Can it really have been like this, or is it just the way I've reconfigured it, stretched out as I am, mushroomed and Django'd, with my brain's wiring still scrambled from the sickness? Could I have lived through this and still be sane?

At some early point when we couldn't begin to imagine how much worse it was going to get, you lay down with a fever, and I read to you, and Simon who seemed to have lost the power of speech was so quiet I sometimes forgot he was there. And we argued and you painted our wall and your second fever burned you into oblivion. And the last thing I could do for you was to carry your body to the designated collection point for a hastily improvised municipal burial, where you and others became landfill while the mourners covered their mouths – me among them – and looked away.

Agnes

I have shown Dell my book, this book that has been my most precious secret. It made me breathless to do it. She wasn't shocked, but only puzzled at this new strangeness. When I read her something I'd written she smiled. 'I see it now,' she said. 'You throw a pebble for someone to catch. Before, when you found meaning in the marks in all those books, I saw only the catching.'

I wonder at myself that Dell could see this at once, when all this time I couldn't. But how could I when no one in the village does?

Then Dell frowned again. 'You put your own words in your book,' she said. 'So why didn't my mother write her own words to me?'

I saw then how impossible it would be for Dell to understand all the ways of the Hall, and it came to me with a sharp pang that I have travelled further than I ever meant to and left behind everything that was once precious to me.

I don't know when I shall see the village again. The cottage where Walt and Janet raised me comes to me sometimes in dreams. More often I dream of the Hall, its dark places, and I must walk endlessly to find what's lost, the passageways tilting so I crawl and cling to keep from tumbling backwards. And my neighbours turn away from me, cold and indifferent. I think often of cousin Annie who would have been my friend if I'd let her, and of Roland and Megan who will be an old married couple by now, but I haven't yet dreamt of them. I dream the stern face of the Mistress. I dream of Brendan falling from the banisters into trees that sprout to meet him from the tiled floor. And one time I dreamt of Sarah, shedding light from one end of the top corridor to where I stood desolate at the other, and I woke weightless with joy, until I remembered where I was and what my life had come to.

I love Dell and Trevor, but I fear for myself out here among the scroungers. And I fear for my child. Meanwhile I gather wood for the fire and help Dell with the cooking. And I teach her the letters and the sounds they make, which she is quick to learn, being eager to understand this oddness of wild words found in patterns of ink, and longing to read for herself her mother's only message.

Later I will teach her writing, which she has her own reason to learn. That torn page she said was her mother's way of passing her the word. And I see now that for the scroungers a word isn't a shape made of letters but something left at the O to be passed on to someone else – that this one has gone east, that one south, that another might be found hunting cattle in such a place or won't be back before the first stirrings of spring – all these words to be stowed in Trevor's head. With writing she can help him. Is this wrong? I am so far from the schoolroom and the study, and so accustomed to this strange book of mine, that my qualms slide away.

But not my fears. I fear that Brendan is dead. I fear that he is still alive and Sarah takes my place in the red room. I fear I shall be found and punished for his killing, that Sarah regrets putting herself in danger for my sake, that she hasn't forgiven me, that she will never forgive me, trapped at the Hall to be maddened by the muttered longings and resentments of the village. I fear that Roland, when he remembers me, thinks only how glad he is that I am gone and he has Megan to love and comfort him.

I write too much about fear, and think about it uselessly. I mean anyway to write less, so that there might be ink when I have urgent need of it.

I've helped Sarah make ink and could do it myself if I were at the Hall. Here in the forest, I've taken Dell to search for the purple galls that swell sometimes on oak twigs and we've left our findings in a lidded pot to seep and grow mouldy. Among the ruins we've found shards of iron small enough to stir into the mix when it's time. I've put aside a piece of cloth that may be fine enough for straining. There's no lack of water. Sarah adds sloe juice, but says water alone will do. But what of the indigo that grows in the windowed shed beside the Hall and deepens the ink's colour? And where will I find an acacia bush like the one that spreads its purple leaves against the south wall beside the study window and spills thick sap under the knife. I'm afraid my ink will come faint and watery from the nib, and fade to nothing, and my writing wasted, and my thoughts forgotten.

And besides, now that I have Dell as a friend, now that Dell knows about the book, now that the book is not my only friend, perhaps I can put it by and maybe not think about it so often and so fiercely. I will try at least.

Jason

Is it October yet? There's no way of knowing. The day's colour faded long ago from the sky, but it's warm still, almost sultry. I'm tired, but too restless for bed. I sit on the front steps of the house and rest against a pillar. I push my hands against the stone and its texture speaks like Braille. I was here before you were born, the house says, and I'll be here after you're dead. And when I'm old I'll shelter your offspring. Your descendants too will be nurtured here, will sit where you sit and see the cottages standing among trees across the empty road, the church tower breaking the skyline to the east where the woodland thickens, a drift of haze softening the edges of the moon.

I'm distracted by human voices. Below in the orchard Aleksy has said something to make Deirdre laugh. So that's where they disappeared to after our spin in the Merc. I see them now. Their outlines shift and mingle in the shadows and their soft laughter joins the other noises – the bird cries and fox barks, the scurrying of badgers, the wingbeats of roosting pheasants.

How close you seem to me right now, Caro, Caroline, though forever out of reach.

The Merc is where we left it, down there tilting into the ditch among the weeds. That's the last of our old life. Somewhere up in the house the monkey is bickering with Django's clarinet, bubbles of noise floating from the high windows. There are footsteps behind me in the hallway and a rushing sound like wind blowing through the grass, but there is no wind.

Abigail speaks to me. 'I brought you a jumper, look.'

'I'm not cold.'

'But you might be later.'

I turn and look up at her and see there's a duvet over her shoulder, dragging on the flagstones.

'Maud's gone to bed. I don't want to sleep in the house. Not tonight.'

She puts her hand out and helps me up. Then without letting go she draws me down the steps and towards the High Wood.

'It's Django's stew,' I say.

'Yes, it's Django's stew, so we don't have to think of another reason.'

'Did you know he'd spiked the food?'

'Spiked – is that what you call it? Because of those sharp-capped mushrooms? I should have known not to eat them. I was so eager for everything to be all right.'

'What are we going to do about Django?'

'He can't hurt us if we don't let him.'

'He could have poisoned us.'

'I'll keep him out of the kitchen.'

'He burnt my books.'

'So that's one thing he can never do to you again.'

'I'm not sure that makes sense.'

'Maybe it doesn't. Ask me in the morning.' She looks at me closely, her eyes fixed on mine, and starts to smile and looks away, because looking and smiling aren't allowed at the same time.

I let her lead me in silence across the lawn and in among the trees until the house is obscured. Her headscarf snags on a twig and for a moment she's tangled. I help her pull her hair free. Then she unhooks the scarf from the branch and pockets it. Where the trees are most ancient and the ground opens up, she throws the duvet down on a bank of leaves and we sit watching bright slivers of sky between trunks of beech and elder.

'I want to tell you about Caroline.'

'Tell me then.'

'We were married for five years and we were going to have a child, a little girl. She was great, Caroline was, really great. She was always full of ideas. She lived in her head. It drove me up the wall sometimes. She'd lose something and not notice for days. It never bothered her. She was much cleverer than me, except about practical things. She didn't tell me much about her childhood, only that she was lonely and read for company. I should have asked her more. But asking questions was more her thing than mine. She was an anthropologist. Do you know what that is?'

'No.'

'It doesn't matter. I don't either, really. She wrote things – books and articles. She wrote all the time, when she wasn't teaching and going to meetings or doing what she called fieldwork. But there was a book she was writing for herself. Nothing to do with her job, just an idea she had. It started with *Jane Eyre* because she loved *Jane Eyre*. She had various copies of it, but her favourite came from her godmother and was about eighty years old. Do you know *Jane Eyre*?'

'No.'

'She wanted to write a kind of history of the way *Jane Eyre*'s been imitated and re-written and generally ripped off. I teased her about it, how far up itself it was – a book about a book and all the other books it's spawned. She didn't mind. She enjoyed being teased. You don't know what I'm talking about do you? Don't listen to me. I don't know why I'm talking so much.'

'Don't stop. It's interesting. I like it when you talk.'

'There were books she liked a lot. One that told the story of Rochester's mad wife, all the things Charlotte Bronte doesn't tell us and Jane Eyre doesn't know – about her being a Jamaican and how she's done in by men. I forget the name of it. And there were books that annoyed her, and books that made her laugh. She loved spotting Charlotte's children, as she called them. Stories about Victorian husbands driving their wives mad and locking them in lunatic asylums. Stories about houses haunted by secrets, and you'd know it wouldn't be over until someone had set fire to the house. I said once it was the houses I felt bad for and she pretended to be shocked. Of course I never actually read them, but she'd be in bed with a book and start giggling or get excited and then she'd tell me. I asked her once why she didn't write a book of her own – a novel, I mean. And she said she didn't have the talent for making things up.

She was better at seeing patterns in other people's stories. But she did once have this idea for a children's story.'

'Tell me.'

'I'm not sure I can remember it all.'

'Tell me what you remember.'

'All right. This girl lives in an orphanage. One day she finds a book hidden in the fireplace where they're too mean to light a fire. It's a beautiful book and she loves it like a friend, like a toy bear or something, hugging it at night. She starts having these strange dreams. Every morning she finds the story of her dream has printed itself in the book in place of what was there before. Meanwhile, in some other country, a wealthy man finds parts of his life disappearing – objects missing from his house, then pieces of his own history. Friends become unreachable and unknown as though they'd never existed. When his son doesn't come down to breakfast, he sends his daughter to wake him. Go and fetch your brother from his room, he says, and she reacts as if he's gone mad. What brother? What room? His piano disappears. He visits a friend, a violinist. He sits to play the friend's piano and he can't play a note. It's as though he's never touched a piano in his life. I can't remember how it ends. Maybe that was going to be the end. It doesn't sound like much of story does it.'

'It's sad.'

'Yes, but Caroline wasn't sad when she told me about it. She was excited. That's the way she was.'

'There's something I must tell you, Jason.'

'You can tell me anything.'

'But this is a secret. I mean I've kept it a secret and I shouldn't have, and now I'm afraid you'll be angry that I didn't tell you before.'

'Why didn't you?'

'Because I was afraid.'

'You're not afraid of anything.'

'I'm more afraid than you know. If you weren't here I don't know what I'd do.'

I wait for her to tell me her secret, thinking she could hardly guess how hard it would be to shock me.

'Do you think sometimes,' she says, 'that we've known each other all our lives?'

'My life stopped, and began again when I woke up in this house.'

'But we knew each other before.'

'Is this about reincarnation?'

'I don't know what that is. But we did know each other. I was in Hebron. I was on the Jesus bus.'

And I *am* shocked after all. 'What do you know about the Jesus bus?'

'Everything. I was there. With my grandma. Grandma Cheryl. We left my mother in London because she didn't want to come. I mean... because she was a streetwalker – that's what Grandma Cheryl said. I think it must have been a hard life. I barely remember her and I never saw her again after we left.'

'Abigail? I don't remember any Abigail.'

'I wasn't Abigail then. Caleb gave us all new names, remember, when we reached Hebron. I was Tiffany before.'

'Tiffany!' I search her face for that child, that pudgy kid bundled up in clothes too big for her and clinging to Penny's skirt. It is her. Now I see it, I wonder that I didn't see it before. 'But how come you're here? It's unbelievable.' It makes me laugh with astonishment.

'No, not unbelievable. I saw the house when you did. When we were getting apples in the orchard. And you said, one day you'd buy it and live in it and I asked if I could come too. I knew if I was ever going to find you it would be here – back along the road from Lloyd's farm. Not that far away. Three days walk, as it turned out. When most of the others were dead and there was no one left to nurse.'

'You grew up on Lloyd's farm.'

'Yes, Hebron.'

'So you knew Penny.'

'Yes.'

'And my mother.'

'Yes.'

'And Derek and Walter and all of them.'

'Walter I remember vaguely. He died when I was quite young. Just after you left. They said it killed him when you ran away.'

'That's a lie. He was dead already. I watched him go.'

'And Caleb – Derek – that's the part I was afraid to tell you.'

'Why? What about him?'

'I was his wife. One of his wives. After your mother died, and your sister ran away, he chose me. Then later a girl called Sarah, and then Maud.'

'Three of you?'

'It was better when it wasn't just me. We took care of each other. I loved Sarah. We were everything to each other.'

'You were all his wives?'

'Yes, like in the time of the patriarchs, Caleb said.'

'I bet he did. Were there any children?'

'No, none of us had children.'

'He was infertile, then, I suppose.'

'Maybe, I don't know if that's the word for it. It's hard to explain.'

'Don't tell me if you don't want to.'

There's a pale movement overhead and I see the owl swooping among the trees to settle on a branch.

'I knew what it was supposed to be like,' Abigail says. 'My grandma told me not to be scared, that it was nice when you got used to it. *All good fun really*, she said, *as long you don't fight it*. She saw me, one day, looking at the stallion in the field across the river with his pizzle hanging under his belly like something that didn't belong to him, and she laughed and said it wouldn't be *that* size. I knew that anyway. I'd seen one of the boys... you know... doing himself behind the barn. But it turned out different than I expected. Caleb never got hard like that. He'd get on top of me, but only to kiss me and rub against me.' She stopped. 'I didn't think I'd tell you this. No reason to tell anyone now. I told Sarah, so she'd know what to expect. And Maud, later on. But I've no reason to tell you.'

'Yes you have. So that you don't have to carry it around all by yourself.' I'm thinking of Penny, of what she told me when I found her squatting in my property with Jack or Zac – that sex with Derek was worse than she'd expected.

'Well, I was supposed to use my hands and sometimes my mouth. It took a long time, longer than the boy behind the barn, a lot longer than the horse, and quite often nothing happened and he'd give up or fall asleep.'

'And what if you didn't? What if you refused?'

'He never forced me. He never hit me or anything. Not for that. But I always did it as thoroughly as I could, and Sarah as well, to keep Maud from having to. Sarah and I could laugh about it. He wasn't bad, Caleb. Just an old man who wanted to feel big and strong when he wasn't any more. But it was difficult for Maud. She never got used to it.'

'And that's why she doesn't talk?'

'*I do* was the last thing I ever heard her say. Are you disgusted with me now?'

'Why should I be?'

'I was always half afraid of you.'

'Why?

'Because you were the bad seed.'

'And Penny was the good?'

'Until she ran away. Then it was a wicked streak you'd both inherited.'

'Not from mum?'

'No, he loved your mum. We all did. Your mother was a living saint. It was your father, with his fleshly appetites and worldly desires, who'd kept her from the path of righteousness until God cast him down from a high place and raised up Caleb to seek Hebron.'

'He fell off a ladder. He wasn't cast down by God. He had a heart attack. I don't know anything about his fleshly appetites. It was Derek who liked Korean tarts. And the extent of my dad's worldly desires was to have mum cook him steak and chips for tea on a Friday night and watch a bit of telly.'

'You miss him.'

'He would have known how to take care of this house.'

'You loved him.'

'Did you believe those stories – about my dad, about me being the bad seed?'

'I never believed anything bad about you.'

I take her hand and she shivers.

'Do you want to go back inside?' she says.

'No. Do you?

'No. And you're not disappointed?'

'About what?'

'That I'm not a virgin.'

'Abigail – you might be the first grown-up virgin I've ever met.'

'You're teasing me.'

'It's hard not to.' I look her in the face. 'I've had sex with other women you know. I was in London for years before I met Caroline. And Caroline wasn't a virgin when I met her.'

'You can tell me that another day. You should stop talking about Caroline now.'

'Why?'

'Because it's time.'

She kisses me. I realise I didn't expect her to be passionate. She's so practical always and so self-contained. And modest, of course, with the headscarf and the heavy skirts – always careful to close the curtain when she washes at the spring. I've never seen her flustered before. There's garlic on her breath. She puts her hand up to my face and I kiss her fingers. The nails are darkened at the rim with soil, and the palms of her hands are rough and calloused. There's a memory of the milking shed overlaid by vegetable smells – roots and rank weeds and the sweeter scent of sage. Unbuttoning her blouse, I see a fine silver chain and a star of David at the end of it.

'It was my mother's.' she says quickly, as though she has to justify this secret ornament. 'She gave it me when Grandma Cheryl took me on the Jesus Bus. So I'd remember who I was, she said.'

'You're Jewish?'

'That I was her daughter – she didn't want me to forget.

What do you mean, Jewish?'

'If Cheryl was Jewish what was she doing on the Jesus bus?'

'Stop asking questions.'

As I free her from her clothes, I find I can trace her day's work across her body, tasting the salt on her skin and the sharper tang of sweat clinging to the intimate crevices, and then sweeter flavours that are only hers and owe nothing to the field or the kitchen. After a while her breath is warm on my face and the sounds she makes in her throat are louder to my ear than the woodland noises and then drown them altogether.

Agnes

It feels strange to write in this book after so long. I'm not who
I was when I last opened its covers. Having a baby of my own
makes me think again about my mother. She knew what it was
to have a baby die. She had suffered imprisonment in the red
room. I see how fear might have grown in her, all her fears for
herself swelling into one monstrous fear that her second child
would come to harm. I'm sad to think that I will never say this
to her. That I know why she slapped me when I paddled too
deep, why she hissed at me when I spoke up too loud or played
too wildly. And I'm sad that she will never know her grandchild.
I have called him Walt, after my father. I think of the village
now as a river that flowed through me, and my life just part of
its flowing. I can't bear to think that it will never flow through
my child, that I have stopped it here, in me, and fear that little
Walt's life will be like a dried up river bed without it.

It was hard having him. Dell helped, and Madge, an old
woman who comes to the O sometimes with pigeons. Madge
has a knack for snaring, but no teeth, so she brings the birds but
only slurps at Dell's gravy and gets drunk on Trevor's brew. The
cramps came on at tea time and came faster and sharper into the
evening, but it was the dead of night before little Walt appeared.
Madge said this was quick but it seemed long enough to me.

I thought at times that the pain would tear me open. At
times my mind went somewhere else and I seemed to be in a
river and the pain was like water rushing through me, wave after
wave, and I must either fight it or drown in it, and drowning
was better.

So lovely it was at last to hold him damp and blooded from
my belly and so tiny in my arms. I've never known a sweeter
thing. For such a time I'd known him, but never yet seen him

face to face. All winter he'd called to me, kicking and turning, nagging me to eat the wild berries Trevor pickles in gin. But when I took his tiny wrinkled fingers and his little eyes blinked open and looked into mine, I came at last to his calling. And I understood Sarah's grief at losing Dell to the scroungers, never to see her again.

Madge took a kitchen knife to the binding, and Walt became his own person.

'Oh, Agnes,' Dell said, 'Look at his tiny noggin, all red and furrowed. Who'd have thought he'd be so lovely.'

Madge took him from me to wrap him from draughts. When it was Dell's turn to hold him, she hugged him and hugged him, saying, 'Look at the little tablet.'

Loving Walt as I do, I find I must try to forgive Brendan. I know I will catch glimpses of him in Walt's face as Walt grows older, and I would be sorry to mind. Even so, I think what Brendan did to me was wrong. I see that now clearer than ever. Wrong to give me this baby, then to punish me for it. To do it to me when I was far from home and afraid of him. And I was always afraid of him, though I called it love. And it was wrong of him to tell lies about my mother. If I killed him I'm sorry, but not too much. I can't wish Brendan safe at the Hall and myself locked away to save him from shame.

I have seen more pictures, but never with such innocent wonder as that first time. I guard myself against their power. I prefer to sit at the back with Trevor, where the light spills from his machine, and help him work. I love to see the long dark ribbon curling off its wheel to wrap itself round another, the pictures so tiny and so delicately made, and so many of them, each one hardly different from the last. I cry to think of the skill of those who made them, all long dead and forgotten.

As for the Jane Writer, it lights the pictures and makes them move, but I'm afraid its name is only the trace of a memory and nothing more. When I ask Trevor he shrugs and says that's what Cat's mother called it and that's what it is.

I've grown used to the work at the O. For a while I could

only waddle like a fat sow, but now Walt is born I help Dell with cooking and banking up the fire. And together we watch the baby. Dell is my friend now and knows everything about me that can be told in words, though nothing of what lies deepest in my heart. She knows that Brendan is Walt's father, which makes Walt almost a brother to her. That Brendan might be dead. That if he's dead, then I am to blame. She was quiet when I told her that – sad and thoughtful. I was afraid she would hate me for it, but she knows what men can do, knows about the dangers of the road, never goes far without a knife in her belt.

When someone leaves word at the O I help her write it. We use the wall for paper and our pen is a stick padded at the end with fur. Our ink is pale and watery but we crush berries into it – blackberry, hawthorn, sloe – and so the word lasts long enough to be passed on, then fades, making space for other words. Trevor can neither read our letters nor understand how their shapes can make a sound, seeing them, I suppose, like the scatter of leaves blown in at the window.

I read to Dell from the books and have found a different way of reading, moving forward from one sentence to the next, content with one meaning at a time, sometimes two, often not even one if the words are hard and their meaning too strange to us. Dell is curious about my own book, but finds my writing in it no odder than many things I do.

And what of the Book of Air? I still love it above all other books that exist or might exist. I still feel Jane's presence sometimes, though I am far from the Study. I still want to believe that everything is in Jane and Jane in everything, but it gets harder. And I wonder if it could ever be true for Dell or Trevor or any of the people who live beyond the village.

Other things I once believed seem just tales to me now. The story of Maud who went at night to the house of windows that is now a ruin. Of how she danced with the Monk by starlight to the jangle of bells. Of how one night she didn't come and the Monk in sorrow tore out his own heart. Brendan said this was good for a winter evening by a cottage fire and I think he

246

was right. And the story of Old Sigh who flew down from a burning tower, without a stitch of clothing on him, to save the Book of Moon. The Mistress told us that one, but I think now it was a story meant only for children.

Jason

I'm woken by the church bells. Abigail is breathing steadily against my neck. We're snug in our quilt, bedded in mossy soil and dead leaves, and the old trees stand around us in the grey light.

A slight movement tells me Abigail's awake. I sense her listening.

'Jason?'

'Yes.'

'Do you hear that?'

'Yes.'

'What do you think it means?'

'Nothing, probably. It means Django's up. Or never went to bed.'

'Do you think we should find out?'

'I'd rather stay here with you.'

'So would I.'

She stirs and we disentangle from each other. I get up and pass her some clothes, her underwear and her skirt, and turn my back to let her dress.

We leave the wood and walk down the woodland side of the brook, hand in hand, pushing through straggly yellow weeds. The Mercedes with its nose dipped towards the water reminds me of our last wild car ride.

'Jason,' she says, 'last night…'

'Yes.'

'When you said am I Jewish, why did you say that?'

'It's a star of David, a Jewish symbol.'

'Because I think I must be.'

'But Cheryl was a Christian. I mean, seriously.'

'Cheryl wasn't anything. She just went along for the ride, and to protect me from my mother's influence.'

'But if your mother…'

'Mum wasn't Cheryl's, not really. Cheryl adopted her. So you'll remember who you are. That's what Mum said when she gave it me. That must've been what she meant.'

'It's possible.'

'But what *does* it mean? That I'm descended from all those Old Testament people, those kings and prophets and high priests, those Israelites wandering in the desert?'

I can't help laughing at the earnest way she says it.

'And I was never meant to be praying to Jesus?'

'Join the club.'

That makes *her* laugh too.

Reaching the road, I climb over the fence. Abigail follows and I help her down. She's preoccupied, thinking about her mother I suppose, and the whole Jewish thing, and I'm wondering what it means, if anything, and whether she wants to talk about it. But turning to the church I see Simon on the tower looking down over the parapet. I don't see any clothes on him. He holds himself against the cold and his little shoulders shake. There's light from the window below him and the shadowy form of the monkey swinging on the bell ropes.

I run round to the gate and into the churchyard and see Django standing on the roof of the nave, straddling the ridge. He's got his clarinet in one hand. There's the bulge in his jacket where he keeps his Bible closest to his heart. He edges forward, moving westward towards the tower. The slates are bright with dew. The stained glass below him flickers with colour – not sunlight but candles. The altar must be covered in them. His foot slips and he recovers, arms out, holding himself steady with a little panting laugh of excitement.

With a few stray notes, the bells fade. The monkey runs out through the porch to meet us, then back inside the church. Up on the tower, Simon begins whimpering. He has his back to Django, but it's obvious that whatever's happening Django is controlling it. Simon is leaning forward, as if nerving himself to take more risk. I hear behind me Abigail's sharp intake of

249

breath. And I hear all the birds of the morning – a riotous clamour – and nothing now to disturb or silence them, no traffic, no tractor or chainsaw, no fighter plane, no road drill, nothing across the wide expanse of fields and woods and wasteland and distant abandoned streets – just birdsong. The air seems dense with the sound, but it's as thin as ever. When Simon leans forward there's nothing between him and the churchyard but a fifty foot drop.

Django's laughter grows and he begins to shout. 'Don't be afraid, Simon. They that wait upon the Lord shall mount up with wings like eagles.'

Simon shivers and lets out another whimper. Then he takes a step up and he's standing naked on the edge of the parapet. My insides react with a lurch as if I'd taken that step myself and was already falling. And I see how this is meant to end.

I make my voice as steady as I can, just loud enough to reach Simon without startling him. 'Simon,' I say, 'step back away from the edge. Whatever he's said to you, you don't have to do this. Step back and wait for me.'

Django's looking at me now, and his face is so full of joy I could punch him. 'Consider not the things of old,' he says, 'For, see, I create new heavens and new earth, and the former shall not be remembered, nor come into mind. Sorrow and sighing shall flee away and the tongue of the stammerer shall speak plainly.'

'Leave him alone,' I tell him. 'You're scaring him.'

'I'm not scaring you, am I, Simon?'

Simon shakes his head, but his eyes are shut and his teeth are clamped together.

The window is brighter now, the medieval saints are stirring into life, and I see that it's more than candles burning. Django's built one of his bonfires on the altar and the whole of the chancel is ablaze.

'Behold,' he says, gesturing at Simon, 'mine elect, in whom my soul delighteth.' He lifts his instrument and plays a little upward run of notes. 'I will cause the sun's shadow to move backward on the sundial. Then shall thy light break forth as the morning, and thy righteousness shall go before thee.'

I don't know if there's a way to stop this without making it worse. I'm measuring the distance I'll have to cover to catch Simon if he falls. Can I move now without disturbing his balance, without prodding Django into greater madness? Would I do better to go inside and up to the tower?

'You shall be like a watered garden, Simon, like a spring whose waters fail not. Your descendants will rebuild the ancient ruins. You will be called repairer of broken walls, the restorer of paths to dwell in. All they that despised thee shall bow themselves down at the soles of thy feet.'

Simon is nodding his head, though his eyes are shut tight. He's heard this before – he already knows what's expected of him.

'Rise on the back of an angel and be seen on the wings of the wind. Fly, Simon. Fly in the midst of heaven.'

Simon raises a foot and puts it out into space and I'm thinking the world's about to end all over again. There's no end to the ending of things. Our life is one long sickening plummet into loss and more loss. I hear footsteps in the grass behind me and a hum of distress, but my eyes are fixed on Simon. Whatever power Django has over him, Simon thinks he can fly, or thinks he has no choice but to behave as though he thinks he can fly. This is what I should have been attending to, only this – taking care of Simon. Because if Simon dies nothing makes sense.

A swallow swoops over the roof of the nave, a blackbird starts up nearby, and I notice the birdsong again that I'd forgotten to hear – a chorus of inattention and indifference.

My body reacts to the explosion. My eyes are shut for no more than a second, but when I next look Simon is gone. I heard a scrabbling sound and the thud of a falling weight, but see nothing now except the sun over the porch roof and the sheen of damp slates. From the neighbouring fields and woods all the birds have taken flight, flitting into the air or rising on slow wings.

Behind me Abigail is talking. 'Maud,' she says. She's calm, but means to be obeyed. 'Maud, give me the gun.'

I turn for a moment and see them, Maud staring in shock, the shotgun sinking in her arms towards the ground. Abigail has one hand on the barrel and the other round Maud's back. Deirdre is behind them and Aleksy further off, still running. The monkey passes me, scampering through the grass towards them.

I turn back to shout Simon's name and his face appears above the parapet. He makes the noise he makes before speaking. I see the effort, the motion in his neck and lower jaw. The first word comes out and it's my name.

'Don't move,' I tell him. 'You're all right. I'm coming to get you.'

I take the stairs two at a time and reach the top breathing heavily. He's kneeling by the door, rubbing himself. 'Uncle n-Jason,' he says, 'There was a bang. I hurt my mm-bottom.'

I take my jacket off and wrap him in it. 'You're freezing,' I tell him. 'You need to come home with us and sit by the fire and have some breakfast. Let's see if those bantams have laid us any eggs.'

I see Abigail and Maud down among the gravestones, clinging to each other. The monkey's chatter rises to a scream. He's found Django sprawled beside the porch, a dark stain spreading around him on the grass. He clambers over the body, making noises of alarm, glancing back to see who's with him. He pulls at the hole in Django's jacket. White flakes come out of it and scatter on the ground. He pulls again and there are more flakes. I think for a moment that Django is stuffed like a toy bear. Then I see that it's paper. The monkey is pulling the pages from Django's Bible, which wasn't quite thick enough to save him. The swallow soars up over the church, drawing my eyes across the trees until I lose it against the sun.

I'm startled by another burst of noise. The chancel windows are shattering in the heat. Some of the roof tiles crack at the far end of the nave and flames appear.

'Come on, Simon. Time to go.'

'But where's...?'

'We'll talk about Django when we're on the ground.'

'He said I had to...'

'Don't worry about it.'

'...I had to...'

'You don't have to do anything you don't want to do.'

'...I had to fly.'

'No one can fly, Simon. Only birds can fly.'

'But Jangle said.'

'Quick, Si, before the fire gets us.'

I lift him and he climbs into my arms.

'If the mmm-bantams have laid an egg, can I have soldiers?'

'No bread, Si, remember. Not this year. Later we'll have bread and you can have all the soldiers you want.'

I take a last look over the parapet and I see the monkey chattering away among the gravestones with Django's clarinet. He crosses the road and scampers across the lawn, diminishing as if into an unimaginable future where babies will be born to replace the dead and everything lost will be found.

Agnes

Since I last opened this book, a horrible thing has happened, and we have left the O, Walt and I, for ever. Dell is with us. Until last evening we had no thought of making this journey. But now we shelter in the shadow of a fallen house and wait for the rain to ease before we set off again on the road to the village. Dell is asleep. Neither of us slept last night. Gideon stands patiently, head down against the wind. Walt lies beside me in his basket while I write. He holds one foot above him and makes small contented noises. He knows nothing of the danger we are in, trusting his safety to my care.

Yesterday at dusk Dell sent me to the canal for water, while she skinned some rabbits. When I had scooped up the last bucket and was loading it on the cart, a boy came, leading a cow along the pathway. The cow tugged a boat. Inside the boat a man stood to steer it with a paddle. I have seen other scroungers travel like this, usually with a horse or a donkey, sometimes with nothing but a pole to push against the riverbed. This cow was white all over like no cow in the village and bigger than any I've seen, with strong muscles in her rump. The boy was so small beside her that I took him at first for a child, until I saw the wisps of hair on his chin. The man shouted something from the boat and I couldn't tell if it was me he was shouting at or the boy. The cow seemed to understand him, anyway, because she stopped and dropped her head to graze at the side of the path. The boy waited, leaning against her side, looking so frail and sickly that I thought he might have fallen over into the water if the cow hadn't been there to support him. The boatman spoke again and I heard enough of his words to know he was asking where a person with a thirst might get a drink.

I told him he could follow me to the O. If I had known what trouble I was bringing to us all, I would have dropped the water and run into the darkest alleys of the forest. But how could I have known?

There was dog chained up on the boat that growled at me, until the man slapped its muzzle. Quick and jerky in his movements this boatman was, in a way I've observed here among the scroungers where a man can't stand easy among his neighbours but must watch for danger. He had a voice with a creak in it like a door shifting in a draught. When he stepped on to the path, his hot stink blew against me.

He took a swipe at the boy, sent him to fetch some things from the boat and set about untying the rope from the beast's harness. He winked at me and more words came out of his mouth. I moved so that the cow was between us, making a show of patting and stroking her. Seeing her so close, I wondered at her bulk and her milky colour.

'You like my Charlie?' he said. 'Got a bunch of them, all Charlies, barned up back home. The lads tend them while I'm on the canal.'

He told me people called him Quinlan. If the boy had a name I didn't hear it. I led the way, pulling the water cart under the trees. Quinlan followed with the cow. He was not much taller than me, but powerfully built. He wore a kind of smock that showed his knees and his huge calves. The boy trailed after with some fish from the canal and a bag of fresh squirrels.

Back at the O, I poured Quinlan a drink and he took a seat by the fire, while the boy stayed outside with the cow. For a while I was busy helping Dell make the rabbit stew. There weren't many wanting food but we thought more might come in later and what was left would keep for another day. When I went back to fill Quinlan's mug, Madge was sitting by him with Walt in her arms. I went back again later with some stew for Quinlan and a cup of the gravy for Madge and I stopped to cuddle Walt and kiss his little squinting face, and I felt Quinlan's eyes on me and saw the way he gnawed without thinking at the inside of his mouth, while his eyes slid up and down.

It was a quiet evening. And when all but a few had left or settled to their beds, I went again to take Walt for his feed. Trev had joined them by the fire, as he does sometimes to show welcome to a stranger. I lifted Walt from Madge's lap and turned away, and felt the hairs rise on my neck as if Quinlan's eyes could reach through the air and touch me.

I sat where I could feel the fire's warmth, but out of sight behind a curtain because I wouldn't have people see me with my clothes unbuttoned. The scrounger women are not so particular, but I still keep to village ways. Walt was in a fussy mood and wouldn't settle, so I put him to my shoulder to rock him and hum a low tune that I remember my gran singing to me.

On the other side of the curtain Quinlan was talking. 'She's not bad looking, and plump enough, with a nice pair of bags on her. A bit pale. But she'll colour up with outdoor work. I'll offer a good price.'

I thought at first it was the cow he meant, and wondered why he would think of selling her and who'd pull his boat for him if he did.

'She's a face filler, mind, I can see that,' he said. 'Don't suppose there's much left for your sows once she's done with the scraps. I'll take her off your plate for all that, and the tadpole with her.' I knew then he meant me. I'm heavy still from carrying Walt and swollen with milk.

I waited for what Trevor would say, but it was Madge who answered. 'And we get what in return?'

'There are plenty can haul water and cook a rabbit stew. You don't need this girl eating double.'

'She's a worker,' Madge said, 'and sharp at everything.'

'And we like her.' It was Trevor at last speaking up for me. 'Dell likes her. She's family.'

'You know how the world goes,' Quinlan said. 'I'm in the leather racket. Charlie leather. Four pelts I give you and you let me take the girl. I've three good lads to help make her welcome. She'll cook for them when I'm on the road.'

'It's a good offer, Trev,' Madge said. 'How many years before that tiddler's grown to pull his weight? And who's to say there won't be more where he come from?'

There was nothing then but the crackle of the fire and the murmur of talk from the others at the O. From Trevor I could only hear sighing. Then he spoke again in a sad, wheedling voice. 'She's happy here, see, her and the boy. I heard your offer, but what's in it for her is all I'm asking?'

'Look, I'm set up. Got the space. Got more meat than I know what to do with. Live in my barn, you do all right.'

'Well you can ask her yourself, I suppose. She came free and can leave free.'

'Wo,' Quinlan said, 'I don't do business with no girl. We spit on it, man to man, she don't need asking.'

I heard Dell calling for me then and was afraid to be found listening. So I took Walt with me on my hip and set about gathering the dishes to be scraped and stacked, all the while dizzy with fear.

I told Dell when we had a moment alone in the kitchen. It put her in a rage, though she kept her voice low. 'I know his sort,' she said. 'You'd be skivvied hollow. See his boy, standing out now in the cold. Dead on his feet. And at least the boy gets snoring time. Cheeses, Ag, you'd be nursing his precious charlies all day and then he'd be slobbering at you. And the lads he speaks of, they'll all want their turn. And what does he want with a kid? You leave here with Quinlan, Walt won't live to see another spring. He'll get plump, all right. He'll be fattened for the pot.'

I told her that Trevor had spoken up for me and said it must be my choice. She calmed down then. But how feeble Trevor had sounded I did not say. Walt began to squirm and whimper, so I sat in a high-backed chair in the darkest corner of the kitchen near the log pile and let him feed. This time he was ready and took it eagerly. I felt the force of his mouth on me and the pulse of it, stronger than my heartbeat, reaching deep down inside. I thought of all the jobs to be done. Tidying and sweeping. Damping the fire in the stove. Taking the stew from the heat before it spoiled. It was a good stew, with parsnips and onions, and a good rich flavour of thyme and rosemary. It had been a quiet night and there'd be plenty for tomorrow. Warmed by the stove, I let my eyes close and gave way to sleep.

I woke to feel the roughness of a man's hand on me. I was uncovered, and still tender from Walt's sucking. Rigid with fear, holding the baby tight, I opened my eyes. There was very little light, only the red glow from the stove. But I could see it was Quinlan. He had pulled his smock up to his waist and stood as naked as Old Sigh, his thing nudging at me and twitching like a creature with its own will. I drew my head back as far as the chair would let me.

'Your turn, sweet heart,' he said, 'your turn to suck.'

I shut my mouth tight then, and my eyes too, and held on to Walt. I hummed maybe in my fear but couldn't think straight to make any other sound.

'Don't be like that,' he said. 'You're with me now. It's settled.' His voice was soft but there was menace in it.

From another room came the clatter of dishes and the scraping of chairs across the floor as Dell and Trevor worked, and from outside among the ruins the soft scrabbling noises of creatures that like darkness. After a moment I heard the hiss of Quinlan's breath. His hand moved and withdrew. I waited sick with terror to feel it again, calloused, palsied, damp with sweat, settling on some other part of me. I remembered Brendan the night he took me from the red room, his hands reaching up under my skirt. But the strange disturbance I felt then was a pale shadow of this fear that seemed to rob me of motion.

When nothing came, I opened my eyes and saw that there was a knife at Quinlan's throat and it was Dell behind him holding it. I watched them in the light of the fire. Dell looked ready to kill, but I could see no fear in Quinlan's face, only cunning.

I looked down only to see if Walt was still sleeping and to lift him closer, but when I raised my eyes again everything had changed. Quinlan had turned about and forced Dell to her knees, gripping her wrist to keep the knife safe. Her cry had brought Trevor running from the outer room. There was a desperate scramble then, all three tangled together, and the firelight throwing their huge shadows on the wall. I stood, pushing my chair back. I could think of nothing except keeping Walt from harm. Laying him in the log basket by the stove, I looked about for something to fight with in case Quinlan should come for me again.

There was a grunt of effort or of pain and Trevor was on the ground, curled up as though winded from a blow. Dell too had fallen, upsetting a table, and lay dazed and breathless against it.

'Now then sweet heart. You come without any squealing, or we unstitch the tadpole and see what his insides look like.' Quinlan was talking to me. He was holding Dell's knife, which was already stained with blood, unless it was only the flame from the stove gave it its colour.

Some power surged through me then, a rage such I had never felt. I reached for the nearest thing, which was the lid of the cooking pot, and hurled it at Quinlan's head. He made to duck, but it clipped his ear and clattered away into the dark. While he was still reeling, I held up the pot, took two steps towards him and threw the stew in his face. I stepped back, letting the pot fall, feeling only then the searing heat of it.

I watched him lumber about, howling, crashing into furniture, blinded by the scalding broth, and had no thought of what to do next, except to find some way to soothe my poor burnt hands. I didn't see where Dell came from, nor what she held beside her, until she was close enough to take a blow at him. It was an axe she struck him with, and I felt the heat of his blood on my face as he went down and was sickened, all at once, by the smell of blood and ash and rabbit meat and rosemary and burning skin.

There were figures then in the doorway, sleepers roused by our noise, gaping and wide-eyed in the glow of the flames. But none of them stepped forward. It wasn't their fight. Dell rolled Trevor on to his back and cried out to find there was a bleeding gash near his heart and not a breath of life left in him.

Some of the men helped us dig graves for Quinlan and Trevor. We carried them to the patch of ground where Cat is buried, which was a garden once I think, though long neglected like the ruins all around. We put Quinlan in a far corner so that their bodies might not be eaten by the same worms. Dell bound two sticks together into a shape like a t to mark the place where Trevor's body lay. I asked her was it for the t of Trevor's name, thinking I might one day show her the difference between a big and a small t, but she frowned and shook her head and said it would be the same for anyone loved and missed. Then she wept bitterly.

She told me it wouldn't be safe for us now at the O. People would come looking for Quinlan. The boys he had spoken of would want to know where he had gone and his boat full of leather. She said we should trust no one, not the men who had helped us, not Madge, not the regulars who had been Trevor's friends. If we meant to go north we should set off south. I saw she was right. So we packed up what food and clothes we could carry, with some precious things of my own to load on Gideon's back. We thought of taking the cow to help with our burden – such a fine strong beast and the boy who tended it nowhere to be seen. But we knew it was too pale and strange and would mark us out on the road. We slipped away while it was still dark.

I think now of life at the O as a dream from which I have woken. I once feared more than anything to watch a flogging at the Hall. But a flogging had its own shape, always the same. You knew the worst of it from the beginning. Even in the red room I knew why they had put me there. I see now that here among the scroungers, at the best of times, everything must be haggled over from day to day and everyone lives by chance like a weed in a cottage wall.

I have lived here no one's wife and free to care for my child without shame. But all the business of calling and being called and then standing on the lawn among neighbours to hear certain texts from the Book of Air was as warm and comforting to me as sunshine, and it seems to me now that shame was its necessary shadow.

After Walt was born no one stood with me to ask, as after any birth in the village, 'What crime was this that lived incarnate in this sequestered mansion? What mystery that broke out now in fire and now in blood at the deadest hours of night?' And no one to explain that through these hard words of Jane's we are reminded that from the moment of our making we are fire as well as air, that Bertha no less than Jane is in all of us, that we are conceived in crime and must live a mystery to ourselves.

I have found the turn of spring with all the birds coming and the bright leaves and the snowdrops pleasant and comfortable, but here, away from the village, it has no meaning. And so with everything. Times and changes are just themselves and nothing more. I see that it is not just the Book of Air that I yearn to read more than one way, but the events of my waking life. I didn't begin to understand this until Walt was born. Even if Quinlan had never come to the O, I would have wanted more for Walt than this thin scrabble for existence.

If we mean to go north. Those were Dell's words. We both knew without saying that with nothing left for us at the O but danger we would try to reach the village. There is danger for us there too, I have no doubt of that, but at least Walt will be safe. My neighbours will surely take the child, even if they turn me out. If I am locked away or killed, perhaps they will raise him at the Hall. If we lose our way in the forest and starve or fall into the hands of ruthless men it will be worse.

I think Dell has her own reasons to come that neither of us will put words to. For myself, I am frightened of the village, and frightened of what I must do when I get there, but driven by a desperate hope. My courage might fade when we come near the Hall and within the Mistress's reach. But we have decided and must take our chances.

Jason

In the dining room, what's left of last night's dinner litters the table – the plates stained with gravy, the wilting flowers, the candles shrunk to dried puddles of wax. The chairs are just as we left them, angled away from the table, one tipped over on to the floor.

I sit with my back to the window. Simon is on my lap. He's wearing my jacket and I hold him close, but he doesn't stop shivering. I'd take him to the kitchen, but Maud's in the kitchen with Abigail. The church is still burning. I can taste the fire. The flames light up the mirror above the mantelpiece and animate the pictures.

There are blackberries scattered on the table. I gather the ones within reach and offer them to Simon, but he shuts his mouth tight and shakes his head. He asks for Jangle and I tell him again that Django's dead.

I hear raised voices in the hall. Deirdre comes in, followed by Aleksy. She asks me what we're going to do.

'About what?'

'What are we going to do about Maud?'

'I don't know,' I say, 'I haven't thought about it.'

'We must do something.'

Aleksy pulls a chair up to the table. 'Maud's young. She'll get over it.'

Deirdre is exasperated. 'It's not about her. It's about Django. She killed him. We can't do nothing.'

'You want we build her a little gaol? We all milk the cows and bring water in for her to sit and get fat? You want to give her ten years maybe? Then for sure she won't kill no one else.'

'Don't be ridiculous.'

'Just give her a good slapping then. What do you think?

262

You want to do it, or how? You want me and Jason to beat her a little?'

'You're really a disgusting human being, Aleksy – you know that?'

Aleksy grins slyly.

Deirdre turns to me. 'I just think we ought to do something, Jason – to show that it's important – to show that Django's life mattered.'

'You never killed no one, Deedee?' Aleksy asks her.

'That was different. That was on the road. That was self-defence.'

'This was no different.'

'She gets away with it and who'll be next?'

'No one will be next,' I tell her.

Deirdre looks at me for a moment and then turns to the window. She speaks more quietly, as if this is an argument she's having with herself. 'She never talks. Who knows what she's thinking?'

Simon frowns and his mouth begins to move. 'What did mmm...' We watch for a bit while he struggles with Maud's name.

Then I answer his question. 'What did she do? She watched out for you, Si. She saved you from a fall. You might be dead if she hadn't.'

'She...' There's a k-word coming. It scratches in his throat like a hairball, until it threatens to choke him.

'Killed Django, yes, but someone had to.'

He frowns at me, struggling with this new thought. 'Why did someone have to?' He pushes my arm away and shuffles off my lap to stand on the floor. 'Why did someone?' I watch the rage gathering in him, tightening his face, pulling him upright.

When Maud appears in the doorway all Simon's red-faced fury is turned on her. 'Why did you?'

Maud turns to Abigail, standing beside her with an arm round her shoulder, then she faces Simon again. 'Because, Simon...'

We've never heard her voice. We couldn't know it would sound just this way – the soft music of it, the faint Welsh lilt – but now no other voice is imaginable.

Maud breathes and tries again, speaking slowly but with gentle urgency. 'Because I wouldn't have him fill you with that book of death.'

Simon glares at her, shaking with rage. 'She must be sent to her room,' he says, 'withouten any ice cream.'

They stand for a moment confronting each other. Then Maud turns and runs. We hear her footsteps on the oak staircase, all the way to the top of the house and more faintly along the passage. A door bangs, and I know which door it is. She's chosen your beautiful bathroom, Caro, to hide herself in. The house creaks and falls silent. Deirdre rests her head against the glass. Aleksy sighs. Abigail says, 'We should have tea,' but doesn't move, and I realise this isn't a proposal, but an expression of loss. A strange peace settles on the room.

Agnes

We rode for two days. It was late afternoon when we saw the village. A fresh spring wind came up to meet us. The hedges were all in blossom, the track skirted with sorrel and thrift, a sight I'd not thought about in my time among the scroungers but had pined for in my heart. Dell, who is not so used to riding, sat behind with Walt. I saw in the distance through the trees the swallows swooping and the cows grazing the meadow, everything in its right place.

When the Monk's Ruin came into view ahead of us, I cut in through the trees and headed for the High Wood, so that we would see the Hall before being seen.

The villagers who had once been my neighbours were gathered on the grass. Seeing them together and the Mistress with them I faltered. If Brendan was dead they couldn't blame me for it, but I had escaped from the red room and defied the power of the Hall. I told Dell, though she seemed less afraid than I was, that everything would be all right and that she should stay by the horse with Walt. If they took me she should do as we had agreed – ride boldly to the oak door and ask to speak to Sarah. If Sarah wouldn't come she should tell whoever would listen that little Walter was Brendan's child and should be taken in for his sake.

I dropped quiet as I could to the ground, pulled the leather bag from Gideon's back and took some steps towards the lawn. The shadow of the Hall reached out to meet me, pointing with its gables and chimneys.

A woman stepped from the shadow of a tree and I saw it was my old neighbour Bessie. She threw her arms around me. 'You here,' she said. 'I never thought to see you again.' Drawing back, she put her hands to my face. 'And are you well, dear

Agnes, and are you home for good? Your cottage stands empty since your poor mother died.'

'I'm home if they'll have me, Bessie,' I said, 'and not lock me up.'

She shook her head and sighed. 'That's more than I know.'

I asked her, 'Why is the village gathered?'

'A terrible thing. Morton is dead and they say Daniel killed him. So he must be beaten, poor boy, and sent out into the forest to scavenge.'

'Dead how? Of what cause?'

'Tal found him in his bed with his throat cut and swears he saw Daniel washing in the brook at midnight.'

'And what does Daniel say?'

'At first he tried to speak but no words came. Now he is proud and silent, and that's enough for them.'

'But he was always so kind.' I couldn't believe that Daniel would do such a thing.

'And such a good father he is to Annie's little girl. And so happy he's been these past months between the child and helping Roland.'

'Helping him with what?'

'I don't know altogether. First it was the murk that must be broken apart, all the pipes inside it, and each part carried up to the turret to be peered at. Then day after day, water to be boiled on the fire.'

'But what's it for, all this carrying and boiling?'

'It's beyond me, Agnes dear. But Roland says it's set down in the Book of Windows if you know how to read it. And so they played like boys. And now this. I should stand on the lawn to watch but I can't bear to watch.' Bessie's tears stopped her talking then. We held each other until Gideon snorted among the trees and shook his mane, and we heard Walt gathering himself to cry out and Dell soothing him.

Bessie looked to see who I'd brought with me. 'Is it a scrounger? And a scrounger's child?'

I waved the question away. I wanted more news. I wanted

to hear how things stood in the village. 'Tell me about Megan. Does Megan have a child yet?'

'You didn't hear, of course. There was no wedding. Megan ran with the other girls to the wood, though the rain had come on hard during the night and the way was all mud. But there was only a tree with bindweed hanging on its trunk, and no husband. Now she keeps away from the Hall when she can. And Roland devotes himself to the Book of Windows, with Brendan gone. So much change, such troubles, and Morton murdered in his bed.'

Her sobbing was drowned by Walt, who had opened his mouth in a pure, clean cry.

Faces turned towards us from the lawn. I heard behind me Dell tramping among the trees, crooning words of comfort, and Walt's noise muted to whimpers and gurgles. Then the Mistress spoke and everyone looked at her again, and Daniel was led out, hooded and naked to the waist.

Someone else was making noise, one of the villagers. It was Annie with an infant in her arms. I saw her stifle her own howling with a hand to her mouth. Her anguish was for her living husband not for her dead father. I was sure of that. And it came to me, not as a thought but as a feeling, a sensation on my skin, that it was true. It was all true. I remembered how Morton had taken hold of me the night I cut myself in the red room. And I knew all in a rush that Annie's baby was Morton's doing. And my mother's baby too, who was born too small to live. Brendan had not lied about that. Daniel, who shrank from speaking, had once spoken up in front of the whole village to save Annie. And now there was another girl growing under Morton's too watchful eye. I saw how Daniel might have wished Morton dead and not left it at wishing.

Walt had started up again, in spite of Dell's efforts to distract him from his hunger. I would have fed him but had more urgent work to do. His wailing had drawn more than looks. Tal had left the gathering and was walking towards us, his face blank as a stone, and Peter trailing after him. There was movement among the villagers, a murmur of voices, and Sarah appeared from among them, hurrying across to where we stood.

People turned this way, and back again towards the Mistress whose voice rose to silence their noise, then this way again, straying towards Sarah, who had never walked away from a flogging however she shrank from it inside, and towards me who was mad and had escaped to live among the scroungers, and was mad still no doubt and stained with scrounger ways.

Now there were more coming. Ada and Miriam hooded as Reeds, their green fronds blowing about them. The voice of the Mistress grew louder and more shrill, but whether calling them back or urging them on I couldn't tell.

As if pulled over the lawn by their long shadows they moved towards us. I told myself not to be afraid, though in truth I was faint with fear at the thought of what I was about to do. I stepped forward with the bag swinging heavily against my leg.

Sarah reached me first, moving with quick light steps. 'Is she with you?' she said, 'is it my child?' hardly stopping to hear my answer before hurrying on under the trees.

I knelt, sinking back on my heels. I heard the gasp of joy from Dell and the comforting murmur of Sarah's voice and Walt grumbling between them. The bag lay open on the ground. A book came into my hand and I tossed it in Tal's path. Another book spun towards the women, landing softly on the grass. A third book for Peter. A fourth and fifth for the women. The books perched on the lawn fluttering, holding themselves to the wind like curlews.

More faces turned from the crowd by the Hall, straining to read the meaning of what I did.

Tal had stumbled in his progress and now stooped to see what lay in front of him. Peter came up beside him, scratching his beard. Miriam and Ada turned this way and that to gather the books that fell flapping at their feet.

I heard Bessie's voice behind me. 'What are they, Agnes?'

A whisper grew among the villagers. Above our heads the branches ducked and strained. The old slates rattled on the roof of the Hall. The people moved back and forth across the lawn while the sky darkened and the wind howled down from the moor to riot in the wood.

Then there was Roland. I stood with my empty bag billowing at my side and waited for him to come towards me. I raised my voice to be heard above the storm.

'So you're the Reader now.'

'What have you done, Agnes?'

'You thought there were only four books. I've brought more to show you.'

'I never thought there were only four.'

'We all did, Roland. You never said different.'

'What does it mean anyway?'

'It means we think fresh about everything. If there are a thousand books.'

'A thousand?'

'Why not? Then there are a thousand ways to think.'

'And this is what the scroungers have taught you?'

'The books taught me this. And my own mind.'

'And what good will it do?' He looked about at the villagers, who passed books and held them open for the air to snatch at, muttering in their agitation. 'They're frightened already, Agnes. This is a hard time for us. You should have waited.'

'For your permission?'

He laughed but I could see it was just to hide his own fear. 'There's still only one Book of Windows.'

'Which will teach you nothing. Not to capture steam nor how to ride without a horse.'

'You don't know that.'

'I know it's just a trick of yours to say otherwise, to have your own way. For years Brendan studied the Book of Windows and he found so little sense in it, it made him mad.' I stopped then, because I saw all at once that Brendan had led a sad and worthless life.

'You haven't asked about Brendan.' Roland looked as if he thought this question would make me stumble.

'Should I have asked?'

'He's not here. I thought you might have wondered what became of him. Unless you already know.'

'I haven't asked about Megan either. Weren't you going to marry?'

'You can't lie to me, Agnes. We grew up together.'

'You grew up at the Hall. I only lit your fires and washed your sheets.'

He smiled at that, because it was my old way of talking, I suppose. 'There are others to do that now,' he said. 'But I'm not as idle as I was. Come to my room and see how I work.'

'Your room in the turret? I've been there before. It's too close to the red room. I'm afraid I might never see the forest again, or the fields, or the geese. How are the geese?'

'The geese are laying and will go on laying without any help from you. Come to my room and we can talk about the books.'

'And if I did come, what would Megan say?'

I saw I had unsettled him at last. 'The night you left.' He looked at the ground. When he looked up again his eyes were fierce. 'Until the night you left, Agnes, I didn't know.'

'What didn't you know?'

'That without you the Hall is an empty ruin and the other villagers worth less to me than a rabble of scroungers.'

I was surprised to feel my heart beat faster to hear him say this, and my breath come less easily. I didn't know what I would say in reply until the words came. 'Then knock on my cottage door and I might answer.'

I made to walk away but was stopped by a thought. When I turned back, three or four women had gathered around Roland, old neighbours puzzled to see me, some holding books awkwardly in both hands, while the air tore at their scarves and the hems of their skirts. Bessie joined them, puzzling at a page of words. They were afraid perhaps the Book of Death was come for them in many faces and the world was soon to end. Behind them on the steps, the Mistress moved her arms through the air but her voice was drowned. Daniel, waiting beside her to be flogged, tilted his hooded head as if to catch a sound that would tell him what was happening to the village.

'I met some scroungers on the road,' I said. My words were for Roland but I didn't mind who heard them. 'They boasted they had killed a villager. An old man who limped in his walk. I thought of Morton. Is Morton dead? They said they cut his throat while he lay in bed asleep and left him to be eaten by rats.'

Roland watched me through narrowed eyes. 'How did they know of his limp if they killed him in bed?'

I looked at the wild sky, then at the women who waited for an answer. 'They followed him home from the forest where he'd been gathering firewood.'

'A loaf of Annie's bread was in the kitchen, Agnes. Did the scroungers tell you that? Cheese and freshly churned butter. In the yard a shed full of chickens. None of it touched. Only Morton, slashed from the ear to the throat, and enough blood to drench the straw and spill down through the floorboards on to his kitchen table. Is there no hunger any more among the scroungers?'

I shrugged. 'Scroungers do what scroungers will, Roland, and there's no accounting for it.'

I left him standing there, and the neighbours gathering round him, and hurried to where Dell stood with Walt, and Sarah clinging to her, while above them the trees tossed and churned. I told Sarah she should come with us to the cottage, but she pulled herself away from Dell and said she must see things right at the Hall. She held me tight for a moment, said she would come to us later, and set off into the storm.

So it was just the three of us again. I led the way on foot back down to the road and over the bridge towards my mother's cottage.

Jason

The fire has died down, and I've come to dig Django's grave. Inside the blackened shell of the church the roof timbers sit precariously in heaps. Embers break here and there into little runs of flame. The walls give off heat and I'm sweating before I've begun.

Django lies in the churchyard where he fell. On one side his clothes have burnt off and his flesh is singed. I chase off a couple of buzzards, throw a sheet over him and weigh it down with stones. Then I cover my face and start digging. While I work, the wind shifts direction and grows stronger. The air is pleasantly cool. I catch the smell of tree bark and damp leaves. Before I reach the water level the rain comes and I'm hoisting shovelfuls of mud.

I'm about done, when I see Abigail on the road. I climb out and let the rain wash the mud off me.

Abigail calls out, 'The others are on their way.' When she reaches me she puts her hand on my neck and kisses me on the mouth. Then she takes my arm and pulls herself close, resting her head against my chest.

I ask her if Maud's all right.

'I think so. The door's still locked. You won't let them hurt her will you?'

'No one will hurt her.'

'We would have come sooner, but no one could find Rasputin.'

'Simon was searching for him earlier. Aleksy told him he must have gone off in search of a girl monkey to mate with.'

'Poor Rasputin. When I went up to talk to Maud, he was playing on your ladder. So I chased him off with a broom and shut the trap door. That's the last I saw of him.'

The rain stops and we watch the sky clear across the valley, and the faint arc of refracted light.

Abigail says, 'You did say you'd finished in the roof?'

'The roof's OK for now. The house will survive the winter, even if *we* don't.'

'We'll be all right.'

'What will happen to us, Abigail?'

'We'll grow wheat and bake bread. We'll make cheese. There'll be hay in the summer to feed the cows for another year. The orchard will give us fruit. The hens and geese will lay eggs. Maud's bees will make honey and wax for our candles. And we'll have children, first Deirdre and then me, and one day Maud. And we'll take care of each other and our children will take care of us.'

'And what will we tell them, these children?'

'That now would be a good time to earth up the leeks.'

'Have we got leeks?'

'They were the first thing we planted, Maud and me. We brought what seeds we could find in Lloyd's barn.'

'You were thinking ahead.'

'I'd been thinking for years, thinking myself out of Hebron.' She reaches into the pocket of her apron. 'I nearly forgot.' She takes my left hand and slips my ring on. 'I thought you'd like to have it with you.'

'To bury Django you mean. You don't mind that I wear it? You know it's my wedding ring.'

'We shouldn't forget the people who were important to us. We hold them close, any way we can.' She puts a hand to her heart, touching through her blouse the star on its silver chain.

Aleksy and Deirdre come, bringing Simon. He stands and watches while we move the stones away, lift Django's body with the sheet still covering it and lower it into the ground.

Simon asks if he can read from his book.

'Course you can, Si,' I tell him. 'Django would like that.'

'This is n-Jangle's... favourite bit,' he says. He stumbles on the first goodnight. The second and third come more easily. Arbitrary words, they seem to me, though by some mystery they have captured his childish imagination. He draws out the last phrase, hushing his friend to an eternal sleep with his finger to his lips, and twitching in his effort to hold still.

That seems good enough for now. Together Aleksy and I shovel the earth back into the grave.

Later, when the leaks have been seen to and the cows have been milked, when Simon's been put to bed and Aleksy is helping Deirdre clean the kitchen, I walk with Abigail in the long grass that used be a lawn. All day I've been aware of a glow, a vividness I hadn't seen in her before. She touches me, and it's as if her whole body is humming with energy, and mine too.

Above us the stars do what stars are supposed to do, what they've always done, though for a century or so it was hard to see them through the glare of cathode and neon and the glow of incandescent filaments.

I miss electricity – there'll always be a hole in my heart where electricity used to be. God knows, I miss plumbing. I miss all the engineered gadgetry of the industrial age. I miss you too, Caroline, but just now you seem a long way off. If I could put everything back the way it was, if I could exchange this little rescued fragment of life for the world we had, in all its astounding, calamitous glory, I wouldn't hesitate. Not for a second. But I have moments of forgetting. A mist crosses in front of it and I begin to lose the sharpness of its outline. I know it will come back to me, the desolation, the knowledge of all that's gone. But for now there's this glimmer of what it might feel like to be glad.

Agnes

So here we are in my cottage and the fire laid and Walt cleaned and fed, and Dell plucking some pigeons for the pan and a start made on the sweeping. And for now no one comes.

I sit at the kitchen table to write in my book. If someone should knock at my door and ask what it means, I will turn to them boldly and say: if Jane why not Agnes?

I have shown Walt my father's things, his knife with its hidden blades, the little wren he carved from a scrap of maple. And the most precious of them – the silver chain he gave me when he could no longer speak, that he had from his mother, that will be Walt's one day to pass on to his child. As delicate as anything ever made, like tiny grass seeds strung together. And the star with six points that hangs from it like a silver snowflake, and the ring, all gold except for a curling rim of paler colour, as though its first owner held it by one edge to dip it in the butter churn.

Little Walt laughed and reached a hand to all the shiny things. He cried when I wouldn't let him play with them or put them to his mouth, but forgot them again soon after. When he's older he'll know how to value them.

So what now? If they went on with Daniel's punishment, Annie will be washing his wounds and the villagers returning mute and fearful to their work. If Sarah is punished for walking away from a flogging, she won't come. If she wants only the study and the Book of Air and nothing more, she'll stop at the Hall. Maybe the Reeds will come in the night and I shall be dragged away and my little boy taken from me. The Mistress will send them, surely, but will they come now at her sending? I saw the whisper scurry across the lawn, the books fluttering from hand to hand. Their certainty is shaken. The world is not as they thought. She may come for me herself and I will invite her into my kitchen, but not to cower at her every word. Knowing this, she surely won't come.

Or they'll all come, the village and the Hall together crowding at my door to know the meaning of these books, leaving Roland to sit alone in the turret, if he likes, and boil his own water.

Unless the books are already gathered into the fire, Sarah locked in the red room, the villagers afraid to raise their eyes from the ground.

Putting these thoughts down on a new page, I see something I hadn't seen before. That when I write about things that haven't yet happened and might never happen I can make them seem true just by writing them. Did Jane know this feeling too – of bringing things into being just by putting the words on paper? It makes me feel closer to her than ever to think she did.

Maybe I can say straight out then that this is how our day ended, with Sarah coming wrapped against the storm to find Dell like her younger self for all her strange manner of speaking. And cousin Annie arriving soon after with her little girl and Daniel unharmed. That it ended with candles lit and a fire to warm the cottage's old stones, and good food from the pot, and tears for bad times past, and laughter that we are all here together to talk about them, and Walt and Eliza cuddled and passed from hand to hand, and wonder that all these things should come about never before guessed at.

And maybe writing this will make it so, even while the sky darkens and the wind howls at my door.

And maybe I can say that before another day passed Roland came himself with some primroses for the mantelpiece and a basket of strawberries to ask if we might forget our quarrel and talk in the old way. And that I told him I had my own cottage to clean now and a child to care for but, if I had time, we might walk out along the river and enjoy each other's company as we once did.

Acknowledgements

First, my thanks to Hayley, Kate, Gareth and all at Clink Street for guiding this book safely into print.

It has taken me a good while to discover how to tell this story. Many people have helped along the way. For answering questions, offering suggestions, correcting errors and supporting in other ways, I would like to thank Michael Buck, Alan Buster, Jane Carol, Russell Kennedy, Shelly Nel, Neil Parker, Richard Porter, May Rigler, Zimmy Ryan, Liz Treasure and Tom Treasure.

Jane Kennedy, who was encouraging me to write before I had begun to think of myself as a writer, has offered invaluable insights.

While preparing The Book of Air for publication, I have benefitted greatly from the encouragement and professional advice of Jenny Rogers and Phil Wilkinson.

I am grateful to my agent Victoria Hobbs for her care and attention in promoting this book and pushing me to make it better, and to my friend and colleague Tahmima Anam who nurtured it from its early days through many drafts.

Finally, my thanks to Leni Wildflower, whose love, companionship and fearless support has made this project possible.

About Joe Treasure

Raised sixth in a family of nine, Joe Treasure enjoyed a capriciously Bohemian childhood. Having received his educational grounding at the hands of Carmelite priests, he escaped to Cheltenham Grammar School where he excelled only in music and art. His architectural ambitions were thwarted by low grades in maths and physics. The local college of further education allowed him to pursue more congenial subjects, after which he surprised everyone, not least himself, by winning a place to read English at Keble College, Oxford.

Settling in Monmouth, Wales, Joe taught English and ran an innovative drama programme. He moved to Los Angeles at the turn of the millennium to join his wife, Leni Wildflower. Temporarily unemployed, he set about fixing up Leni's house and turned to writing fiction.

In 2004, at the end of George W Bush's first explosive term in office, they relocated to London where Joe studied creative writing at Royal Holloway. He wrote *The Male Gaze*, a novel that drew on his American experience, mingling social comedy with political drama. Offered a two-book publishing contract with Picador, he went on to explore the divided loyalties of an Anglo-Irish family in *Besotted*, a novel that celebrates the enduring bonds of brotherhood.

The Book of Air is Joe's first venture into speculative fiction. He and Leni currently live in Balham, London.

Jason —

Lightning Source UK Ltd.
Milton Keynes UK
UKOW03f0618100417
298756UK00004B/259/P